ALASKAN HIDEAWAY

BETH CARPENTER

MILLS & BOON

First Published in Great Britain 2018
by Mills & Boon, an imprint of HarperCollins*Publishers*
1 London Bridge Street, London, SE1 9GF

Alaskan Hideaway © 2018 Lisa Deckert

ISBN: 978-0-263-26514-9

38-0718

MIX
Paper from
responsible sources
FSC™ C007454

FSC
www.fsc.org

This book is produced from independently certified FSC™ paper to ensure responsible forest management.

For more information visit: www.harpercollins.co.uk/green

Printed and bound in Spain
by CPI, Barcelona

To Rosemunde Pilcher, Sue Grafton,
Agatha Christie and all the other writers,
living and dead, who have brought me endless
hours of pleasure with their stories.

And to all the readers who share my passion
for the written word. Happy reading!

CHAPTER ONE

SNOW CRUNCHED UNDER Ursula's ski poles as she pushed up the rise and stopped at the top of the hill to catch her breath. She'd earned an Anchorski second-place medal in the over-fifty age group a few winters ago, but that didn't mean she could keep up with her eight-year-old goddaughter. From somewhere nearby, a raven cackled as though amused at these earthbound creatures with boards strapped to their feet.

Up ahead, Rory picked up speed as the slope grew steeper. She crouched into a tuck, her corn-silk hair lifting from her shoulders and streaming behind her. At this rate, she'd be airborne before she reached the bottom of the hill.

"Remember, pizza," Ursula called. The little girl instantly spread the tails of her skis and slid to a stop.

She looked back at Ursula and frowned. "I know what a wedge is." Of course, she did. Rory had been on the ski trails before she could walk, riding in a pulk behind her parents. She didn't need anyone to remind her to shift her skis in "pizza" position to slow herself or "hotdog" to speed up.

"Sorry. I forget you're an expert. But I'm not as fast as you. Slow down a little so I can keep up. Okay?"

"Okay." Rory flashed a smile before she resumed skiing, and Ursula's heart melted. Rory's smiles had been all too rare lately. After a week including a discouraging meeting with Rory's teacher and a glowing article about the new resort in Seward that was bound to cut into Ursula's business, this was exactly what they both needed. Time outside, space to move and breathe. Somehow, nothing seemed quite as overwhelming in the outdoors.

The trail ran between a cluster of spruce trees and a huge boulder making a sharp bend toward the right-of-way across Betty's place. Movement caught her eye, and Ursula looked over to watch a rabbit disappear into the woods. She rounded the bend and turned her attention back to the trail.

What in the—? A gate Ursula had forgotten existed blocked the trail at the bottom of the hill. Rory had spotted the gate first and was standing in the middle of the trail. Ursula slowed but couldn't stop in time to avoid a slow-motion crash, and they both skidded downhill in a tangle of arms, legs, skis and poles, coming to rest a couple of feet from the heavy gate.

Ursula sat up. "I'm sorry. Are you okay?"

Eyes wide, the girl nodded and stared at the gate. "Why is that there?"

"I don't know." The top rail sported a new sign: Private Property. No Trespassing. A thick chain looped around the fencepost adjacent to the gate. On the far side, someone had gone to considerable trouble shoveling the snow away so the gate could swing shut. It had always been open during the six years Ursula had been operating the inn. Betty had enjoyed watching the skiers and hikers pass through on the way to the main trails. She used to sit outside on nice days and wave at them.

Ursula got to her feet and jabbed her poles into the snow before offering Rory a hand up. The wooden sign pointing toward Fireweed Trail was missing, too. This was no misunderstanding. The shortcut she and her guests took across her neighbor's property to the cross-country trails was closed.

This wouldn't do. Not only did she and Rory enjoy Nordic skiing, but access to trails was one of the main draws for her bed-and-breakfast inn, especially in the winter. Across the snow-covered meadow, a steel-gray SUV with a propeller-shaped medallion on the grill backed up to Betty's porch, its liftgate open. A real estate agent, no doubt, finally getting the place ready to sell.

It had been almost two years since Betty Francis, Ursula's friend and neighbor, passed away at the age of eighty-nine and left her cabin to her granddaughter, Danielle. Except for a monthly cleaning service, the cabin had been deserted ever since. Ursula was surprised it had taken Danielle this long to list the property. She'd seldom found time to visit even when her grandmother was alive, with her busy career writing cookbooks.

Rory's lip quivered. "Does this mean we can't ski anymore?"

"Of course we can ski. We can get to the trails by Marge's place if we need to, but maybe if we ask nicely, they'll let us through today." If they could get the agent's attention, anyway.

Either way, the gate wouldn't stay closed for long. The credit union had already preapproved Ursula for a loan. Assuming the asking price was anywhere near reasonable, Ursula was ready to buy Betty's cabin and the land around it. With that new resort going in, she needed something special to entice guests, and with this property she could give her guests something the hotel couldn't.

A man stepped to the edge of the porch and looked their way. Ursula waved, but he didn't respond. She held her hand against her face like a phone to let him know she wanted to talk, but he just crossed his arms over his chest and stared at them. Great sales technique.

Ferocious barking interrupted her thoughts. A black-and-white dog tore through the snow. All at once, Ursula was glad for the heavy gate. She liked dogs, but the pit bull charging toward them didn't evoke her usual warm and fuzzy response. She clutched her ski poles, just in case she needed them to fend it off. Rory squeaked and hid behind her.

The dog roared and leaped at the gate, shaking the heavy iron, fell to the snow and leaped again. Ursula knew fleeing would only engage the dog's chase response, so she slowly eased away from the fence, staying between Rory and the dog. What kind of realtor brought a vicious dog along on his visits?

Cupping her hands around her mouth, she shouted, "Call off your dog." She wasn't sure if he could make out her words from that distance or not, but if he did, he chose to ignore her.

Fine. She turned and urged Rory back up the hill. "We're okay. The dog can't get through the gate." The barking continued long after they had rounded the boulder and disappeared into the forest. Eventually, Ursula heard a distant whistle and the dog quieted. By that time, they were halfway home.

Once they made it to the B&B parking area, she and Rory released their bindings and stepped out of their skis. When she laid a hand on Rory's shoulder, she could feel the girl shaking, whether from fear or anger Ursula wasn't sure. Ursula was leaning their skis against the wall on the porch when she heard a chattering noise. A squirrel dashed across the porch and tried to run up Rory's leg, but the ski bibs she wore were too slick.

Rory giggled. "Hi, Frankie." Giving up on climbing her leg, the squirrel ran up the porch post to stand on top of the railing. Rory stroked a finger along his back. "I couldn't find you yesterday. Where were you?"

Ursula smiled at their reunion. Animals were Rory's soft spot, and she'd been fascinated with Frankie from their first meeting. "He comes and goes. He was probably just off playing with his friends." She patted her coat and found a few sunflower seeds in the breast pocket, which she handed to Rory. The squirrel took them from her hand, stuffed them into his cheek pouches and scurried away. Good old Frankie. Unlike a certain realtor, he didn't bite the hand that fed him. Rory watched him disappear into the forest.

Ursula put an arm around the girl's shoulders. "What do you say we get a cookie before we drive over to Marge's house to ski?"

Rory shrugged, her features once again settling into that bland expression she wore too often. "I don't want to ski anymore. Can I watch a movie?"

Ursula sighed inwardly. That's all Rory had wanted to do at first, to watch the same dozen movies over and over. Recently, she'd seemed a little more engaged, but here they were again. Eventually, Ursula was going to need to put some limits on screen time, but after the gate and the dog, she understood why Rory needed this. Saturday night used to be movie night for Rory and her parents, when they would pop popcorn and cuddle together on the couch. Wrapping herself in her mother's blanket and watching movies made Rory feel closer to them. But it had been four months since the accident, and Ursula was starting to see traces of the bundle of energy Rory used to be. The ski outing had been going so well, until the stupid realtor ruined it.

Ursula forced a smile before opening the door, for the sake of her guests as well as Rory. People came to the B&B to relax, and she made it a point never to add to their stress. "You can watch a movie if that's what you want." The faint odor of maple syrup from this morning's breakfast still hung in the air. The couple staying in the Rose room sipped coffee and gazed out the windows, watching the birds flutter between Ursula's collection of bird feeders. Good thing they weren't skiers. The family in the Shooting Star suite had gone into Seward for the day.

Ursula greeted her guests and followed Rory to their private quarters in the back of the inn to change. When the zipper on her ski boot stuck, she jerked it free and dropped the boot on the floor with a thud. That realtor was just plain rude. He could have at least given her warning before he closed the shortcut, not to mention controlling his dog.

But getting mad wouldn't accomplish anything. Betty's granddaughter had chosen to hire him, so if Ursula wanted that property, she was going to have to work with him. Once he'd had a chance to put up a for-sale sign, she'd call and make an appointment to tour the property.

Not that she needed a tour. She'd visited Betty often, especially as she got older and her health was failing. Ursula knew the cabin far better than some realtor. She knew the roof was only four years old but the water heater was getting toward the end of its life, that the thermostat in the oven ran fifty degrees low, and that the sun filled the living room with light in March once it was high enough in the sky to clear the mountain. And she knew exactly where on the five-acre property she would situate the RV park—on the other side of a stand of spruce, out of sight from the house but an easy walk away.

It would be the perfect complement to her bed-and-breakfast inn, great for family reunions or gatherings, where guests could choose to either stay in her comfortable rooms or bring their own RVs and still have facilities to get together for meals and fun.

She returned to the living room to help Rory find the movie she wanted. She could do this. Rory was slowly getting better, and eventually she would revert to her bright cheerful self despite this temporary setback.

And soon, Ursula would have the land she needed. The realtor was an aggravation, but on the bright side, his presence meant she was one step closer to putting her expansion plan into action. And Ursula always tried to look on the bright side.

"GOOD GIRL. You ran off the evil intruders, didn't you?" Mac rubbed behind the dog's rosebud ears. She wiggled in delight. "We don't want a bunch of nosy people poking around here, do we? No we don't." He'd been a little surprised at the dog's performance. She wasn't usually so aggressive. She must have found something sinister about the two skiers, which was odd since one of them was a child. Not that people were above using children in their schemes. He'd had photographers try the "my kid lost a baseball in your yard" trick more than once.

The whole point of this impromptu move to Alaska was to get away from people. Especially some members of the tabloid press. Bunch of vampires, feeding on sensationalism without giving a thought to the pain they inflicted with their questions. Even if he'd wanted to feed their appetite for new information, there was no more to give. The police and the private investigator he'd hired had hit a dead end, leaving nothing but questions and conjecture.

The dog pushed her head harder against his leg, letting him know he hadn't done nearly enough to reward her for her stalwart defense of their new home. He bent over and tickled that itchy spot under her chin. If it weren't for her, he didn't know if he would have survived the last couple of months. She'd been his constant companion, even on the long drive up the Alaska Highway, curled into a ball in the back seat amid the moving boxes.

He glanced toward the car, and the dog took the opportunity to make a quick swipe across his nose with her tongue. When he jerked his head back, she opened her mouth in a doggie grin. He swore she laughed at him sometimes. Hers was the only laughter in his life right now. He patted her rump and lifted the last box from the car.

Mac closed the liftgate with his free hand, crossed the porch and stomped the snow off his boots before stepping into the house. He added the box to the stack half filling the living room and let his gaze drift around the room.

A plaid recliner, an orange vinyl couch and a coffee table made from a crosscut log and moose antlers huddled up to a woodstove. Across a shaggy gold rug, an ancient console television the size of a washing machine jutted into the room. Bookshelves lined the wall behind it, a row of *National Geographic* magazines taking up one entire shelf. Everything in this room was almost as old as he was. But it was functional, and that was all he cared about right now.

Might as well unpack. He lifted a heavy box, set it on the coffee table and pulled his grandpa's knife from his pocket. After slitting the packing tape, he opened the box to reveal a stack of books, all identical. The cover featured the silhouette of an armed man crouching. Blood-red letters formed the title.

A knot tightened in his stomach. He closed the box and set it on the floor of the coat closet near the front door. A swift kick shoved it into the back corner. He trudged across the room and sank into the recliner, letting his head sink into his hands. Senseless evil. It was all too real.

The dog whined and pushed until her front half was on his lap. She nuzzled his face just as she had so many times before. How could he, of all people, have missed the signs? He should have seen it coming, should have done something to stop it. But he didn't, and she was gone. He screwed his eyes shut, willing himself into control. A single tear escaped, but the dog's tongue erased the evidence. After a moment's struggle, he was able to breathe again.

Why would he think moving would make a difference? He was old enough to know better. You couldn't run away from yourself.

URSULA SPRINKLED A little more flour on the countertop and returned to pummeling a lump of bread dough. She had a bread machine, but after yesterday's aggravation, she had an urge to knead it the old-fashioned way. At least the dough cooperated, yielding a smooth-textured pillow under her hands.

A knock sounded at the door she kept closed between the kitchen and dining room to discourage guests from bumbling in and upsetting her cooking routine. She reached for a towel, but before she could wipe her hands, the door opened and Marge, her neighbor and proprietor of the Caribou B&B on the other side of Betty's place, popped her head in. "Busy?"

"Hi. Just finishing up. Come sit, and I'll make coffee."

"I'll do it." Marge reached into the cabinet for the canister. Ursula oiled a bowl and dropped the dough inside, setting it on the stove to rise. She washed her hands and pulled a pitcher of cream from the refrigerator while Marge poured them each a cup of coffee. Marge let herself through the divider gate Ursula had set up to keep the cat out of the kitchen and plopped down on the window seat beside him. He opened one eye and regarded her briefly before returning to his nap.

Marge grinned. "I thought the cat was temporary."

"He was supposed to be, but I put up a notice on the library bulletin board and nobody's breaking down the door to adopt him." Ursula settled into a chair across the table from her.

"I could have told you nobody would want an old tomcat with a missing ear and half a tail. At least he looks like a good mouser."

Ursula sniffed. "I wouldn't know. The Forget-me-not doesn't have mice. But Rory likes him."

"Rory likes every animal, the uglier the better." Marge chuckled, but then her face sobered. "Is she doing any better?"

"I thought so. But her teacher called me in for a meeting this week. Rory's distracted, doodling instead of listening."

Ursula sighed. "It's almost like I'm pushing a boulder up the hill and every time I get anywhere, it rolls down again."

"Well, I think you're a saint for taking her in."

"I'm not a saint. I've loved that little girl from the minute she was born. Coby and Kendall were so happy."

"I know. You've told me the story. But her own grand-parents–"

"When Rory was tiny and I was helping out, Kendall told me a little about her parents and the way she was raised. From what she said, it's a good thing they're not around Rory. After losing her mom and dad, the last thing Rory needs is to be stuck with people like that. She needs to be-long. And she belongs with me."

Marge nodded and sipped her coffee. After a moment, she looked up. "Oh, I almost forgot what I came to tell you. Did you hear the news about Betty's place?"

"I haven't heard anything, but I saw the Mercedes parked out front, so I guess Betty's granddaughter is finally put-ting it up for sale. The real estate agent was standing on the porch, but I couldn't get his attention."

Marge's lips curved into her *I know something you don't know* smile. "That's not an agent. That's the new owner."

"What?" Ursula set down the creamer without adding any to her coffee. "But it wasn't even on the market. Are you sure?"

"That's what I heard. From Penny."

Shoot. If Penny said so, it was a done deal. Married to the only attorney in town and heading up the tourist infor-mation center, Penny knew everything happening in and around Seward. And since she and Marge had been best friends since kindergarten, Marge knew most of it. Ursula tapped her nail against her coffee cup. "After Betty's fu-neral, I told her granddaughter I was interested in the prop-erty once she was ready to sell."

"Maybe he offered her more."

"I never got the chance to make an offer."

Marge shrugged. "I don't know what to tell you."

Ursula added cream to her cup and stirred. "So who's the new neighbor?" Based on his behavior, not someone interested in making friends. A loner? Perhaps he'd decide a cabin situated between two bed-and-breakfast inns wasn't remote enough. "Maybe he'd be interested in a quick resale."

Marge leaned closer. "Penny's being mysterious. She knows, but she won't tell me the owner's name. She says I'd recognize it if I heard it." She dropped her voice to a stage whisper. "What if it's a movie star?"

Ursula snorted. "What would a movie star want with Betty's old cabin? She didn't even have cable."

"Well, he could get it installed. Besides, he probably wants it as a remote getaway, to recharge after filming a movie. They must get tired of always being on."

"If a movie star wanted an Alaskan getaway, he'd buy a luxury fishing lodge on the Kenai, not a rundown cabin along the Seward highway."

"Who knows what they'd do? He didn't look familiar to you?"

"No. Of course, I only saw him from a distance and he was wearing a coat."

"Not that you'd recognize him anyway. You hardly ever watch movies that aren't animated. You've probably had famous actors staying with you and never even known."

"If I did, they didn't let on. But seriously, I doubt Betty's granddaughter rubs elbows with actors. Doesn't she live in Kansas?"

"Wichita. You're probably right." Marge sighed, but then her face brightened. "Although, if a celebrity from California wanted to stay under the radar, buying a cabin in Alaska from someone in Kansas would be a great way to throw the paparazzi off the track."

Ursula laughed. "I can't argue with your logic. So how

long do you think it will take your movie star to get tired of the cold and dark, and sell me the property?"

"If he's used to California winters, he'll have cabin fever in no time."

"I can only hope. In the meantime, I need to talk him into opening the gate to the ski trails."

"He blocked off the trails?" Marge's face grew serious. "But Betty and her husband let that trail cut through their property probably forty years ago. Don't you have some sort of legal access?"

"I don't know. It never came up when Betty was alive. I'm not sure it was ever set down as an official right-of-way."

Marge sipped her coffee and considered. "You'll still chip in to maintain the trails, won't you?"

"Of course. I promised I would, and it's not your fault if he cuts off my access."

"That's good, because I didn't budget for your share of the grooming." Marge paused. "Your guests can park at the Caribou and ski from there if they want."

"Thank you." It wasn't ideal. Marge might be a friend but she was also a competitor. Ursula didn't want her guests wondering why they should patronize the Forget-me-not and drive or hike half a mile down the road to access the ski trails at the Caribou B&B when they could just stay there instead. But it was nice of Marge to offer. "Let's hope it's not necessary. Tomorrow, I'll drop by and explain about the ski trail access. I'm sure he'll be reasonable."

"What if he isn't?"

"He will be. I'll take cinnamon rolls and welcome him to the neighborhood. Movie star or not, I'm sure he'll want to get along with his neighbors."

Marge didn't look convinced. "Well if you figure out who he is, get his autograph for me."

"We'll see." Ursula had no intention of bothering their new neighbor with autograph requests. "If he seems busy,

I'll just leave the food, mention the ski trails and hint that if he ever decides to sell, I'd be interested."

"You really think this RV park thing is a good idea?"

"Yes, I do. In order to compete with the new resort they're building in Seward, I need to offer something they can't. It will be good for the Caribou, too, since you're next door. This way groups can vacation together even if they don't all have RVs."

"We can always lower our room rates. The resort will probably charge a pretty penny."

Easy for Marge to say. She and her husband inherited their B&B from his grandparents years ago. They didn't have a mortgage to consider. "I need to make at least enough to cover Sam's loan payments and ongoing expenses."

"There is that. You wouldn't want to drag down Sam's finances. Especially since they have a new baby."

"Exactly. And if Sam sold the inn, I'd have to move back to Anchorage. I don't want Rory to have to change schools again, when she's just starting to make friends. Let's just hope our mysterious neighbor is open to possibilities when I stop by tomorrow with the rolls."

Marge adjusted the position of her coffee cup. "I hope he's not gluten free. Most of those actors are, you know. He's probably on some weird acorn and kiwi fruit diet or something."

Ursula shrugged. "I guess I'll find out tomorrow."

CHAPTER TWO

URSULA PULLED TWO pans of cinnamon rolls from the oven and set them on a wire rack to cool. The divine aromas of yeast, butter and spice filled the kitchen. She eyed the pans doubtfully. Everybody liked bread, right? Occasionally she had a guest with special dietary needs, but the odds of her new neighbor not appreciating a plate of homemade cinnamon rolls had to be low. And even if Marge was right and he was an actor from Hollywood who didn't eat gluten, he'd surely appreciate the gesture.

Movie star. She shook her head and smiled. Why would someone famous want to buy Betty's cabin? It only had two bedrooms. The kitchen hadn't been remodeled since the forties. Neither had the bathroom. The guy probably asked Penny's husband, Fred, not to spread his name around to avoid a pesky relative or debt collector.

Could someone really do that? Keep your name a secret? Property tax records were public, weren't they? Ursula opened her laptop and did a search for Kenai Peninsula Borough's tax records. She located the property on the map and clicked on it, but the record hadn't been updated from Betty's name. Ah, but she had a source. The assistant at the tax assessor's office had stayed in the inn for several weeks while she house-hunted.

Ursula picked up the phone and called. After exchanging pleasantries, she got down to business. "So, Michelle, I seem to have a new neighbor. I was trying to look up his name on the tax records, but they haven't been updated yet."

"Why don't you just ask him?"

"Well, I was hoping to do some background research first, to—"

"Sorry. Can you hang on a minute? Someone's in my office." Michelle didn't bother to put the phone on hold, and Ursula tapped her fingers while listening to a long conversation about the probable whereabouts of someone's stapler before she came back on the line. "I'm sorry. What was your question?"

"I just wondered if you'd received the paperwork on the new owner of the property next door." Ursula read the parcel number from the form.

"Let me look." Papers crackled. "Here it is. It's an LLC."

"What's that?"

"A limited liability company. This one's called R&A Holdings."

"Does that mean he's running a business there?"

"Not necessarily. Some people hold their assets in LLCs for other reasons."

"Doesn't he have to give a name or something?"

"Not on my records. Sorry. Guess you'll just have to do it the old-fashioned way and introduce yourself."

"I guess so. Thanks anyway."

"You're welcome. Stop by next time you're in town and we'll grab coffee."

"I will. Talk with you soon." Ursula hung up the phone and stared at the wall. This could be good news. Her new neighbor was a limited liability company, not a movie star. Probably a flipper, with plans for a quick remodel and resell. If so, this could work out just fine. He would probably be thrilled to make a small profit with no work, and she could get started on the RV park. Win-win. First thing tomorrow, she would pay him a visit.

MAC'S EYES FLEW OPEN, his dream shattering into fragments. Thanks to the heavy curtains covering the small bedroom window, only the charging light from his cell phone broke up the darkness. After a long day of unpacking and moving boxes, he'd fallen asleep almost immediately, but it wasn't long before the dreams came. He could never remember them, just bits and pieces. A scream of pain. Crimson drops of blood on a white sweater. His own heart pounding and an overwhelming sense of powerlessness.

It was in the darkness he felt the full weight of his mistakes. He'd failed her. Failed to understand the magnitude of danger she was in. Ignored his own instincts. Told himself she was old enough to make her own decisions. Maybe she was, but he should have tried harder to guide her, should have been more supportive. Should have made it clear she could count on him if things went wrong, and there would be no *I told you so*. Should have said *I love you* more often. Because now it was too late.

Eventually, he gave up trying to sleep and moved into the living room. The dog lifted her head from her bed beside the woodstove and thumped her tail against the floor. Mac added a couple of logs to the stove and stoked the fire. He selected a branch from the woodbin, picked up his grandfather's pocketknife from the table and settled into a chair beside the stove. A warm muzzle rested on his foot.

The wood stripped away in long curls, landing in the kindling box at his feet. Once the branch was smooth, he began to whittle, a notch here, an arch there. As he worked, the terrors of his dream worked their way out of his head and into the wood. As the last log in the stove fell into a pile of embers, Mac laid the carving aside and yawned. Maybe now he could sleep.

ONCE SHE'D FED her guests and cleaned up the breakfast dishes the next morning, Ursula arranged the extra cinnamon rolls on a pretty blue-and-white plate she'd picked up at the church rummage sale. She wrapped them carefully and glanced at the clock on the stove. Was nine too early to drop in on a neighbor? It shouldn't be. And she didn't want to wait too late, for fear he'd be out shopping for building supplies.

Today, instead of taking the ski trail, she walked the quarter mile along the highway to his driveway, carrying the plate. A strip of duct tape covered Betty's name on the dented mailbox. An Anchorage newspaper waited in the tube below. Ursula tucked the newspaper under her arm and followed the drive to another gate that Betty had never used. Ursula gave a soft testing whistle, but no guard dog appeared to challenge her, so she unlatched the gate and slipped inside, closing it behind her.

The sun never made it over the mountain this time of year, but the sky was growing brighter and she didn't need her flashlight to make her way along the driveway toward the porch. No lights shown in the cabin windows; hopefully she wasn't wasting her time. An unfamiliar pedestal table rested beside Betty's old Adirondack chair on the porch.

The steps crackled in the cold as she climbed them. Frantic barking erupted inside the house, punctuated by thumps of a canine body slamming repeatedly against the inside of the door Ursula hoped was securely latched. No need to knock, anyway. She held the plate in front of her and practiced her most welcoming smile as she waited for her new neighbor to call off the dog and answer the door.

And she waited. Eventually, the dog gave up on breaking the door down. Instead the heavy curtains in the window pushed upward, and a black-and-white head appeared. The dog tilted its head, watching her. Obviously, the dog's owner wasn't home.

Ursula set the rolls on the table, pulled a notepad and pencil from her pocket and jotted a short message of welcome and her phone number. As she bent to tuck it under the plate, she noticed a whimsical carving around the table pedestal of a chubby puppy chasing its tail. She smiled. Maybe her new neighbor wasn't the curmudgeon he seemed.

She headed home at a brisk walk, breathing in the crisp air. Behind the fence, spruce trees sagged under their load of snow. It was a lovely winter day, with not a breath of wind. The porch table reassured her. After all, how bad could a man be who loved puppies? He'd find the rolls and call her, and they could get this all straightened out. Everything was going to be fine.

MAC WATCHED HER go from behind the curtain. Figured. He'd driven thirty-nine hundred miles to get away from people, only to have some strange woman pounding on his door three hours after he'd finally managed to fall asleep. Well, she didn't literally pound, but she might as well have considering the barking fit her visit inspired.

To add insult to injury, the bounce in her step as she strolled along his driveway seemed to indicate she was enjoying her morning, in contrast with his pounding head and gritty eyelids. A cold nose pressed into his hand. He turned to greet the dog. "I see you've been hard at work already."

The pit bull wagged her tail and jerked her head toward the empty bowl in the kitchen. He took the hint and filled it with kibble before starting a pot of coffee for himself. While it brewed, he dropped to the rug for his usual round of push-ups. He used to go out for a run every morning before breakfast, too, but the paparazzi put a stop to that.

Once he'd completed fifty push-ups, he got up and pulled the curtain aside to make sure the woman was gone and had latched the gate behind her. The dog scratched on the door, so Mac opened it to let her out and stepped onto the porch, shivering in the cold. A newspaper and plate of rolls sat on the table—cinnamon pecan, according to the cutesy label shaped like a daisy. Underneath, he found a note asking him to call her.

Just what he needed—some nosy neighbor trying to woo him with homemade treats. He'd sworn the local lawyer to secrecy, but somehow word must have gotten out he was here. Well, she wasn't the first woman to make a play for him since he'd become successful, and like all the others, she was doomed to disappointment. He whistled for the dog and returned to the cabin, dropping the note into the trashcan under the sink. He started to pitch the rolls in after it, but his stomach growled, reminding him he'd not yet had a chance to buy milk for his raisin bran.

No sense letting good food go to waste. He picked up a roll and bit into it. Cream cheese frosting melted in his mouth. He chewed, savoring the blending of fresh bread and sweet cinnamon. Quite possibly the best cinnamon rolls he'd tasted since he was a boy, visiting his grandmother's house. He took another bite. These might in fact edge Gram's off the middle podium. Shame he wouldn't be getting any more once she figured out he was a lost cause.

He poured a cup of coffee and sank into a chair at the scrubbed pine table, pushing aside a pile of mail he'd found in a box when he unpacked. A return address caught his eye. A bill from the private investigator. Chandler had sounded almost apologetic about billing him for the hours spent following leads that went nowhere, but Mac didn't care how much it cost, how many possibilities turned out to be dead ends. They couldn't quit. Not until they found Andi's killer. Eventually, they would. People didn't just vanish.

He set the bill aside to pay later and slid the newspaper from its sleeve. A subscription offer fluttered to the ground. He opened the paper and took another bite of cinnamon roll. And another. There was something restful about perusing local politics and events that didn't concern him. By noon, he'd written a check to the investigator, unpacked all the boxes marked kitchen, called to subscribe to the Anchorage newspaper and wiped out the entire plate of cinnamon rolls. He washed the plate and set it in the drainer to dry. His family used to eat off blue-and-white plates not too different from this one when he was a boy.

His job was to wash dishes, and his mother would dry. She'd wipe each plate, stack them in the cupboard and sigh because there were only seven. He'd heard the story a dozen times. How her cousin had taken home a plate of leftovers one evening and moved off to California without ever returning the plate, leaving her with an incomplete set. He was never clear exactly why Mom couldn't have asked for the plate back or bought another one, but she didn't. Instead, she mourned the loss nightly.

He eyed the plate in his drainer. According to the note, the woman lived in the big house on the next property over. He needed to drive into Seward that afternoon to buy groceries. He could easily drop off the plate on the way. But his polite gesture could be misconstrued as a friendly overture, which posed a danger to his privacy. If he ignored her, she'd leave him alone.

And that was really Mac's only goal in moving to Alaska. To be left alone.

URSULA HAD WAITED three long days, but the call never came. How was she going to convince the guy it was in his best interest to sell if he wouldn't talk to her? Her cinnamon rolls seldom failed, but maybe he really didn't eat gluten. Time to pull out the big guns.

She took a jar of smoked sockeye she'd canned last summer from her pantry. Chopped green onions, lemon juice, cream cheese and a few secret seasonings turned it into her special salmon dip. She filled a crock and tucked it into her backpack, along with a bag of moose jerky, and strapped on her snowshoes.

A fresh snow had obliterated the tracks on the ski trail since their aborted outing a few days ago. No doubt the groomer had laid fresh tracks on the main trails but he could no longer reach her property with the gates closed. Getting them opened should be her first order of business.

She reached the gate, relieved to see the SUV parked between the house and the garage. Good. He was home. Hopefully, the dog was in the house with him, but if not, she had a plan B. Ursula rattled the gate and waited.

Sure enough, a black-and-white blur bounded toward her, almost disappearing into the deep snow between leaps. The dog must be in great physical condition to be able to bark and run at the same time.

The pit bull reached the gate and bounced into the air, almost head high, barking. Ursula wasn't sure this was going to work, but she had to try. She laid down her ski poles to take off her backpack. The barking stopped. She looked up. The pit bull still watched her. Ursula reached toward the poles, and a low rumble emanated from the dog's throat.

Aha. "Bad experience with a stick? Poor puppy." Ursula left the poles lying on the ground and spoke in a gentle voice. "Don't worry, sweetie. I'd never hurt you." She unzipped her backpack, pulled out a stick of jerky and tore off a bite-size piece. "Would you like a treat?" She tossed the bite to the dog.

The dog jumped into the air to catch the tidbit. Tail wagging, it waited expectantly. Ursula smiled. "That's a good boy." She checked. "Girl, I mean. Want some more?"

The pit bull cocked her head. Ursula tossed another bite. The dog came closer and stuck her nose between the gate and the fence, wagging her tail harder. Ursula handed her another bit of jerky. The dog licked her hand and gently took the meat from her. "All that bluster is just for show, isn't it? You're really a marshmallow."

The dog wagged in agreement. Leaving the ski poles behind, Ursula pulled the chain up over the post to unlatch the gate and slipped inside. She fastened the gate behind her and gave her new best friend another bite of jerky. Together, they crossed the meadow between the gate and the house, Ursula on snowshoes and the dog crashing through the snow beside her.

Before she reached the house, Ursula noticed a light in the window of the oversize detached garage. When Betty's husband built it forty years ago, he'd included a woodworking space as well as room for cars. The light was coming from the workshop area.

The dog headed straight for the workshop and squeezed through a new dog hatch cut into the outer door. The door must not have been completely latched, because it opened when the dog pushed against it. Ursula removed her snowshoes, pulled the crock of salmon dip from her backpack and followed the dog inside.

The workshop featured an arctic entry, a small alcove inside the door leading to another door off to one side to keep the wind from blowing in every time someone opened the door. The inside door stood open, and the dog padded on into the main room. A bench against the wall held a box full of carved wood. Curious, Ursula picked up one of the pieces.

The polished wood retained the natural curves of a tree limb, but a face peered out from the wood grain—an inquisitive gnome with shaggy eyebrows and a long beard. The piece gave the impression that the face had been in the wood all along and just needed a skilled craftsman to let it out. A quick glance showed maybe a dozen similar carvings, each face unique. Enchanting.

The sound of the dog's toenails clicking across the concrete floor of the shop reminded Ursula why she was there.

She returned the carving to the box and stepped inside, inhaling the piney scent of fresh sawdust. At the far end, a man perched on a stool. His profile revealed a strong brow and a determined jawline. A few gray threads wove through thick brown hair that could have used a trim. His full concentration was on the blade he was using to remove chips of wood from the chunk in his hand. The dog, lying on a cushion at his feet, wagged her tail when Ursula appeared. The man looked up and seemed anything but pleased to see her there.

Before he could speak, Ursula jumped in, determined to be friendly. "Forgive me for just walking in. The door was open."

He didn't smile back. "The sign says No Trespassing."

"Oh, but I'm your next-door neighbor." She took a step closer. "Ursula."

He remained where he was. "How did you get past the dog?"

"We're friends. Aren't we, sweetie?" The dog trotted over to her and nudged her hand. Ursula smiled. "She likes my jerky."

The man let out a huff of exasperation. "What do you want?"

Ursula licked her lip. "I came to see you. That is, I brought you some salmon dip. It's homemade, from Copper River sockeye I smoked myself." She held out the crock. "I hope you found the cinnamon rolls I left a few days ago."

He made no move to accept her offering. "No, thanks. I'm busy right now, so—"

Okay, the friendly approach wasn't working. Time to get down to business. She straightened to her full height. "This won't take but a minute. What are your plans for the house? Are you fixing it up to sell? Because if you are, I'm interested in buying."

"No. I have no plans to sell."

"What if I'm willing to pay, say, ten percent more than you did? That's a decent rate of return for a quick investment."

"Not interested." He returned his attention to the carving in his hand and flicked away a stray curl of wood.

For the first time, Ursula noticed more of the carved faces lying on the workbench beside him. Unlike the ones she'd seen in the box, these seemed tortured, in pain. The half-finished carving in his hand appeared to be screaming. She looked away. "If you do decide to sell, will you let me know before you list the property?"

"Yes. Fine. If I ever do, you'll be at the top of my list. What was your name again?"

"Ursula. Ursula Anderson."

"All right, Ms. Anderson. But don't hold your breath." He pushed his knife blade against the wood.

"Your carvings are amazing. I saw the ones on the bench in the entryway. Is there a name for that sort of sculpture?"

He concentrated on a cut he was making before he replied. "People call them wood spirits."

"Wood spirits. That's perfect." She stepped closer and touched one lying on the workbench that appeared to be weeping. The wood was cool and smooth under her finger. "How do you decide what sort of face to carve?"

He gathered up the carvings and set them out of her reach. "I don't have time for a discussion right now. If you'll excuse me…"

She held up a hand. "Just one more little thing and then I'll let you be. I don't know if you know, but I run a bed-and-breakfast inn. The main skiing and hiking trails are just behind and to the east of your property, and there's always been a right-of-way through your back corner connecting the ski trails to the trail across my property."

"No. I don't know anything about that."

"Well, there is. Your gates are cutting my guests off from the trails. I'd much appreciate it if you'd open them."

He stared at her as if she'd suggested he cut off his foot. "You want me to let a bunch of strangers traipse across my property?"

"Only that little corner in the back."

"That rather defeats the purpose behind private property, don't you think?"

"Not at all. I'll make sure my guests understand they are to stay on the trails and not disturb you in any way."

He stood, towering over her by a good six inches. "But I am disturbed. You're disturbing me right now. One of the main selling points of this property was that it's completely fenced and private."

"Betty lived here for fifty years. She always kept the trail open, and never had a problem."

"If you haven't noticed, I'm not Betty."

"I've noticed." Ursula couldn't keep the frustration from her voice.

"Good. I'm glad we understand one another. Now, Ms. Anderson—"

"Ursula, please." One more last-ditch attempt at friendly conversation.

"Ursula. Could you please take your salmon and your jerky and any other bribes you might have in that backpack of yours, and let yourself outside the fence before I have you arrested for trespassing?"

She bit back a retort. "I'll go. But if you change your mind—"

"I won't."

"If you do, I'm the Forget-me-not Inn. You can get my number or email from the website."

"Goodbye."

Ursula gave the dog one final pat and left, shutting the door with more force than was necessary. She strapped on her snowshoes and returned the salmon dip to her pack. Looked like her guests arriving that evening would be getting a little extra treat to help make up for not being able to ski from the inn to the trails. At least she hoped it did, because it didn't look like she was getting those gates opened anytime soon.

She wasn't giving up. There had to be some way to convince the old grouch that a few skiers in the back corner of his lot weren't going to kill him. She'd even have offered to pay an access fee if he'd let her talk. What was his problem anyway? He may have been a natural-born people hater, but there was more to his story than that. The agony in those wooden faces told her so.

"SOME GUARD DOG you are," Mac growled. The pit bull hung her head and crept closer to him, liquid brown eyes begging for forgiveness. Mac laughed. "You don't even know what you did, do you?"

She wagged her tail and licked his hand. The dog might put on a good show of ferocity for people ringing the doorbell or walking by, but she'd never actually met a person she disliked. And she seemed especially fond of this Ursula person. Of course, she was easily bribed.

Pushy woman. And yet Mac couldn't help feeling a twinge of guilt for the way he'd treated her. She wasn't a reporter, using him as a way to sell papers. She just wanted access to the ski trails. She wasn't going to get it—Mac had no intention of allowing strangers on his land and he needed the fence for the dog—but it wasn't an unreasonable request. And she had dropped off those amazing cinnamon rolls.

His mouth watered, thinking of them. She probably made an excellent salmon dip, too. It was bound to be better than the bologna sandwich he was probably going to have instead. He loved Copper River salmon. One of his favorite restaurants in Tulsa always had a special promotion in May when the first Copper River salmon arrived. Maybe the neighborly thing to do would have been to accept the food and politely refuse her request.

Listen to him—as susceptible as the dog about food bribes. Ursula seemed like a nice woman. She had the sort of face he liked, intelligent eyes with crinkles at the corners as if she smiled often, a faint sprinkling of freckles across her nose.

But even if Mac had wanted company, he was in no shape to be around other people. He was better off alone. And everyone else was better off away from him.

CHAPTER THREE

MAC ALMOST MADE it through the night, but early in the morning, the dreams came. He sat upright in bed, waiting for his heart rate to return to normal. No more sleep tonight. He fed the dog, did his push-ups and started a pot of coffee. The blue-and-white plate still resting in the drainer scratched at his conscience. He was well within his rights to refuse to sell his property or allow strangers to cut through it, but that plate bugged him. He could almost hear his mother sighing.

You'd think one more feather on top of the load of guilt he was already carrying wouldn't be noticeable, but it was. Fine. The rooster-shaped clock on the kitchen wall read five twenty-five. He could drop off the plate now and eat his breakfast with a clear conscience. Relatively.

After dressing and bundling up in a down parka and wool hat, he grabbed the plate and set off. The dog scratched on the window and barked. He hesitated. This errand required stealth. "If I take you, will you be good?"

Her body wiggled in agreement. He returned to rub some balm on her paws. He'd picked it up in Whitehorse when he'd noticed her feet seemed sore after playing in the snow, and it seemed to work well. He clipped a leash to her collar and set off once again. Surprisingly, he didn't need his flashlight. Once his eyes adjusted, the moon reflecting off the snow provided plenty of light for him to make his way to the road and along to the Forget-me-not Inn sign.

He followed the drive, flicking on his light when he

reached the trees. After a few minutes, he came to a clearing. Moonlight illuminated a cedar building crowned with steep gables. A bench, small tables and several rocking chairs were scattered across the wide front porch. A snow shovel leaned against the wall.

He'd just leave the plate on the bench beside the door. He commanded the dog to sit-stay and started for the porch. As he reached the second stair, the front door opened and Ursula stepped outside, shaking dust and gravel off a rug and all over him.

"Oh my goodness, I'm sorry." Her voice was apologetic, but the corners of her mouth twitched.

"No problem." Mac dusted his coat with his free hand. "I was just returning your plate."

"That's thoughtful, but you didn't have to do that." She smiled, and it was like a sudden flash of sunshine, warming him. Her silver-shot hair fluttered in the breeze. "Come on in."

"No, I need to go." He handed her the plate. "But I did want to thank you for the cinnamon rolls. They were delicious."

"I'm glad you enjoyed them." She accepted the plate. "Seriously, come in for a cup of coffee. I just took a batch of blueberry muffins from the oven."

"I don't think—"

A squirrel scurried onto the porch and ran right up Ursula's leg and body to sit on her shoulder. Ursula absentmindedly pulled an almond from the pocket of her jeans and handed it to the squirrel, who accepted it and stuffed it into his cheek. "What if I promise not to mention gates or property?"

Mac stared. "That's a squirrel."

"What? Oh, yes. This is Frankie."

"You have a pet squirrel?"

She chuckled. "He's not a pet, exactly. Frankie was orphaned, and I bottle-fed him until he was old enough to forage on his own. He stops by often to say hello."

The dog had been trying her best to stay as instructed, but seeing the squirrel was too much. She bounded onto the porch. The squirrel took a flying leap to the railing, dashed up a pillar and jumped onto a tree limb. Within seconds, it was twenty feet into the tree. The dog gave a final bark, came back to Ursula and nudged her hand in greeting and then ran through the open door into the inn.

Before Mac could apologize, Ursula laughed. "Well, what are you waiting for?"

He followed her inside. She hung his coat on a hook and led them through an expansive dining and living room into a kitchen, which somehow managed to look functional and cozy at the same time. A collection of African violets bloomed in shades of purple and pink on a shelf under a grow light. Ursula opened a gate, which separated the kitchen from a small dining area. A cat, curled up on a chair cushion, took one look at the dog and took refuge on top of a corner cabinet.

The dog stiffened, but Ursula made an uh-uh noise and shook her head. She pulled a dog biscuit from a cookie jar on a shelf by the back door and soon had the pit bull lying peacefully on a rug. She nodded at the cat. "That's Van Gogh."

"Van Gogh?"

"He's missing an ear."

Mac chuckled, and soon found himself sitting at a wooden table sipping an excellent cup of coffee. Fruit-scented steam rose from the muffin on the plate in front of him. Considering he'd only intended to drop off the plate, he wasn't sure how he'd wound up here, but maybe it wasn't too surprising that a woman who could pacify pit bulls and tame squirrels could maneuver him wherever she wanted him. She slipped into the chair across the table. "So, as I said, I'm Ursula Anderson."

"Mac. Macleod."

"Nice to meet you, Mac. And where do you hail from?"

"Oklahoma." He bit into the muffin. Jammed with sweet blueberries, with a hint of something else, maybe orange? The woman had a way with baked goods.

She raised a delicately arched eyebrow. "I'm surprised. I knew cowboys from Oklahoma when I was growing up in Wyoming. You don't have much of an accent."

"I've lost it over time, living in Tulsa. People from all over the country live there."

"So what brings you to Alaska?"

Mac paused before his next bite. Here was an opportunity to make his point. He met her eyes. "Solitude."

She nodded. "I got that. I apologize for bursting in yesterday, and realize I was overstepping. I'll try not to bother you again." She nodded at the plate she'd set on the table. "Thanks again for returning that."

He shrugged. "My mother would turn over in her grave if I didn't."

"I think I'd have liked your mother." Ursula's eyes crinkled in the corners. "What would she say if she knew you'd threatened to have me arrested for trespassing?"

"I didn't exactly…" She gave him the same look his mother used to when he was trying to talk his way out of trouble. He had to laugh. "Okay, I admit it. She'd have given me an earful."

Ursula laughed. "Now you sound like an Okie cowboy."

"I suppose that's because I am one. Or I was, until I was seventeen and we moved to town."

"Did you raise cattle?"

"Yes, Herefords." At least until that last year of drought, when Dad had to sell off the herd, bit by bit. And then they lost the bull. But Mac didn't want to think about that. "Were your family ranchers in Wyoming?" he asked quickly.

She met his eyes and paused, just long enough for him to wonder if she'd read his mind, before she gave a gentle smile. "My father was a mailman and my mother taught school. After I graduated from high school, I worked in the office for an oil company, where I happened to fall in love with a certain roughneck. Tommy believed Alaska was the land of opportunity. So we got married, packed up a truck and headed to Alaska."

"And was it? The land of opportunity?"

"It was for us. We had a wonderful life here." She rubbed the bare ring finger of her left hand. "I scattered Tommy's ashes on Flattop. That's what he wanted." Suddenly she smiled. "Look at that." She inclined her head toward the dog.

Mac turned. The cat had come down from the cabinet and was gingerly touching noses with the pit bull, who thumped her tail against the floor. After a moment, the cat rubbed against the big dog's face and then curled up against her. The dog seemed fine with that.

Ursula chuckled. "That's quite a ferocious beast you have there. What's her name?" She took a sip from her cup.

Mac glanced down at his plate. "Blossom."

Ursula snorted and almost choked on her coffee. Once she quit coughing, she grinned at him. "Blossom? Really?"

Mac shook his head. "I know. My daughter adopted her as a puppy. Andi happened to be volunteering at the shelter when they brought in this half-grown pit bull. She'd been starved and beaten, but Andi was convinced with love and care she'd blossom into a great dog. She was right."

"She certainly was. Blossom is the perfect name for her. Where's your daughter now?"

Mac kept his gaze on the dog. "She's dead." It was the first time he'd ever said it aloud to someone who didn't know the story. His daughter was gone. Forever.

Ursula laid her hand over his and squeezed. "I'm so sorry."

Mac nodded, unable to speak. That familiar wave of grief washed over him, but in a way it was a relief, to acknowledge what he'd lost. For some reason it was easier with Ursula, maybe because she didn't know him, didn't know the story, had no preconceived ideas. She didn't rush in with some platitude or awkwardly edge away as though grief was contagious. She simply accepted what he told her.

Ursula looked over at Blossom, snoozing on the rug with a cat under her chin. "Your daughter must have been a gentle person, to raise such a gentle pit bull."

"She was." Mac swallowed the lump in his throat, remembering. "She was too gentle for her own good sometimes. Always saw the best in people, even when they didn't deserve it."

"If everyone could be like your daughter, the world would be a better place."

"Yes it would." If only there were no predators, no evil. But they were there, preying on the innocent, and it was her very goodness that had cost Andi her life. Her murderer had disappeared, but eventually they would find him and he'd go to prison for the rest of his sorry life. Mac would make sure of it.

But today—today he could talk about the daughter he loved. He told Ursula stories, about Andi as a girl, giving away her school supplies to other kids. About how she would make him chicken soup when he had a cold. About how she'd volunteered at the animal shelter, and done every walkathon and fund-raiser that came along. "When she was seventeen, she spent two weeks with a team in Peru, building a new dormitory for an orphanage."

"Wow. How did she learn about building?"

"We'd both done some weekend work building houses

locally. Andi was pretty handy with a nail gun. I was all set to go, too, but she wanted to do it without me."

"Brave girl. At seventeen, I'd never been more than a state away from Wyoming. Didn't her mother worry?"

Mac shook his head. "Her mother died when she was a baby. I worried. But Andi was fine."

"She sounds like a special person."

Mac sighed. "She was."

Ursula refilled his cup. Mac realized he'd monopolized the conversation but she didn't seem to mind. On the wall behind her, a calendar featured a picture of the inn. An emerald green mountain rose behind it. The setting was spectacular, summer or winter. He could see why people wanted to stay here. "How many rooms do you have in your inn?"

"Six. Besides my private quarters." She nodded toward the back door leading from the kitchen.

"You run it by yourself?"

"I have a housekeeper three times a week. I do the rest."

"Sounds like a big job."

"It is, but I love it. I've been running the inn for about six years now."

The back door opened and a blond girl about seven or eight peeked through the crack. Ursula smiled at her and held out her arms. The girl ran over and climbed into her lap.

Ursula stroked her hair from her forehead. "You're up early. Did we wake you?"

The girl gave a sleepy nod. An ache formed in Mac's chest. She didn't look much like his daughter. Andi had brown hair and eyes, while this girl was fair, but the way she cuddled against Ursula while watching him through her lashes brought back memories.

"Sorry, sweetie. Mac, I'd like you to meet my goddaughter, Aurora Houston. Rory, this is our new neighbor, Mr. Macleod."

"You can call me Mac."

The little girl watched him for a moment before her eyes opened wide. "You're the old grouch who blocked the ski trails."

"Rory, you shouldn't say–"

"But that's what you said. That the old grouch wouldn't open the gate and we have to go all the way over to Marge's to ski."

"No. I, uh…" Ursula's cheeks flushed a charming shade of pink. Who knew women still blushed? It was all Mac could do to keep a straight face. "That is, yes, I did say that but it was wrong. I was frustrated, but Mac has every right to decide how to manage his property, and I apologize to you both for what I said. Besides, he needs to keep the gates closed to keep the dog in." She pointed toward Blossom.

"A dog!" Rory scrambled off her lap and dropped onto the rug beside the dog and cat.

Mac had to smile. Andi would have had exactly the same reaction. "Her name is Blossom."

She stroked the dog's head, and Blossom thumped her tail. Rory looked up. "Look Ursula, she's really nice. She must have just been having a bad day when she saw us before."

"I think it was the ski poles. She's afraid of them."

"Oh, that's right." Mac had forgotten. "My housekeeper mentioned she always has to put the dog out before she sweeps because Blossom doesn't like the broom."

"Why doesn't she like poles?" Rory asked.

"I'm not sure," Mac responded, "but I suspect someone was mean to her when she was a puppy and might have hurt her with a stick. It's funny, because she doesn't seem to mind if I carry sticks and poles."

"That's because she knows she can trust you." Ursula smiled at him. "And I do apologize for calling you an old grouch."

She'd only spoken the truth, but she was obviously trying to set an example for her goddaughter. "Apology accepted."

Ursula glanced at the clock. "Oops, time flies. Rory, you need to get dressed for school while I get your breakfast ready."

"But I want to pet Blossom."

Mac stood. "It was nice to meet you, Rory. Blossom and I need to go, but maybe you can see her another time."

"Go on, sweetie." Ursula allowed her to give the dog one last hug before she shooed her through the door. Ursula turned back to Mac. "Thank you for returning the plate."

"No problem. Thanks for the muffins. And...everything."

"You're welcome. Stop by anytime, if the solitude gets to be too much for you."

"Thanks, but I'll be fine."

"Yes, you will be." Odd phrasing, but then he realized she wasn't just being polite. She acknowledged his loss and believed he would get through it. He wasn't nearly so sure, himself. He looked back just before he stepped out the door. She gave him one last smile. "Goodbye, Mac. Take care of yourself."

THE CELL PHONE RANG, again. Mac considered ignoring it, but Ronald would just keep calling. Persistence was a good trait in an agent, most of the time. "It's Mac."

"So you're still on the planet. I assume you made it to Alaska okay?"

"I did."

"Everything all right with the cabin?"

"It's fine."

"Good. Danielle gave me the address, and I arranged for them to install Wi-Fi."

"You what?"

"It's DSL. They're supposed to be there between ten and three today."

"You don't have to babysit me," Mac growled. He wasn't keen on working around an installer's schedule. He was running low on essentials like coffee and pickles and needed to run into Seward. "I could have picked up the modem myself next time I'm in Anchorage."

"But when would that be? I feel responsible, since I'm the one who mentioned if you wanted to get away, one of my clients had a cabin in Alaska she planned to sell. I didn't think you'd take me seriously."

"How can I take you seriously, when you put me at the mercy of some internet installer?"

"I need to be able to reach you out there in the wilderness."

"The cabin is only fifteen minutes from town, and only two hours from Anchorage. I have cell phone coverage, which you obviously know since you're talking to me."

"I just want to make sure you don't go dark. You might need to email me about royalty questions or something."

Mac didn't bother to point out he could email from his phone. They both knew it wasn't email Ronald was worried about; it was the manuscript due in a few months. Mac had already told him it wasn't going to happen. Ronald had mentioned the possibility of a deadline extension, hoping Mac would pull out of his funk, but Mac knew he couldn't write that book. Not after what happened to Andi. He wasn't sure he'd ever write again. But there was no use retreading that discussion now. Ronald would have to face facts eventually. "Fine. I'll get internet. Bye."

"With all that solitude, have you had a chance to—"

"Goodbye, Ronald." Mac ended the call. Pain in the butt. Still, Ronald was the closest thing Mac had to a friend these days. If it made him feel better, Mac would hang around and wait for the installer. Meanwhile, he'd make a list.

He found a pen in a kitchen drawer and pulled an envelope from the wastepaper basket. Milk, bread, coffee, pickles, musta—the pen gave up the ghost midword. Somewhere in this house were a handful of pens and pencils he'd thrown into a box. But which box? There were still at least a dozen stacked in the second bedroom.

He shrugged. Since he wasn't going anywhere until the internet guy showed up, he might as well finish unpacking. In the first box, he found T-shirts, underwear and socks. Good, because he was almost out of clean clothes and until he bought laundry detergent, he couldn't wash. Now if he could find a pen to add it to the list.

The next box held an assortment of items nested in newspaper. He unwrapped his favorite coffee cup and one of Blossom's chew toys and then a silver frame. He ran his finger over the smooth edge.

The photo was of Andi, the summer after her senior year of high school, bathing an elephant. He smiled. Andi had been fascinated by them since he read her a book about an elephant when she was about four. She used to insist on reading it almost every day. When she was in high school, he heard about a sanctuary where she could spend a weekend interacting with pachyderms, and knew he'd found the perfect graduation gift. When she opened the envelope, she'd squealed and given him a big hug. That was a good day.

They hadn't all been good. Somewhere in middle school, Andi seemed to go from sweet little girl to moody teenager overnight, and as a single dad, Mac was clueless on how to handle the drama. Maybe he'd had more rules than she'd have liked, but how could he not? He didn't want to see his little girl hurt. Even so, she managed to get that big heart of hers broken more than once before she left for college. Although tempted to put out a hit on the culprits, Mac only killed them off in his books. That showed a certain restraint, didn't it? He'd often wondered if the lack of a mother to talk to made all Andi's problems loom larger than life, or if it was just typical teenage angst.

Maybe it was his overprotective tendencies when Andi was a teenager that made her so insistent on her independence as an adult. Maybe if he'd been a little more relaxed, she would have confided in him, let him help her when she got into trouble. He set the photo on his nightstand.

The next item in the box was a plain brown envelope with Andi's name on it. Her personal items. Mac swallowed. These were the things she'd had on her when the police found her. Silver earrings, a watch and a charm bracelet.

The bracelet had been her mother's. Mac bought the silver chain with a jingle bell heart charm while he was on shore leave in Thailand and sent it to Carla, hoping it would make her smile. He never knew if it did. A year later, after she died, he found it in her jewelry box, beside her wedding ring.

When Andi was five, Mac had come across the bracelet again and decided to give it to his daughter. He'd added an elephant charm after she saw her first live elephants at the zoo, and many more charms over the years. Andi had loved that bracelet. She'd worn it every day. Mac set the envelope aside.

The next item he unwrapped turned out to be a clutch of pens and pencils in the lopsided mug Andi had made in pottery class and given him for Father's Day one year. He carried it into the kitchen and used one of the pens to finish his shopping list. He was flattening out the newspapers to add to the recycling bin when an opinion piece caught his eye.

The article questioned the ethics of releasing violent books and movies, and whether society as a whole became more violent when exposed to fictional violence. As an example, the columnist used a popular movie involving a serial killer, saying that although the main character was on the side of good, the serial killer was a complex and powerful character in his own right. Some moviegoers might identify with the villain more than the hero, which could encourage them to act upon their violent tendencies.

Mac read the entire article twice. Then he picked up the paper and ripped it in half. And ripped those pieces in half, again and again, until the newspaper page had been reduced to confetti at his feet. He hoped to God the person who wrote that article was wrong. Because the movie he'd mentioned was based on one of Mac's books.

URSULA DROPPED A birthday card for a friend in her mailbox and put up the flag before heading out to Anchorage to stock up on essentials and visit her adorable grandson. She pulled onto the highway and headed toward the turnoff to Mac's cabin. Should she stop and offer to pick up anything he needed in Anchorage? She'd always collected Betty's prescriptions for her. It would be the neighborly thing to do.

But who was she kidding? Mac was perfectly capable of running his own errands, and judging by the lean muscles of his forearms, healthy and fit. He said he'd once been a cowboy, and she could picture it. As they'd talked yesterday and he'd started to relax, a hint of Oklahoma drawl crept into his speech. Now, she was hoping for another chance to talk with him, and not about selling her the property or allowing the trail to cut through. She'd seen the pain in his eyes when he talked about his daughter.

The man was suffering. And she suspected it wasn't just the pain of loss. She'd been there, when Tommy died. She knew how hard it was to go on while missing someone you loved. But there was something else going on inside his head, and she was afraid she recognized it. His eyes held the same haunted look as her father's had after her little brother died. That look had never gone away.

She slowed, debating whether to check on him. But Mac was clear. He was after solitude. She had no right to badger him while he grieved. If he wanted to be alone with his daughter's dog, she wouldn't bother him.

The sound of frantic barking changed her mind. Blossom was at the fence line near the road, dashing forward and jumping back. She seemed to have some sort of animal cornered. Ursula pulled her car over and jumped out, running along the driveway and slipping through the gate for a closer look. A bald eagle had somehow gotten a wing caught in the fence. Blossom jumped back, a trickle of blood running from her nose. Those talons could be lethal.

The eagle screeched. Ursula plunged into the snow and struggled toward the fence. "Blossom. Come."

The dog looked toward her but didn't seem inclined to leave the fight. Ursula stopped and used her most commanding voice. "Come. Now."

From the corner of her eye, Ursula saw Mac running toward them, but she kept her gaze on Blossom. With one last defiant bark in the direction of the eagle, the pit bull bounded through the snow to Ursula. "Good girl." Ursula grabbed her collar and bent to inspect her nose.

"What's going on?" Mac pushed his way through the snow toward them.

"Blossom was in an altercation with an eagle."

"Eagle?" Mac caught up with Ursula. "Is everybody all right?" He peered toward the fence.

"Blossom has a nasty scratch on her muzzle, but she'll be okay. Judging by the way the eagle is holding his wing, it's broken."

"Oh, no." Mac's eyebrows knit together. "Can it live like that? Or would it be kinder just to…"

"I'm on my way to Anchorage. If we can get it out of the fence, I can take it to the bird rescue center there."

"There's a bird rescue in Anchorage? That's great." He reached for Blossom's collar. "Let me lock up the dog, and I'll be right back."

"Bring wire cutters. There should be some in the tool chest under the bench seat in the kitchen. And a heavy blanket or rug. When animals are hurt, they sometimes lash out at people who are trying to help them."

Mac gave her an odd look but obeyed. A few minutes later, he returned with the things she'd asked for, plus a large dog kennel. "I thought you could transport it in this."

"Good idea." She studied the bird, who stared back, unblinking. When she took a step closer, the eagle gave a jerk but couldn't seem to get loose from the fence. "Do you think you can throw the blanket over it and hold it still while I cut the wire?"

Mac nodded. "I think so. Here, I brought us both leather gloves. Why don't you try to distract it from the right, and I'll approach from the left?"

The distraction plan was only marginally effective, but after three tries, Mac was able to throw the blanket over it and hug the bird so that it couldn't get its beak or talons loose to fight them. Ursula went to work, cutting the thick wires that formed the fence.

"I've dealt with a few animals tangled in fences on the ranch, but a bald eagle is a first for me." The bird struggled, but Mac managed to maintain his hold. "How do you think it happened?"

"Some of these wires are rusted. I suspect a rabbit or something ran through this break in the fence to get away from the eagle. He must have hit it pretty hard." Ursula cut the last wire.

The eagle flapped the now freed wing awkwardly at Mac's face, but he hung on. "Can you open the kennel?"

Ursula unlatched the kennel door, and together they shoved the bird inside, blanket and all. Ursula latched the door shut. The eagle shook the blanket off and glared at them. Mac lifted the kennel, carefully avoiding putting his hands too close to any airholes, and carried it to Ursula's Subaru. She opened the back, and he slid the kennel inside.

He turned to face her. "Thank you. Blossom could have been hurt a lot worse if you hadn't stopped."

"No problem. I think she'll be fine, but if you want to have her checked out, there's a vet in Seward."

"I will if I think she needs it. I hope the eagle will be okay."

"Me, too. I'll let you know."

THE SCRATCH ON Blossom's muzzle wasn't too bad. Mac had just finished cleaning it, despite Blossom's protests, when the internet installer arrived. While Mac had waited for him to finish, he'd gotten caught up in a book on the history of the Alaska gold rush he found on the living room shelf. He didn't remember about the groceries until later that afternoon, so he locked Blossom in the cabin and drove into Seward.

He returned to find the empty dog kennel in his driveway. A roll of lamb wire rested beside it. That was nice of Ursula. He hadn't even thought about how he was going to repair the fence. Funny, back when he was a kid on the ranch, one of the constant chores was working on fences. Life seemed to have come full circle.

Once he had the groceries put away, he'd give Ursula a call to find out what the rescue people said about the eagle. He opened the liftgate and reached to load the kennel. A note was taped to the top. *I have your dog. —Ursula.*

What? He'd left Blossom in the house. He drove the rest of the way down the driveway and unlocked the front door. No nails clicked across the floor to greet him. The back door was also locked. The windows were closed—it was winter after all. So how did Blossom get out?

The key. That was the only answer. Ursula had known exactly where he would find a toolbox containing wire cutters. He hadn't even realized the built-in bench lifted up, much less that there was a toolbox underneath. She was obviously friends with the woman who had owned the place before him. Ergo, she would have a key.

But why would Ursula take Blossom? It wasn't as though he'd neglected her. He was only gone an hour or so. Ursula had to know he'd never let anything happen to Andi's dog.

Maybe that's what she was counting on. She'd fed him muffins and listened to him talk the other morning to get him to trust her. She'd helped with the eagle and even brought him wire to repair the fence. Now she was going to "rescue" the dog, because she knew Blossom was important to him. And he would be so grateful, he'd give her access to the trails, or maybe even sell her the property. Classic manipulation.

But she'd missed one little detail. She should have left the back door open. Mac couldn't be expected to believe Blossom had closed and locked the door behind her. Yeah, if Ursula thought her little plan was going to work on him, she had another think coming.

He jumped into the SUV and turned around. Could she have arranged the injured eagle, too? He couldn't imagine her trapping an eagle and somehow getting it stuck in the fence without injuring herself. But then, the woman had a tame squirrel. For all he knew, she might have a pet eagle trained to pretend it had a broken wing.

He pulled up in front of her porch, jumped out and ran up the steps. He reached up to pound on the door, but paused to take a breath. Better to let her carry through on this charade, see exactly what she was up to. He rang the bell.

A minute later, Ursula's smiling face greeted him. "Oh, good. You got my note. Come in."

He stepped in far enough to allow her to shut the door. Across the room, Blossom lay on a rug in front of the fire, getting belly rubs from Rory. She rolled to her feet and ran to greet him, pushing her head against his hand. He rubbed her ears.

Rory chased after her. "Me and Blossom were playing. And I gave her a dog biscuit. But I didn't share my cookie 'cause chocolate is bad for dogs."

Ursula put an arm around the girl's shoulders. "I found Blossom running along the highway. She must have taken advantage of that hole in the fence. You found the fencing I left?"

"Yes." Mac kept his gaze on the dog, so Ursula wouldn't read his face. "Thank you."

"You're welcome. I'm pretty sure there's a roll of bailing wire in your toolbox. If not, I have some you can use."

"Uh-huh. How much do I owe you?"

"Don't worry about it. I was picking up a few other things."

He met her eyes. "I pay my debts. How much for the fencing?"

Oh, she was good. Her expression was the perfect mix of surprise and hurt at his brusque tone. This wasn't playing into her plan to have him indebted to her. "About twenty dollars, I think. I'll find the receipt."

"And the key."

"Key?" Wide-eyed innocence. She could be a professional actress with those skills. Maybe the whole time she'd let him babble on about Andi, she'd known exactly who he was and what happened. Getting him to sell his property might not even be her end game. She might be planning to sell his story to the tabloids.

"The key to my house. You have one, don't you?"

"Oh. Yes, I do. I'll get it." She left him standing beside the door and disappeared into her kitchen, returning a few minutes later carrying a key and a slip of paper. "Nineteen ninety-five. Here's your key." A paper tag attached to the key identified it as "Betty's House."

Mac nodded. "Is this the only copy?"

Ursula narrowed her eyes. "As far as I know. I only have it because I used to water Betty's plants when she visited her granddaughter in the lower forty-eight. I don't know if she gave keys to anyone else."

Mac nodded. "I'm having the locks changed anyway, so if you find other copies, you can throw them away." He put a subtle emphasis on find. She noticed, judging by the way she stiffened. He opened his wallet and pulled out a twenty. "Thank you for picking up the lamb wire."

"I'll get your change." She turned.

"That's okay."

She ignored him and crossed the room to fish a coin from a pottery bowl on the mantle. She returned and handed him a nickel. "I pay my debts, too."

"I'm sure you do." He slipped the nickel into his pocket. He should go, but he had to ask, "What happened with the eagle?"

"They think he'll make a full recovery and they'll be able to release him eventually."

"That's good news."

"Yes." She stood perfectly still, watching him. The girl looked back and forth between them, her eyebrows drawn together as though she couldn't quite decipher what was happening.

"I appreciate you both taking care of the dog." Which he did. Even if Blossom had never been in any real danger, at least they had cared for her. And the little girl had no way of knowing what her godmother was up to. With a smile for Rory and a curt nod for Ursula, he stepped through the door. Blossom cocked her head and stayed where she was, obviously reluctant to leave. He had to call her twice before she came and jumped into the SUV.

He glanced over at the inn before he put the car in gear. Ursula stood on the porch with Rory in front of her, her arms wrapped around the girl's shoulders. He couldn't quite read the expression on her face, but what should it matter? If he had his way, he'd never see either of them again. Mac shifted into gear and drove away.

CHAPTER FOUR

MAC SAT IN his living room, holding his knife in one hand and a piece of birch in the other, but he wasn't carving. Instead, he stared at the flames dancing behind the glass window of the woodstove. Was he missing something? Ursula's reaction when she handed him the key didn't quite fit. She'd looked…hurt.

He shrugged. Of course she did. She was an expert manipulator. She knew exactly what buttons to push, what expressions to adopt. He'd learned a few things in the little over half a century he'd been on earth, much of it from sad experience. Fame and money attracted con artists and moochers like ants to a picnic. He seldom even wasted the energy resenting them, just wrote it off as an occupational hazard.

So why was he so disappointed in Ursula? Maybe it was because she'd seemed real. She was attractive, but not in an obvious way. Just classic bone structure, healthy skin and an infectious smile. He liked her hair, the way she'd left in the natural silver, short but still feminine. She was a good listener. And she seemed to care. Of course, that was stock in trade for people like her. Listen, learn and take advantage.

Blossom rose from her bed and stretched, head low over her front paws, tail poking into the air. She padded into the kitchen and took a long and sloppy drink from her bowl. Her nails clicked across the vinyl floor into the laundry room beyond, where she made a scratching noise.

Mac stood and followed her without bothering to slip on

his shoes, wondering why she didn't scratch on the front door. When he got to the kitchen, enough light filtered into the laundry room to see her on her back legs, pawing at the back door latch. What was she up to?

He'd noticed the levers on the doors looked much more modern than the rest of the house. Probably easier for arthritic hands to operate than the original doorknobs. Within a minute, Blossom had managed to catch the lever with her paw and pull it down. The door swung open, and she ran outside. When the heck did she learn to do that?

He flipped on a light and went to examine the door. Before he reached it, a gust of wind banged it shut. Just as he thought, the latch was turned to the lock position. What he hadn't realized was the inside lever still operated. He reached outside without letting the door shut and tried it. Sure enough, from the outside, it was locked.

Blossom pranced to the door, head held high. Mac let her inside and locked the door behind her, this time using the deadbolt. He hadn't bothered with the deadbolts before, since he didn't have a key, but that was before he realized he had a canine Houdini on his hands. Tomorrow, he'd call a locksmith. And fix that hole in the fence.

He followed Blossom into the living room. "You have some 'splaining to do, young lady."

She wagged her tail, reminding him of Andi when she was five and had just learned to tie her own shoelaces. Blossom seemed so pleased with herself, it was almost a shame he had to shut down her new game.

And it was an even bigger shame he'd jumped to conclusions. There wasn't much he hated more than the taste of crow, but he was going to have to eat a big helping.

"THERE'S ANOTHER EXTENSION cord in the hall closet if you need it." Ursula held a folding table steady while her friend Catherine folded out the legs.

"Thanks. I'm sure someone will need it. You'd think after doing this so many times, we'd have it down, but someone always forgets something." Catherine grabbed the far end of the table and together they set it in place. "There. That's the last one."

Ursula checked her watch. Four o'clock. Some of the quilters would no doubt take off work early on a Friday afternoon. "They'll be arriving soon. I've got a big batch of brownies in the kitchen."

"The girls will love that." The doorbell rang. "I'll get it. It's probably our guest speaker. She's going to talk about wool appliqué."

"Okay. I'll put those brownies on a platter." Ursula started for the kitchen.

Catherine opened the door. "Well, hello there, beautiful," she crooned in her dog-and-baby voice. Ursula was betting dog. Possibly a black-and-white pit bull.

She paused at the kitchen door listening to the murmur of voices. She wasn't sure if she wanted it to be Mac or not. She thought they'd made friends, but she'd sensed a definite hostility when he picked up Blossom yesterday. That hint of cowboy drawl was gone, and he was back to his formal voice. She couldn't imagine what she'd done to upset him, after helping him with his eagle, picking up wire to fix his fence and rescuing his dog from traffic. Maybe he was embarrassed about the dog getting out. Or maybe he was just moody.

Whatever his reasons, she had better things to do with her time than spend it with a bad-tempered hermit. She'd be better off staying far away from him. And yet, she couldn't stop thinking about him. Ursula sighed. Who was she kidding? She'd seen his pain. She could no more walk away from him than she could have left the eagle in the fence to die. And just like with the eagle, if she wasn't careful, she was going to get hurt.

"Ursula. Your friend Mac is here to see you." The lilt in her voice made it clear Catherine would be demanding details later. Ursula crossed to the door.

Mac stood on the porch, holding what looked like the local grocer's entire stock of mixed flowers. "Hi. Do you have a minute to talk?"

"I'll just go see about those brownies," Catherine murmured. "Come on, Blossom. I'll bet we could find you a dog biscuit."

"Come in." Ursula stepped back from the door to allow Mac inside.

He handed her the cellophane-wrapped bundles. "For you."

Ursula gathered the three, no, four bouquets in her arms. "Thank you, but why are you bringing me flowers?"

"I want to apologize." Actually, from the pained expression on his face, the last thing he wanted was to apologize, but he was doing it anyway. This should be good.

"Come with me." Ursula led him through the maze of tables and power cords littering the living room.

"What's going on?"

"A quilt retreat. Twice a year, Catherine and a dozen or so of her friends reserve the whole inn and spend the weekend sewing. It's a lot of fun."

"Do you quilt?"

"I dabble, but I'm not a serious quilter like these ladies. My job is to keep everyone fed and happy." Ursula gestured for him to sit on the couch near the fireplace and laid the flowers in a basket on the coffee table. She sat in a chair directly across from him and leaned forward. "Okay, shoot."

"Shoot what?"

"The apology. You said you wanted to apologize. I'm ready."

He chuckled. "You're not making this easy."

"Well, I'm curious exactly what you're apologizing for.

Blocking access to the ski trails without giving me notice? Siccing your dog on me? Threatening to have me arrested for trespassing? If it involves this many flowers, it must be serious."

"Actually, none of those things. Well, all those things, but they're not the main reason I'm here." He took a long breath. "I was rude to you yesterday because I blamed you for something of which I've since learned you were innocent."

She raised an eyebrow. "Say again?"

"Yesterday. When I found your note that you had the dog." He explained, and as he talked, Ursula started to smile. By the time he'd finished, she was laughing out loud.

"You really thought I'd sneaked into your house and kidnapped your dog just so I could bug you about the right-of-way." She shook her head. "You have some imagination."

"Occupational hazard, I suppose."

"What occupation is that?"

"I'm a writer."

"Are you? That's exciting. What do you write?"

"Thrillers."

"Ah. I don't read a lot of those. Too scary. I would have thought growing up on a ranch, you'd write Westerns."

Mac shook his head. "No. Growing up on a ranch means I know too much to write pretty little stories about cowboys."

"That bad?"

"No." He paused and just for a moment his gaze went past her toward some remembered place. "Rather wonderful actually. It was losing the ranch that was hard. My dad never really got over it. He died young. They both did." He gave a sudden smile. "But I didn't come to talk about myself. I came to say I'm sorry."

"I accept your apology."

"Good. Well then, if I can find my dog, I'll let you get back to what you were doing."

"I'll get her." She gathered up the bouquets before starting for the kitchen. "Thank you for the flowers. They're lovely."

"I'm glad you like them. Thank you for delivering the eagle and picking up the fencing wire. And for your patience."

"You're welcome. See you around." Before she could get to the kitchen, the door opened and Blossom ran past her to Mac.

Catherine followed, carrying a tray. "Mac, take one of these brownies before you go. Ursula made them. She's a fantastic cook."

"Yes, I know." Mac nodded before accepting a brownie and taking his leave.

Ursula carried the flowers into the kitchen. She was on a step stool, retrieving vases from the highest shelves when Catherine bustled in. "So what was that all about?"

Ursula grabbed a ceramic jar and set it on the counter before answering. "You mean you weren't standing in the kitchen with your ear pressed against the door?"

"I was but he didn't talk loud enough. Spill. Why are good-looking men bringing you bucket loads of flowers?"

Ursula shrugged. "It was one man and who knows why he does what he does?"

"So you admit he's good-looking."

"He is. He's also my new neighbor."

"Maybe he wants to be more than your neighbor."

"Just the opposite, I think." Ursula stepped down. "He's bribing me to leave him alone."

"If that were true, wouldn't he have brought a cactus?"

Ursula laughed and filled the vases with water. "He's as prickly as a cactus, but it seems his overachieving conscience won't let him get away with being rude. Thus, the flowers. Now that he's apologized, he can go back to brooding in his cave."

"We'll see."

"Yes, we will." Ursula trimmed the stems of one bouquet, stuffed it into a vase, fluffed the flowers and handed the arrangement to Catherine. "Here, you can put these out for your quilters to enjoy."

IT DIDN'T TAKE long for the locksmith to do his thing. Once he'd gone, Mac made sure the deadbolts were latched and slipped the new keys onto his key ring. The leather fob had worn to the point that it was hard to read the *M* stamped onto it. Another of Andi's craft projects, back before she realized leather came from cows.

Mac picked up his phone and dialed the familiar number. He was in luck. Detective Russ Ralston was in.

"It's Mac. Just checking in to see if you've found any new evidence."

"Sorry, nothing." He sounded almost as frustrated as Mac felt.

"Have you checked out that tip from—?"

"You know I can't share details. Rest assured, we're following up every lead. That reward you offered has generated plenty of interest. So far none of the calls have panned out, but we're still working on it. We won't give up until we find him."

Mac believed him. Russ was a longtime acquaintance and had a daughter two years younger than Andi. He was taking Andi's murder as a personal affront. Not that Mac was relying entirely on police resources. The private investigator he'd hired was canvassing everyone even remotely connected to Joel Thaine, Andi's boyfriend.

Mac never liked him. The first time they met, there was something…off about the young man. Nothing he could put a finger on, just the feeling Thaine was playing a part, saying what he was supposed to say to his girlfriend's father. Come to think of it, Blossom didn't care for him, either.

They met on Andi's birthday. She said she had plans

for the evening, so Mac had stopped by her apartment that afternoon to deliver her present. Andi had been happily unwrapping her gift when her new boyfriend walked in unexpectedly, and Blossom barked at him. At Andi's rebuke, Blossom quit barking, but she planted herself between Andi and Thaine, and judging by his stiffness, Thaine wasn't any fonder of the dog than she was of him.

At the time, Mac had written off his own unease. He was annoyed to be interrupted in the middle of giving her a gift and didn't like that Thaine seemed to have his own key. As far as Mac knew, they'd only been dating a couple of weeks at that point.

He'd tried to feel Andi out when he took her to lunch the next week, but she was defensive, saying Mac never liked any of her boyfriends. And she had a point. Andi had a habit of dating fixer-uppers. He guessed it was part of her save-the-world campaign. Andi said Thaine was some sort of professional photographer, although Mac was unable to find any evidence he'd ever made money at it. Anyway, Andi made it clear that if Mac wanted to spend time with her, he needed to respect her choices. So he did.

It hadn't mattered. She still withdrew. She skipped many of their weekly phone conversations and when they did talk, she chattered on about frivolities and never gave him the chance to ask how she truly was. She always seemed to have a prior engagement when he'd invite her for a meal. Mac only found out Thaine had moved in with her when his housekeeper, whose son lived in the same apartment building, happened to mention it.

How could Mac have missed the signs? Abuser 101—isolate victim from her friends and family. Mac should have picked it up from the beginning, when he saw the friction between Thaine and Blossom, but he told himself lots of people were nervous around pit bulls. Then there was that last phone call. "Dad, can you take care of Blossom for a few days? I'm going to this women's retreat thing, and they don't allow dogs."

He'd seen her request as an olive branch, Andi's way of saying he was back in her good graces. She'd seemed jittery when she dropped off the dog, but more hurried than scared. She said she'd lost her cell phone, and would call him when she got a new one. She didn't volunteer any details about the retreat or why she was going, and Mac hadn't pushed. He figured they'd talk when she got back. She hugged him goodbye. That was the last time he'd laid eyes on her.

Judging by the calls to the reward line, it was the last time anyone laid eyes on her except for her killer. Thaine was a clever one. He didn't offer any false alibis the cops could shake. He said he'd spent the day driving around, looking for subjects to photograph. When they asked to see the pictures, he said the light was poor, so he'd made mental notes and planned to come back to the most promising sites later. Perfectly nebulous, and impossible to shake.

He set the perfect tone as concerned boyfriend, not overdone, not too casual. He hadn't been seen in the company of other women. He'd managed to drop hints that cast doubts on Andi's emotional stability without seeming disloyal. Mac could almost buy it, except that some of the phrases coming out of Joel's mouth bore a striking resemblance to popular fiction. He was definitely playing a part.

Finally, they'd found her, inside her partially burned-out car behind an abandoned homestead. When they went to question Thaine, he was gone. The contents of Andi's bank accounts had vanished along with him, no doubt funding his escape. But he couldn't hide forever. Mac would make sure of that.

SATURDAY EVENING, and the quilting retreat was in full swing. The hum of sewing machines filled the room, punctuated by voices and laughter. Over in the corner, Catherine wielded a rotary cutter like a surgeon, slicing and dicing colorful fabrics into shapes. In the dining area, Ursula set a large salad on the buffet table and put breadsticks in a warming tray. Ordinarily, she only provided breakfast, but on quilt weekends, she did all the food so the quilters could concentrate on their art.

Rory shadowed Ursula as she moved between the kitchen and dining area. The change in routine and a room full of people had her sticking close. Ursula smiled at her. "Whew, quilting weekends are a lot of work. I'm glad I have you to help. Could you please fold the napkins like this? Then we'll set the tables." Ordinarily she would set silverware and napkins on the buffet table, but Rory would be happier if she kept busy.

Catherine crossed to the dining area and inspected the napkin Rory had folded into a precise triangle. "Nice job, Rory. Something smells good. When will dinner be ready?"

Ursula checked her watch. "Soon." She moved one of the bouquets from the buffet table to the center of the largest dining table.

Mary, another longtime quilter, wandered over. "The table looks nice. I love all the flowers."

Catherine chortled. "Ursula's boyfriend brought them."

Mary raised her eyebrows. "Boyfriend, hmm?"

Rory stopped folding napkins and looked up. Ursula had to put a stop to this before she got any ideas. "No. Not a boyfriend. A new neighbor thanking me for watching his dog."

"But he brought you flowers," Mary pointed out. "I never get flowers for watching my neighbor's dog."

"And he smiled at her, a big one, before he left," Catherine tattled.

"He did not." Even as the words left her mouth, Ursula knew she was just feeding into their teasing.

"He did," Catherine insisted. "I saw it with my own eyes.

He took a brownie and grinned like a smitten teenager. That's flirtatious behavior in my book."

"He's not a boyfriend," Rory declared. "He's a grouch, like Oscar the Grouch."

"Oh, really?" Catherine snickered. "He didn't seem grouchy to me."

"He blocked the ski trail, and he acted mad when he took Blossom home. He's a grouch."

Ursula rested her hand on Rory's head. "Remember what I said? That we shouldn't call people names like that?"

"But you said it—"

"I know. And I also said I was wrong, and I apologized. Just like Mac apologized when he brought these flowers yesterday."

Rory frowned. "So he is your boyfriend?"

"No." Ursula flashed a look of exasperation at Catherine for starting this whole mess, but Catherine didn't appear the least bit repentant. "Mac is not my boyfriend. He's our neighbor and friend, and we should be nice to him just like we're nice to all our other neighbors. That's all. Okay?"

Rory nodded and went back to folding the napkins, but she looked a little doubtful.

Ursula began distributing silverware around the tables. "You might give everyone a ten-minute warning. I just need to bring the lasagna out."

"Will do." Catherine and Mary went to spread the word.

Rory carefully set the napkins beside the forks, just as Ursula had shown her. "His dog is nice, though."

Ursula pulled serving utensils from the drawer. "Whose dog?"

"Mac's. He's grouchy, but his dog is nice. Maybe if he was your boyfriend, he'd bring Blossom over to play."

Ursula laughed. "He's not, so it's a moot point."

"What does moot mean?"

"That it's something you don't need to worry about, because it's never going to happen."

AT THE QUILTERS' REQUEST, Ursula and Rory joined them for dinner. Afterward, Rory escaped to watch a movie. Once Ursula had finished cleaning up, she strolled around the room, looking at everyone's projects. One of the newest quilters was sewing strips together to make a log cabin baby quilt, in pretty shades of yellow, peach and green. Mary had captured the skyline of Mount Susitna in her wall hanging and was using freehand machine quilting to add texture. One of the other ladies—Susan, if Ursula remembered correctly—had pieced strips of deep pinks and purples onto a fleece backing and was cutting them into a curved shape.

"What are you making?" Ursula asked.

"Dog jackets. This one's for my friend's Chihuahua. Their fur isn't quite suited to Alaska."

"Gorgeous colors." Ursula smiled. "I know of a dog who could use a jacket like this, but I suspect her owner would be embarrassed to be seen with a dog in a pink coat."

"Yeah, it's a guy thing." Susan laughed. "I did one for my son's pit bull out of fleece. What size dog is the one you're thinking of?"

"She's a pit bull, as well."

"I have the pattern here if you want to copy it."

"Thanks. I think I will." Blossom could use a jacket. Unlike huskies with their double coats, Blossom's short fur was better suited to warm weather. She needed an extra layer of insulation. Ursula would just have to make sure not to let Catherine find out she was sewing for Mac's dog, or the teasing would never end.

CHAPTER FIVE

SUNDAY AFTERNOON, THE quilters had packed up their sewing machines and stashes of fabric and gone home. Rory had accepted an afternoon playdate with another girl from Sunday school, a hopeful sign. Ursula carried a load of sheets to the laundry room. Five bedrooms cleaned, and one to go.

She thought briefly of leaving the last room for her cleaner to handle the next day, since only two of the rooms were scheduled for Monday night, but no. She couldn't rest until all the rooms were ready to go, just in case. Once Ursula finished the last bedroom, then she would reward herself by sitting down with a cup of coffee and enjoying the flowers Mac had given her.

In the Rose room, she pulled off the quilt, stripped the sheets from the bed and spread a clean sheet over the mattress. After tucking in the corners on the near side, she circled the bed. A book had fallen and was caught between the bed and the nightstand. Probably Mary's.

Ursula finished tucking in the sheet before bending to retrieve the book, a thick hardback. The cover looked familiar, one she'd seen on various endcaps here and there. A thriller, judging by the figure on the front. No signature on the fly page. She turned it over.

Mac's face looked back at her. R.D. Macleod. Of course.

He'd said he was a writer, but Ursula had been mentally spelling his name McCloud, and he'd introduced himself as Mac, not anything beginning with an R, so she'd never made the connection. Marge was right; he was famous. Not a movie star, but a household name. His books were everywhere, and Ursula knew at least one had been made into a movie, maybe more. So what in the world was he doing at Betty's place?

He said he wanted to be alone. Somehow, it was all tied up with the death of his daughter. But why come to Alaska to grieve? Maybe he was here to write a book about Alaska, but somehow Ursula didn't think so. Not after seeing those faces he carved. Something niggled in the back of her brain, some mention of R.D. Macleod, but she couldn't bring it to the surface.

He looked younger in the photo. Well, maybe not younger exactly, just not as weighed down. He'd posed outdoors with a Kansas prairie behind him, looking off into the distance as though he saw things most people couldn't. Now his focus was inward, like he no longer cared what might be out there.

She finished the room and carried the book to the kitchen. While the coffee brewed, she called Mary. "Hi, it's Ursula. I found a book in the Rose room. Did you happen to lose one?"

"Oh, the R.D. Macleod? I didn't realize I left it behind. I finished it, though, so you can keep it or pass it on, whatever. I love his books. So sad about his daughter, wasn't it?"

"What about his daughter?"

"Don't you remember? It was all over the news. She went missing, and they finally found her body about a month ago. Everybody's speculating on whether the boyfriend did it or what. Apparently he's disappeared. Her father has offered a big reward and hired investigators, but they haven't found the boyfriend yet."

Yes. That was where she'd heard the name Macleod. "I do remember, I just didn't remember it involved this writer."

"Horrible thing for a parent to have to experience. So much sadness in the world." Mary sighed. "Anyway, don't worry about returning that book. I think the quilt retreat went well, don't you?" Mary chattered on about the weekend, with Ursula making agreeable noises at the right intervals. Lucky for Mac that Mary hadn't been there when he dropped by with all the flowers, if he wanted to remain anonymous. Eventually, Mary wound down and Ursula wished her a good night.

Slowly, she hung up the phone. No wonder Mac was hurting. His only daughter. Murdered. He was weighed down with grief, and she suspected, regrets. When a child died, regrets were inevitable, even if that child was an adult. Ursula had seen firsthand what regrets and blame could do to a person. To a family. When she lost her brother, she lost her father, too. He'd gone into the darkness and never came back. Worse, he'd dragged Ursula and her mother in with him. It wasn't until she married Tommy that Ursula realized how much joy was missing from their lives. And she'd vowed never to let that joy slip away again.

She didn't want to see Mac go down the same road as her father. But experience had taught her she could only help people who wanted to be helped. Maybe Mac was beyond saving. Maybe not. In the meantime, she'd do what she could, starting with a coat for Blossom, to bring a little warmth into his life.

Two DAYS LATER, Ursula slowed as she approached Mac's front porch, the dog jacket in her hands. It had turned out well, two layers of black fleece with warm batting in between and red piping around the edges for style. Nothing gaudy, just a simple layer to protect Blossom from the cold.

But what would Mac think? Here she was, butting into his life again. He was perfectly capable of buying a dog jacket on his own if he wanted one. He might suspect she was making excuses to talk to him.

Was she? She stopped before stepping onto the porch. She had no intention of nagging him anymore about the ski trail. He'd heard her request, and he'd chosen to decline. That was his right. No, it wasn't the closed gates driving her to him; it was the memory of those wood spirits she'd seen him carving. The pain on their faces. Mac's pain.

She'd looked up a few of the news stories over the last couple of days and seen photos of Andi Macleod, a pretty young woman with soft brown eyes and a sweet smile. The disappearance of an attractive woman, daughter of a celebrity, seemed to be an irresistible draw for the media. When her body was finally discovered, they'd gone wild.

They stood on the lawn of an attractive brick home she assumed was Mac's to pronounce solemnly that police were still investigating the death of his daughter, and to speculate about the whereabouts of her boyfriend. They'd interviewed Andi's former friends and coworkers, who expressed shock and sorrow and had nothing but good things to say about her. Mac had given statements through a spokesman, but that didn't stop them from filming him driving away in a car. She could only imagine what it must have been like for him. No wonder he ran away to Alaska.

Ursula had also been staying up later than she should reading his book, a fast-paced story of a man charged with stopping a serial killer. The recurring main character, Quillon Ashford, had long ago failed to prevent his wife's murder. Now, driven by regret, he devoted his life to stopping killers. Although the story had been written well before Mac's daughter died, Ursula had to wonder if the character wasn't semiautobiographical. Something told her this wasn't the first tragedy in Mac's life.

She wanted to help him. But was it the ultimate arrogance to think she could have any impact? Of course Mac was devastated after losing his daughter. Anyone would be. If anything happened to Rory, or to her grown son, Sam, or his wife or child, it would tear her heart out, and the kindest words wouldn't bring them back. Mac was old enough to know what he needed, and he'd made it clear he wanted to be alone. Who was she to say differently?

She would just leave the dog jacket on his porch, and he could do whatever he wanted with it. But she'd forgotten about Blossom's sharp ears. As soon as Ursula stepped onto the bottom step, the barking began. Two heavy thumps against the door, and then Blossom was in the window, pushing her head beneath the curtains. As soon as she spotted Ursula, she stopped barking and pricked up her ears. Clearly, she remembered the jerky.

"Hi, sweetie. Hope you enjoy this." Ursula laid the jacket on the table, pressed a gloved hand against the window to greet Blossom and turned to go. She'd only made it a few steps when the door opened behind her.

"Ursula?"

She turned. "I didn't mean to bother you. I was just dropping off something for Blossom." The dog squeezed past him and ran to Ursula. She rubbed her ears.

"What's this?" Mac stepped outside and picked up the coat.

"A dog jacket. I imagine Blossom gets cold if she's outside for very long."

"She does." He unfolded the coat and held it up. A trace of a smile crossed his face. "That's very nice. Thank you."

"You're welcome. Well, I'll see you around." She turned to go but his voice stopped her.

"Would you like to come in?"

"I, uh, don't want to intrude."

"Come inside. You need to show me how this works."

"Oh, okay." She followed him through the door. Other than an untidy pile of wood shavings in a box at the foot of his chair, the room looked exactly as it had when Betty lived there. Exactly. Mac had done nothing at all to personalize the space.

He took her coat and hung it in the front closet. "Have a seat. Coffee?"

"I'd like that. Thanks. Here, Blossom. Come try on your new coat."

Blossom allowed Ursula to lay the coat across her back and adjust the fasteners around her chest and middle. As soon as Ursula released her, she trotted into the kitchen as if she wanted to show off her new jacket to Mac. He assured her she was beautiful, gave her a dog biscuit and carried two mugs of coffee into the living room, handing one to Ursula. He'd even remembered the cream. "How's business at the inn?"

Okay, they were going to make small talk. At least he was talking. She accepted the cup and set it on the coffee table. "Not bad. Not like summers, of course, but steady. I just hope I can keep it after the new hotel opens."

"Is that what they're building just this side of Seward? It's huge."

"I know. It's supposed to be a luxury resort with a spa and indoor pool and three restaurants."

"Seems a little much for a town the size of Seward."

"It's tied in with the cruises. I gather they intend to sell it as part of a package deal."

"Are many of your customers from the cruises?"

Ursula nodded. "Quite a few. That's why I was hoping to expand."

"I don't understand. I thought you were afraid of losing business."

"Yes, so I wanted to open an RV park here next to the inn. It would draw a different sort of guest than the resort, and I could host large groups where some had RVs and some didn't. I need to make sure I can pay the rent on the inn."

Mac sipped his coffee. "If competition from the resort affects your business, it seems to me your landlord should be amenable to a reduction in rent. If you can't make a go of it at the current rate, no one else can either. That's always the risk when you invest in a business."

Ursula shook her head. "I don't want Sam losing money on the deal."

"So the landlord is a friend?"

She laughed. "I guess you could say that. I raised him from a pup."

"Your son."

"In every way that matters. Sam bought the inn six years ago to keep me entertained. Oh, he tried to pretend it was a business investment and I was doing him a favor, but he'd never shown any inclination toward investing in real estate before. He and his wife had their first child this past summer. The last thing they need is a drain on their finances. Until they've paid off the mortgage on this place, I need to make sure I produce enough to cover expenses."

"But wouldn't buying this property put you further in the hole?"

"I had a loan all lined up. The RV park revenue would easily cover the loan payments and supplement the income for the inn."

"I see."

She suddenly realized how this sounded. "I'm sorry. I didn't bring Blossom that jacket as an excuse to lay my tale of woe on you. I understand why you don't want to sell, and I'm okay with it. I'll come up with another way to compete with the new resort."

Mac paused before he spoke. "I honestly don't think you'll have any trouble competing. You have a beautiful location, and there are plenty of people who would rather stay in a small, personal business than in a huge corporate chain. And you could offer special activities like mystery weekends."

"Mystery weekends?"

"You know. Where you assign each guest an identity

and they interview each other to try to discover who committed the murder."

"Have you done one?"

"No, but I've seen them auctioned off at charity events. They're always popular."

"Interesting. I've never thought of anything like that."

"I know of a writer who creates theme weekend packages with scripts, costume suggestions and even food ideas. I can find her website for you, if you like."

"That would be great. Thank you."

Mac nodded. "I'll email you in a few days. I assume your inn has a webpage."

"Yes. Forgetmenot dot com." Ursula spied another of those carved branches in the box with the shavings. A half-revealed face gazed up at her, a sideswept beard following a natural curve in the wood. The facial features had been roughed in, but didn't yet show emotion. Ursula set her cup on the coffee table and reached for the sculpture. "These are fascinating. How did you learn to carve like this?"

"My grandfather. When I was ten, he gave me his pocketknife. He said a man with a knife and a chunk of wood need never be bored."

"How interesting. Do you still have your grandfather's knife?"

"I do." He reached into his pocket, pulled out a pearl-handled pocketknife and held it out for her inspection.

"Nice. I have a ring that belonged to my grandmother, but it's hidden away in a safe-deposit box. It's wonderful that you create such fascinating art with your grandfather's gift."

Mac laughed. "I wouldn't call it art. More like the woodworking equivalent of doodling. I find it soothing, almost a form of meditation."

"It would be amazing to be able to create something like this. How do you do it?"

Mac reached into his woodbin and pulled out a short

length of branch. He opened the pocketknife, revealing a blade narrow from years of sharpening. Within minutes, he'd stripped the bark from the branch. "First, I take a look at what I have to work with. See how this one has a funny little knot here that sort of looks like a mouth?"

He used the tip of his blade to sketch wide eyes and raised eyebrows above the round knot. "Then I shape the features, a little at a time." He whittled away small chips of wood, letting them fall into the kindling box at his feet. A turned-up nose began to appear from the wood. "Here. Give it a try."

"Me?" She stared at the chunk of wood he was holding out for her.

"Yes, you. Here. Hold the knife like this." He placed the knife in her hand, curling her fingers around the handle. "Careful—it's sharp. Hold the wood so that you're not cutting close to your fingers."

Ursula placed the blade against the wood and pushed, chipping out a tiny piece.

"No, you're going against the grain." Mac moved to sit beside her on the couch and covered her hand with his. "Smooth shallow cuts." He guided her hand to push along the grain, removing slivers of wood and starting to round out one of the cheeks.

"Oh, I see." Ursula tried a few more strokes on her own. "This is fun."

"I thought you'd like it." Mac continued to watch as she worked, occasionally giving her instructions or guiding her hand. The face grew more animated, a child's face, lips pursed in an O. It was crude, nothing like the ones she'd seen in Mac's workshop, but it had a certain charm.

Without lifting her gaze from the wood, Ursula spoke. "Someone left one of your books behind at the B&B, and I saw your picture. When you said you were a writer, I didn't realize you were R.D. Macleod."

Mac grunted. "Here, take a little more off below the chin."

She did as he instructed. "Once I realized who you were—"

"You tied me to all those news stories about my daughter."

"Yes." She stopped carving to lay her hand on his. "I'm so sorry." She turned to look at him. "I wasn't sure if I should mention it, but I didn't want to feel like I was hiding something from you. We don't have to talk about it if you don't want to."

"Good." He stared toward the woodstove for a minute before he pulled his hand from under hers and reached for the carving. "Here, let me show you how to add some texture to the hair." They continued work on the wood spirit. Mac didn't speak, other than the occasional instruction, but he didn't withdraw, either. Ursula followed his lead.

The clock in the bookcase chimed. Ursula looked up. "Goodness, I didn't realize it was that late. I have to go. The school bus will be dropping Rory off in twenty minutes or so." She got to her feet and handed him his knife. "Thank you, Mac. I enjoyed the lesson."

He followed her to the door, dog at his heels, and held her coat while she slipped it on. "Your goddaughter lives with you permanently?"

"Yes." Ursula zipped her coat. "She lost her family in October of last year. Carbon monoxide from a faulty furnace."

"I'm sorry."

"Thanks." She pulled on her gloves. "Rory's had a tough time of it, but I think we're starting to see a little light at the end of the tunnel."

"I hope so. She's a sweetheart." Mac held the door for her. "Blossom and I thank you for the coat."

"You're both welcome." She stepped onto the porch. "Take care of yourself."

Mac shut the door behind her.

MAC WOKE IN the dark. The last snatches of a dream escaped before he could catch them, but to his surprise, he realized it had been a pleasant dream. He checked the time on his phone. He'd slept undisturbed through the night. He couldn't remember the last time that happened.

His thoughts drifted to Ursula's visit yesterday, and to the girl he'd met in Ursula's kitchen. He tended to forget his wasn't the only tragedy in the world. That little girl had lost everything. Everything except her relationship to Ursula, that is. Mac was starting to recognize what a valuable thing that was.

He stood and stretched. Beneath him, the floor creaked, summoning Blossom from her bed in the living room. Her nails clicked against the floor in the hallway. When she reached the end, she bumped her head against the bedroom door to knock it open. She'd discovered right away that the latch on that door often failed to catch.

She joined Mac in his stretches, pushing her chest low in a deep bow before hurrying over to greet him. He fondled her ears. "Good morning."

He dropped to the floor to do his push-ups. Blossom stood in the doorway, head bobbing up and down as she watched him. As soon as he reached fifty, she began jerking her head toward the hall. Subtle. Mac laughed. "Are you saying you're ready for breakfast?"

She was. Mac fed the dog and started a pot of coffee. Once Blossom had wolfed down her kibble, she padded to the door. Mac strapped on her new jacket, flicked on the outside light and let her out. Snowflakes like tiny feathers drifted through the air. Mac grabbed his coat, slipped into his boots and stepped onto the porch to watch.

His porch light illuminated only a few feet of falling snow, like a spotlight on a ballerina pirouetting across the stage to the music of exquisite silence. He couldn't have said what sounds were missing, only that the snowfall dampened all ambient noise. He was alone in a world without sound, without color. And yet it was beautiful.

The spell was broken when Blossom crashed through a drift and galloped up the stairs, her mouth open in a doggy grin. She wiggled and jumped, begging for a game. Amused, Mac tried to gather up a snowball, only to find the snow too powdery to pack. Instead, he broke an icicle from the porch overhang and tossed it like a stick. Blossom pounced on the snow where it had fallen and dug frantically, almost burying herself in the process. After a moment, she emerged victorious, the icicle in her mouth.

He threw it for her once more before the cold drove him indoors. By the time he'd showered, shaved, dressed and eaten breakfast, the snow had stopped and the sky lightened. Mac bundled up and went out to wrestle the snowblower from the garage. It took a few tries to get it started, but eventually the engine leaped to life and Mac started the long process of clearing his driveway.

It was slow, mindless work, but Mac found the steady progress satisfying. He piloted the machine up and down his drive, pitching a plume of snow in an arc over the existing berms lining his driveway. Blossom frolicked nearby, occasionally leaping into the air to try to catch the stream of snow in her mouth.

The snowplow drove past, clearing the highway toward Seward. Blossom barked and would have run toward the road, but Mac called her back. She gave one last woof and bounded toward him, shaking the snow from her coat. Mac had found fifteen minutes was her usual limit before she wanted back into the house, but with her new winter coat, she seemed happy to remain outside with him indefinitely. He didn't know why getting her a coat hadn't occurred to him before. It was nice of Ursula to think of it. Even nicer of her to sew a custom coat especially for the dog.

Ursula seemed to have a gift of knowing exactly what was needed. Cinnamon rolls when he was hungry. A listening ear when he needed to talk. A coat for the dog, nuts for the squirrel, brownies for the quilters. Maybe it was a skill developed from running her B&B, but he suspected empathy was a fundamental personality trait of hers. He could have done a lot worse than her for a neighbor.

And now he'd discovered she was raising someone else's child. He'd assumed when Ursula introduced the girl as her goddaughter that she was visiting, but it sounded permanent. Ursula Anderson was an exceptional woman.

Up at the road, he saw a couple hiking along the shoulder, skis propped over their shoulders. No doubt guests at her B&B, heading out to the cross-country ski trails. A twinge of guilt disturbed what, up until that moment, had been a pleasant morning. Closing that shortcut across his property meant that Ursula's guests had to hike along the highway to the trails. If they'd had direct access in the past, they were sure to complain about the change to their friends, which was bound to have a negative effect on Ursula's business, eventually.

But just because the former owner had agreed to the shortcut didn't obligate him. He needed the fence to keep Blossom contained, as well as to keep people off his property. So far, no reporters had managed to track him to Alaska, but it was only a matter of time before they did. Bottom line, it was his land. He'd returned Ursula's plate and apologized to her for thinking she dognapped Blossom. They were square. He was not going to feel guilty about the gate.

He finished clearing the driveway and shoveling the steps. Somewhere along the way, his good mood had deserted him. His stomach growled. That was it. Low blood sugar. He'd just taken the first bite of his ham and cheese sandwich when his phone rang. Ronald.

With a grunt, he set his sandwich on the plate and answered the phone. "What?"

"Good afternoon to you, too. Just thought I'd check in, see if everything went okay with the internet."

"It's fine. Everything's fine. I was just about to eat…"

"Sorry. Okay, I won't keep you. I just wanted to see if you'd made any progress on that manuscript."

"No."

"Oh. Well, I had a talk with the publisher and they're willing to be flexible on the deadline if—"

"Not happening." Ronald wasn't used to taking no for an answer, but Mac was tired of having this conversation. "I've already given you the check returning the full advance. Tell them I'm not going to write it. I'm done."

"But it's already half-written. You can use this book to wrap up the series, if you want, just to complete the contract. What about your fans? Don't you owe them some sort of closure?"

Low blow. Mac knew he owed his living to his fans, and he'd always treated them with respect. Their letters of support when Andi disappeared were one of the few things that gave him any comfort. But he couldn't write. He'd tried. He'd stared down at his computer, trying to make the words come, but he couldn't stand to crawl inside the killer's head, couldn't immerse himself in the violence. Not now.

His publicist could handle this. "I'll draft up a statement and send it to Laura apologizing for leaving the readers hanging. She'll know how to spin it. They'll understand."

"I wouldn't count on it," Ronald warned. "There will be some unhappy people on social media when this goes public. They love Quillon Ashford, and you're killing him."

"Duly noted. Anything else?"

"I guess not."

"All right. I'll get that statement to Laura by tomorrow and tell her you need a copy before it goes public. Goodbye."

Mac ended the call and pushed his sandwich away. It was official. He was no longer a writer. No longer a father. He was nobody. He had nobody.

When Mac was seventeen, his family had been hanging onto the ranch by their fingernails after three years of drought. Mac's father had been forced to sell off most of their cattle, but he'd resolved never to sell the bull. That prize bull was going to be the making of their ranch when the rain returned.

But that all changed the day Mac tried to herd the bull away from the cows to a different pasture. Dad had told him to wait until he got there but, full of typical teenage arrogance, Mac was sure he could handle the job alone. The bull had other ideas. Mac's father arrived just about the time Mac got bucked off his horse and the bull tried to drive him into the ground. A single shot from his father's Winchester saved Mac's life and sealed the ranch's fate. His father found a job in town, but he was never the same. Ten years later, cancer stole Mac's mother from them, and her husband followed shortly behind her. Technically the cause of his death was pneumonia, but Mac knew he'd died of a broken heart.

Mac's parents were gone. His wife was gone—lost to postpartum depression. And now his daughter was gone, as well. Everyone he'd ever loved was dead.

Blossom laid her head in his lap. He wasn't sure if she sensed his mood or just wanted his sandwich, but either way her message was clear. Without Andi, Mac was the most important person in Blossom's world. He took some comfort in that.

CHAPTER SIX

THREE DAYS LATER, Mac finished nailing the last of the fence panels he had installed along the edge of the trail. He grabbed the top of the panel and gave it a shake. Concrete anchors at the base of the poles held firm. Once the ground thawed, he'd have a fencing contractor replace it with a permanent installation, but for now this should keep the dog in and still let the skiers use the trails.

Blossom galloped along the fence line where he'd cleared the snow. She grabbed a stick and brought it to him, begging for a game. He played fetch with her for a few minutes until a raven landed on one of the new fenceposts and cackled at them. Blossom dropped the stick to bark and throw herself against the fence until the raven relocated to a dead tree across the ravine. Good. If that didn't topple the fence, it should hold until spring.

Now, how best to let Ursula know the trail shortcut was once again available? After his insistence at keeping it closed, he didn't want to make a grand announcement, as though he expected her gratitude. If anyone owed, it was him.

He had promised to find that website about mystery weekend kits. He took Blossom inside and removed her coat and his. The email address for Ursula's inn was easy enough to find. He sent an email with a link to the mystery website, along with a brief mention that the gates to the ski trails were open.

He sat down in his chair and pulled out his knife to put

the finishing touches on the wood spirit Ursula had started the other day. A pixie face, eyes wide in wonder. When Andi was little, sometimes they'd go outside on summer evenings, just after sunset. Her mouth would pucker and her eyes open wide like this when she watched the nighthawks perform their aerial acrobatics, dipping and swerving as they chased mosquitoes.

Blossom raised an ear, then trotted to the door. A moment later, someone knocked. Funny she didn't bark. Mac answered the door to find Ursula on the other side. Blossom apparently now recognized her step. For once, Ursula wasn't offering food, just a big smile. "Mac, I got your message. What's this about opening the gates?"

"I'll show you." Mac grabbed his coat. "Follow me." The three of them trooped along the path he'd beaten in the snow to the back corner of his property. "I decided if I used solid panels, I could let your skiers through and still maintain privacy."

"Wow. How did you—oh, I see. They're attached to concrete footers. That's clever."

"I suppose you'll have to wait for a snowfall to cover the trail where I had to dig it out to build the fence."

"No, the groomer can take care of that. I'll give him a call and let him know the trail is open again."

"Good. Then you're all set."

"This was a lot of work." She turned to face him. "You didn't have to do this."

"I know. But I realize you're trying to run a business, and I felt bad for disrupting it."

"Oh, Mac." She reached out to lay a gloved hand on his arm. "Now I feel bad."

"What for?"

"Because I feel like I manipulated you into this. Don't get me wrong. I'm happy we'll be able to access the trails directly again. But I've since realized I was being selfish, expecting you to keep the shortcut open. It upset me to discover the gate closed, and I felt like someone had taken something from me. But it's your property, not mine. And now I've guilted you into building a fence."

"I thought this was what you wanted."

"It was. It is." She smiled. "I'm thrilled. But, Mac, you had no reason to feel guilty. Betty chose to allow that shortcut, and you didn't. There's nothing wrong with that."

"So you're happy about the trail, but you're unhappy because I did it for the wrong reasons?"

She chuckled. "It sounds ridiculous when you say it like that. Let me start again." She cleared her throat. "Mac, your generosity is overwhelming. Thank you."

"You're welcome."

"To show my appreciation, I'd like to make you dinner tomorrow night."

"I happen to be free."

"Hmm. I could make halibut, although if you grew up on a ranch, I'm guessing you prefer beef."

He laughed. "I am quite fond of halibut, but as it happens, meat loaf is my favorite all-time meal."

"Meat loaf it is. Six thirty okay?"

"I'll be there."

"Great. And bring Blossom. Rory misses her."

MAC ARRIVED RIGHT on time, clutching a bottle of wine in one hand and Blossom's leash in the other. "In accordance with advice from a local wine expert, I brought a Bordeaux to go with the meat loaf."

"How thoughtful. Where did you find a wine expert?"

"The cashier at the liquor department at the grocery store had strong opinions."

"Jimmy?" She chuckled. "I heard through the grapevine he accidentally doubled his order on the Bordeaux, and he's been recommending it to everyone. I happen to be quite fond of Bordeaux, though, so thank you."

"Are they here?" Rory burst through the kitchen door. "Blossom!"

Mac unsnapped the leash, and the dog dashed across the room, their greeting involving a frenzy of face-licking, hugging, tail-wagging and giggles.

Ursula hung up Mac's coat and led the way through the great room and into the kitchen. "I hope you don't mind eating in here. I don't have guests tonight, so we could use the dining room if you like but it's a little cavernous for three."

"This is fine. In my experience, the best meals always take place in the kitchen."

Rory and Blossom followed them. Ursula opened the gate to let the dog into the dining area. Blossom hurried over to sniff noses with Van Gogh, who had been sleeping on the seat of a chair. Rory stroked the cat's back with one hand and hugged the dog with the other.

Ursula handed Mac a corkscrew. "Dinner's almost ready. If you'll open the bottle, I'll get some glasses."

Mac poured the wine and carried his into the dining area where Blossom was now lying on her back on the rug, encouraging Rory to rub her tummy. Van Gogh rubbed against Rory and then against Blossom, purring loudly. Mac chuckled. "You're quite the pet whisperer."

"What's that?" Rory asked.

"That means you know how to treat animals, and they trust you."

"Blossom likes it when I rub her here."

"She does. Let me show you her secret spot." Mac knelt beside Rory and scratched Blossom's belly between her front legs. Her back leg twitched.

Rory's eyes opened wide. "Let me try." She scratched, and the dog's leg shook harder. Blossom raised her head to look at her leg as though she couldn't understand why it was moving on its own. Rory laughed. "Why does she do that?"

"She can't help it. It's like laughing when you get tickled."

"Daddy used to tickle me sometimes." Ursula held her breath, expecting tears, but Rory spoke matter-of-factly, still smiling. "It was fun."

They continued to talk about what kinds of toys Blossom liked and what tricks she could do while Ursula got dinner on the table. Since losing her parents, Rory sometimes acted shy with adults she didn't know well, but she chattered away with Mac as though they were old friends. Ursula almost hated to break up the conversation, but dinner would get cold. "It's ready. Time to wash up."

"I'll show you where." Rory took Mac's hand and led him through the doors to the bathroom.

Rory entertained Mac all through dinner, talking about the art project she was doing in school, and how they couldn't go out for recess yesterday because of the moose on the playground which was good because she'd been in trouble for not following directions and had to stay in five minutes late, but since everybody had to stay in the teacher forgot all about it and today she got to go outside with the rest of the class. She only paused long enough to gulp down her dinner while Mac asked her questions.

Ursula listened in amazement. She would have had to drag this information from Rory, piece by piece, but with Mac it all came pouring out. She would follow up on that not following directions comment later, but right now she wasn't willing to let anything spoil the mood. Mac listened, only shifting his attention away from Rory long enough to accept Ursula's offer of second helpings. Finally, when Ursula was serving dessert, Rory seemed to run out of things to say.

Ursula smiled at her. "Do you want whipped cream on your pudding?"

"Yes, please. Can I squirt it?"

"Go for it." Ursula handed her the can of cream. "Mac, would you like coffee?"

"Do you have decaf?"

"I do." She made coffee while Rory built a mountain of whipped cream on top of her pumpkin custard.

Mac laughed. "I'd like cream on mine, too, please, but only about a third that much."

Rory concentrated, the tip of her tongue caught in the corner of her mouth, and managed to create pretty mounds on top of Mac's and Ursula's ramekins before tasting her own. "This is good."

"Thank you, sweetie. Did Mac tell you he fixed the gates so we can take the shortcut to the ski trails again?"

"You did?" Rory dropped her spoon, slid from her chair and hugged him. "Thank you."

Mac seemed surprised by the hug, but not displeased. "You're quite welcome."

Rory grabbed Ursula's arm in excitement. "Can we go skiing tomorrow after school?"

"If the groomer's had a chance to set track. If not, we could snowshoe."

"You'll come with us, won't you?" Rory bounced on her toes, waiting for Mac's response.

"Me? I don't know how to cross-country ski."

"You don't?" Rory was aghast. "Everybody knows how to ski."

"Where I used to live, snow didn't last long. I've done some downhill skiing but never cross-country."

"Can you snowshoe?"

"I've never tried."

"It's easy. I'll show you how."

"I don't have snowshoes."

"Actually, you do." Maybe Ursula shouldn't put him on the spot, but it was so good to see Rory excited about something. "There are snowshoes hanging on the wall in your garage."

He chuckled. "In that case, I guess I'm in."

"Yay!" Rory beamed at him. "You'll like it. It's fun."

"Sweetie, you need to finish eating and get to work on your homework," Ursula said. "You have a math worksheet, remember?"

"But Blossom's here." Rory tried the sad eyes but Ursula didn't back down. Rory sighed and finished her dessert. "Don't leave before I can tell Blossom goodbye, okay?"

"All right," Mac promised. Rory stopped to rub the dog's ears before disappearing through the door.

Ursula set a cup of coffee in front of him. "Thank you for your patience. I haven't seen her talk this much in a long time. Not since..." She trailed off.

Mac gave her a sympathetic smile, but didn't answer. After a moment, he tried a bite of dessert. "Say, this is good. It's almost like crème brûlée, but with pumpkin and pecans."

"I'm glad you like it."

"The whole dinner was excellent. Best meat loaf I've had in a long time. Your husband was a lucky man."

"I was the lucky one."

"How long were you married?"

"Eighteen years. Sam was a senior in high school when Tommy died."

"I'm surprised you never remarried, especially with all the men here in Alaska." He looked up. "Sorry, that was an inappropriate comment. Pretend I didn't say that."

Ursula laughed. "It's okay. I had a few men who showed some interest but it always felt...forced. Maybe I was spoiled." She smiled and shook her head. "I felt like I'd had my allotment. One happy marriage per customer."

"So you found the perfect man."

"Tommy?" She laughed. "He was far from perfect. He flipped channels between different ballgames so I could never figure out who was playing. He would only eat three vegetables. And he couldn't dance to save his soul. Worse, he didn't know he couldn't dance."

Mac chuckled. "So what was it about this ungraceful, channel-flipping, meat-lover you found so attractive?"

She thought back about all the things that made Tommy special. "He was smart. He liked to look at a situation from different angles, to come up with original solutions to problems. And he was kind. The sort of man who stops to help stranded motorists and takes in stray dogs." She stared at the wall, picturing Tommy's face. "But mostly it was because of the way he loved me. Every time he walked into a room where I was, his eyes would seek me out and he would smile, as if seeing me was the highlight of his day. Losing him was the hardest thing I've ever survived." She turned her eyes to Mac. "But you know what I'm talking about. You lost your wife, as well. Is that why you never remarried?"

"It wasn't the same."

"No. You had a baby daughter. That makes it doubly tragic."

"It was tragic. But not for the same reason." Mac sighed. "Just the opposite, really."

"I don't understand."

"I was in the navy, assigned to an aircraft carrier, but stateside at the time. Carla and I had been dating for a few months, but the relationship was nearing its expiration date. She was bored, and frankly, so was I. But I was two months away from shipping out, and she was keeping me on the line until she could find a better prospect. Then she discovered she was pregnant."

"Oh, dear."

He gave a wry smile. "That's not exactly the way she worded it. Motherhood was the last thing she had in mind, but I persuaded her to marry me, so she could live on base and get medical care, even while I was away. I did my best to be a good husband for those two months but…" He shrugged. "We lived together in reasonable harmony until my unit shipped out. Six months later, the navy informed me I was a father."

He set down his spoon before he continued. "My wife sent a picture taken in the hospital. She was smiling, holding this tiny bundle with a red face and a swatch of dark hair. Carla looked so happy. Three months later, she left the baby with a sitter and drove off a bridge."

"Oh, no. Was it an accident or…?"

He shrugged. "Nobody knows for sure, but when I went home I discovered she'd been suffering from severe postpartum depression. And I'd had no idea."

"So sad."

"My fault."

"How could it be your fault?"

"I convinced her to have the baby. Convinced her to marry a man she didn't love. I swore to love and honor her, but I wasn't there when she needed me."

"You were on duty."

"Yes, but I still should have known. We wrote letters, talked on the phone when we could. I should have realized something was wrong."

Ursula shook her head. "So you'd never met your daughter in person?"

"Not until I came home for her mother's funeral." He looked down at the table. "The first time I saw that little face, I fell in love. I got a hardship discharge so I could care for her."

"Is that when you started writing?"

"No, I'd been writing for years. I'd had a few short stories published while I was in the service and written two novels that will never see the light of day. Once I left the navy, I worked the security desk for a big office building. I took the night shift, which allowed me to be with Andi during the day and gave me time to write. It was two years before I sold my first book, five before I quit that job and took up writing full-time, when Andi started kindergarten."

The door opened and Rory ran into the room, waving a paper. "I finished. Can I play with Blossom now?"

Ursula held out her hand. "Let me check it over while you give Blossom a dog biscuit and tell her good-night. It's time for your bath and bed."

Mac followed Rory to the dog-shaped cookie jar. "Why do you have dog treats? You don't have a dog, do you?"

"I allow guests to bring dogs if they like, and sometimes dog-sit for my son."

"Sam's dog, Kimmik, is a chocolate Lab. He's not really made of chocolate, though. He's just brown," Rory explained as she let Blossom take the biscuit from her hand. "He likes to play fetch."

"So does Blossom. Maybe after snowshoeing tomorrow, you can throw the ball for her."

"Okay!"

"Good job on the math worksheet." Ursula put her hands on the girl's shoulders and squeezed. "Bath time now. Say good-night to Mac and Blossom."

"Good night." She hugged Blossom once more and trotted off to the bathroom without further argument. Miracles never ceased.

"I guess we'd better head home, as well," Mac said. "Thank you for making me meat loaf."

"You're welcome." Ursula had packed up the rest of the meat loaf and another helping of dessert while Mac was talking with Rory. "Here's lunch tomorrow."

"Mmm. The only thing I like better than meat loaf is meat-loaf sandwiches, but I feel bad taking all the leftovers." He grinned. "Or am I not allowed to feel guilty about that, either?"

She laughed. "I realize guilt is a hot button for me. It's

just that I've seen guilt drag people down and destroy families."

"Surely guilt is positive. It might be a good thing for society if people felt more guilt about their misdeeds."

"Yes, if someone has been cruel or negligent, they should feel guilty. But you had every right to close the gates on your property. I'm the one who pushed for something I wasn't entitled to. If anyone should feel guilty, it's me."

Mac shook his head. "How's this? I saw how hard you work and how you take care of people, and I wanted to help, so I found a way to open the trail. Just a neighbor helping a neighbor. Okay?"

Ursula smiled. "Okay. This neighbor thanks you."

"Oh, and speaking of neighbors," Mac dug a card from his pocket, "here's my cell phone number. You know, in case you need to call on a neighbor."

"Thanks."

Mac shrugged on his coat and they stepped onto the porch. "It's nice out here, tonight. Not so cold."

Ursula gazed up at the sky. "No stars. It's getting ready to snow." She pulled her phone from her pocket and clicked on something. "Hmm, the forecast is for seven or eight inches, starting around midnight. Last I heard, they thought this storm would miss us. We might have to delay that snowshoe outing. You probably shouldn't plan on going anywhere tomorrow."

"Why? Won't they plow the highway?"

"Eventually. But with that much snow, it might take a while. Better to be prepared."

He hefted the plastic box. "Meat loaf for sandwiches and dessert. I'm good. Let it snow, let it snow, let it snow."

CHAPTER SEVEN

As IT TURNED OUT, the meteorologists were wrong. The promised eight inches of snow had already grown to ten by the time Mac let Blossom out the next morning. It had topped a foot and was still coming down when Mac went out to shovel the steps and the path to the garage. Shoveling while it snowed was bound to be an exercise in futility but he figured he'd better get a jump on it before it got too deep to handle. He'd wait until it stopped to fire up the snowblower and clear the driveway.

He added a smear of horseradish sauce to his meat-loaf sandwich for lunch and enjoyed it so much he made and consumed another. He'd earned it, shoveling all that snow.

Two hours later, the steps had disappeared under another six inches, and Mac was strapping on Blossom's coat so they could go out to shovel again when the lights blinked and went out. Great. At least he had the woodstove to keep the house warm, although that might mean sleeping on the couch.

He finished another round of shoveling. The snow had stopped, but the electricity was still out. With no microwave to nuke a frozen dinner, that probably meant another meat-loaf sandwich. He could think of worst fates.

Now for a cup of coffee. Oh, right—no electric coffee maker. He weighed his options. The snowplow hadn't been by, so he wasn't getting into Seward. The woodstove didn't get hot enough to boil water. He hadn't brought camping equipment along so he didn't have a portable stove. Or a barbecue grill. What was he thinking, moving to the middle of nowhere without an emergency backup plan? Obviously, he wasn't thinking.

Ursula seemed like someone who would own a spare camp stove, although he hated to impose on her again. But they were neighbors, and they'd agreed that neighbors help each other. Blossom nudged his hand, reminding him her afternoon dog biscuit shouldn't depend on his ability to make coffee. He tossed her the treat. "So what do you think? Should we call Ursula?"

At the mention of Ursula's name, Blossom wagged her tail. Mac dialed the number. The phone rang several times and he was getting ready to leave a message when Ursula's voice came on the line.

"Mac?" She sounded flustered.

"Yes, it's me."

"I was just about to call you. Your power's out, too, right?"

"Yes."

"I'm having some trouble here. Do you know anything about engines?"

"A little." Having grown up on a ranch, Mac had worked on truck and tractor engines, but it had been a long time since he'd gotten grease under his nails. "Why? Are you going somewhere?"

"Not in this snow. No, I'm having trouble getting the emergency generator started. Could I possibly impose on you to take a look?"

"Sure, I could do that."

"Thank you." He could hear the relief in her voice. "The shortest way here is along the trail with snowshoes."

"Rory hasn't given me my snowshoe lesson."

She laughed. "It's not hard. Just strap them on your boots and take it slow. Oh, wait. Why were you calling in the first place?"

"I was hoping to cadge a cup of coffee, or maybe a spare camp stove," Mac admitted.

"I cook with propane, so I'll make you coffee and then you can borrow my camp stove. Better yet, bring Blossom and your stuff and plan to stay over. Your cabin is all-electric. I have a propane furnace, so if we can get the generator going to run the fan, we'll have heat here."

His kitchen was already growing dark. He was tempted. "Do you have room?"

"Plenty. I had one reservation and they cancelled. I don't know if you heard, but there's an avalanche blocking the Seward highway, so nobody's getting to or from Anchorage for a while. Power lines are down all over, so they might not get to us for a couple of days."

"I hadn't heard. Okay, I'll bank the fire so the plumbing doesn't freeze and be over there as soon as I can make it."

ONCE SHE KNEW Mac was on the way, Ursula abandoned the dead generator and returned to the house. Rory was where she'd left her, drawing pictures at the kitchen table by the light of a battery lantern, but she looked relieved when Ursula walked in.

Ursula checked the heat under the stockpot simmering at the back of the stove. "I can't make the generator work, but Mac said he'd come over and see if he can get it running."

Rory added a tail to the horse she'd drawn. "You know, Mac's nice. He's not a grouch at all."

"I agree. Do you want to help me get the house ready for the generator?"

Together they made the rounds, turning off or unplugging all the electronics and most of the lights. The generator was powerful enough to power the furnace fan, refrigerator and freezer, but not a lot extra, and Ursula had been warned power fluctuations were bad for televisions and computers. She'd already explained to Rory that the television wouldn't be available even when they got the generator started. That is if Mac could get it running.

Rory wrapped her arms around herself. "It's getting cold in here."

"Let's go put on some more clothes." Once they'd bundled up with thermal underwear and extra sweaters, they carried in a load of logs from the woodpile, and Ursula soon had a blaze going in the great room fireplace. Van Gogh appeared from wherever he had been hiding and curled up on Rory's lap on the rug in front of the fire. Ursula switched on several battery candles and scattered them around the room.

"There. Now we're nice and cozy. Maybe we'll make popcorn in the fireplace tonight." Rory seemed to be buying Ursula's attempt at making this all a fun adventure. In truth, she was worried. They weren't going to freeze, but if they couldn't get the generator going they might be in for an uncomfortable few days. She could only hope Mac knew more about diesel generators than she did. She had the generator checked every autumn before the snow fell, but this year the guy who usually did it was out of state on some family emergency when she'd called, and she'd forgotten to follow up.

Mac should arrive soon. She left Rory by the fire and went to the kitchen to light the burner under the teakettle and dig a French press from the back of the cabinet. While waiting for the water to boil, she scrounged a motley collection of candles from the pantry and set them on a tray to distribute around the inn, just in case.

She heard Rory running toward the front door. Before Ursula could make it from the kitchen, Rory had already let Mac inside and was brushing sticky snow from Blossom's coat all over the entryway rug. Ursula didn't care; she was just thrilled to see them.

"You made it." She was surprised at the relief she felt. She had no guests to worry about, and it wasn't as though she and Rory would die without electricity. They could stay warm by the fire and had ice chests to keep the refrigerated food cold. If necessary, she could put the frozen food outside until power returned and melt snow on the stove if the pipes froze. But it still felt good to have an ally. "You must have figured out the snowshoes."

"I did." Mac puffed. "Snowshoeing is hard work. Between that and shoveling, I've had my workout today. Now, where's this generator?"

"In the back, but come in first for that cup of coffee. The kettle's on. Once you've warmed up, we can take a look."

"I didn't have to go to school today," Rory told Mac. "It's a snow day. But Ursula said we have to wait to go snowshoeing 'cause she had a bunch of stuff she had to do with all the snow and no 'lectricity. I helped her carry the wood for the fire."

"Good for you. Ursula's lucky to have you." He and the dog followed Rory toward the hearth.

Ursula hung their coats and his backpack on hooks near the fire to dry. "Have a seat. I'll bring the coffee in here. It's the warmest spot in the house. Rory, do you want hot chocolate?"

"With marshmallows?"

"Of course. Mac, coffee or hot chocolate?"

"Coffee for me, but are you sure you don't want to get the generator going first?"

"It can wait a few more minutes." Besides, if she didn't stop and regain her composure first, she might just take a wrench and beat the stupid thing into a modern sculpture. "I'll be right back."

She arranged a tray with mugs of coffee, Rory's hot chocolate and a plate of oatmeal cookies she'd taken from the freezer that morning and carried it to the great room.

Mac cleared space on the coffee table for her to set the

tray. He picked up a mug and took a sip. "Thank you. I needed this."

"Have a cookie. They're cranberry oatmeal with almonds."

"You don't have to ask me twice."

Blossom had stretched out on the hearthrug, with Van Gogh pressed against her belly like a cat-skin blanket. Rory sat beside them, stroking the dog's head. Blossom opened one eye to watch Mac eat the cookie, but apparently deciding he wasn't likely to share, she shut it again.

Ursula handed Rory her cup and a cookie before sinking into one of the chairs. She sipped her coffee, feeling some of the tension slip away as she watched Mac devour another cookie. He looked right at home in the firelight, wearing a wool shirt in a classic black-and-yellow plaid.

"Is that your family tartan?"

"Aye, 'tis the Macleod dress." Mac grinned. "Are you Scottish?" He handed her the plate and she took a cookie.

"No, just an admirer of beautiful fabric. Do you have a kilt, as well?"

He laughed. "I don't. Andi tried to talk me into getting one when we visited Scotland, but I just can't see myself in a skirt."

"When did you go to Scotland?" She nibbled on the cookie.

"The summer after Andi's senior year of high school. I wanted to see our ancestral home. She wanted to meet cute Scottish boys. We compromised."

"Oh?" She had a feeling Mac would not have been a permissive father, especially when it came to boys. "How?"

"She agreed to accompany me to castles and museums, and I agreed not to accompany her to a cèilidh she attended with a distant cousin. And she didn't have to taste haggis."

"Sounds like a fair deal to me."

"What's haggis?" Rory asked.

"Oatmeal and sheep liver cooked in sheep stomach."

"Yuck!" Rory shuddered. "Did you eat it?"

"I did." Mac grinned. "It's not quite as bad as it sounds."

Ursula laughed. "I don't see how it could be."

Mac stood and reached for his coat. "Well, now that I'm fortified with caffeine and cookies, let's take a look at that generator."

MAC ZIPPED HIS coat while Ursula gave careful instructions forbidding Rory to touch the doors of the fireplace. "You can dog-sit Blossom while Mac and I are outside, okay?"

"Okay." Rory set her empty cup on the table and draped herself across Blossom with her arms around the dog's neck. Blossom thumped her tail against the ground.

"Thanks." Mac smiled as Blossom raised her ears as if considering whether she should beg to go with him, and then lowered them again, content to stay by the fire with Rory.

They were halfway to the door when Ursula paused and looked back. "Rory, no treats for the dog while we're gone."

"Aww."

"Too many treats could make her sick. Promise?"

Rory gave a dramatic sigh. "I promise."

Satisfied, Ursula turned and led him through the back door to the generator. An open toolbox lay nearby. She aimed a powerful flashlight at the engine while he bent over to inspect it. It was trying to start but he couldn't get it to catch, and working in the cold and dark wasn't helping. Ursula stamped her feet. Mac's felt frozen, too.

He straightened. "It might be a blocked fuel supply line. Do you have any spray lubricant?"

"I think so. Come with me and tell me what you need."

He followed her into the still-warm garage. The can of lube he needed was right in front on one of the shelves, although he was almost tempted to pretend he couldn't find it just to enjoy a few more minutes of warmth. But the sooner they finished, the sooner they could return to the fire. He grabbed the can.

Twenty minutes later, Mac had cleared the line and reassembled the generator. "Here goes nothing."

"Fingers crossed." Ursula bounced on her toes as she waited.

Mac pressed the starter, and the engine roared to life. He grinned and turned toward Ursula. She threw her arms around his neck. "Thank you, Mac!"

Considering how many layers of clothes they were both wearing, there was no way he could have felt her body heat, and yet the hug warmed him. She stepped back, still beaming. "You're a miracle worker."

He tipped an imaginary hat. "Aw, shucks, ma'am."

She laughed. "Come on, cowboy. I left a pot of beef stew simmering on the stove, and you've certainly earned your keep tonight. Let's go in where it's warm."

They picked up the tools and dropped them off in the garage on their way into the house, where they found Rory and Blossom engaged in a rowdy game involving a tennis ball and a lot of running and giggling. The flickering light of the fire and candles created shadows where the girl and dog would hide and then reappear into the light. Blossom had the ball in her mouth, but it wasn't clear who was chasing whom.

Ursula stopped with her eyebrows raised and watched as they dashed under one of the dining tables in the great room. Mac expected her to call a halt to the roughhousing, but she just laughed and removed a glass bowl from the buffet table. "I'd better take this to the kitchen for safekeeping. You and Blossom need to run off your energy, because supper's in fifteen minutes, okay?"

"'Kay." Rory vaulted over the couch. Blossom, who wasn't allowed on furniture, barked and ran around to meet her on the other side. Ursula smiled and shook her head.

"Come on, Mac. Let's have a glass of that Bordeaux while the wild things play in here."

He followed her to the kitchen, where she put away the bowl and stirred the soup while he poured the wine. He handed her a glass, and she clinked it against his. "To good neighbors."

"Good neighbors, indeed." Mac sipped his wine.

In the other room, a loud bark was followed by a squeal and more giggles. Ursula winced. "We usually have rules about running in the house, but since I don't have guests and she's been shut in all day long, I figure today is an exception."

"It's a snow day. Everyone knows the usual rules don't apply to snow days."

"I was hoping you'd say that."

The stew was excellent. Of course, based on his experience with Ursula's cooking, Mac had expected nothing less. She served it with crusty bread that was probably homemade and more cookies for dessert. He fed the dog and insisted on helping wash the dishes, while Ursula dried and Rory wiped the table.

Rory came to tug on Ursula's hand. "Can I watch a movie?"

"No. Remember I told you no television when we're on generator power."

"Then what are we gonna do?"

"Do you have a deck of cards?" Mac asked.

"Sure." Ursula found a deck in one of the kitchen drawers.

Mac sat at the table. "I know a game called concentration."

"What's that?" Rory asked.

"I'll show you." Mac shuffled and laid out the cards in rows. "Turn over two cards. If they match, you get to keep them. If they don't, turn them back over. The person with the most matches wins. You go first."

Rory turned over a queen and a five. "They don't match."

"That's okay," Mac said. "Remember where you saw them and turn them back over."

Ursula came to sit with them. "May I play?"

"Of course." Mac smiled. "You're next."

Ursula turned over a two and a seven. Mac turned an ace and a queen. "No match."

Rory bounced in her seat. She could hardly wait for him to turn the cards back over before she flipped the queen she'd uncovered and the one Mac had turned. "I got a match!"

"Good job. Since you made a match, you get to go again."

They played on, the tip of Rory's tongue peeking from the corner of her mouth as she memorized the positions of all the cards. At the end of the game, she was the clear winner with fourteen matches. Ursula had four and Mac had eight.

"Wow." Ursula shuffled the cards. "I don't know how you remembered where all those cards were hiding."

Mac smiled. "Amazing, isn't it? Andi used to beat me regularly when she was this age. Must be something about a young mind and visual memory."

"Who's Andi?" Rory asked. "You talked about her before."

Mac's heart tightened, but he kept smiling for Rory's sake. "My daughter, Andrea. Everyone called her Andi for short."

"Rory is short for Aurora," Rory explained.

"Aurora is a beautiful name."

"Does Andi live in your house?"

"No." Mac sucked in a slow breath. Ursula was watching him with sympathetic eyes. "Andi died."

The corners of Rory's mouth turned downward. "Do you miss her?"

Mac nodded. "Every day."

"My mom and dad died, too. And my grandma."

"I'm sorry."

"I miss them, too." Her eyes glistened with unshed tears. "Ursula says it's okay to be sad sometimes because you miss people, but they don't want you to be sad all the time. They want you to be happy, 'cause they love you. Laughing makes angels happy. And even though you can't see them anymore, you can still love each other."

"Yes." It was all Mac could choke out.

Rory slipped off her chair and came to hug him. "We can be sad together."

Tears now flowed freely from Ursula's eyes. Blossom got up from the rug where she'd been lying to push her head between Mac and Rory and lick Rory's tears away. Rory giggled. "Blossom says we should stop crying."

Mac stroked the dog's head. "She's probably right."

Ursula reached for a box of tissues and everyone took a moment to blow noses and wipe cheeks. Rory settled into her chair at the table. "Do you want to play again?"

"Okay." Mac began laying out the cards. "But this time I'm going to win."

AFTER THE NEXT GAME, which Mac did indeed win, Ursula flicked on a battery-powered radio to check on the news. Crews were still working to clear the avalanche, and the road into Seward was not yet plowed. School was cancelled.

Rory cheered. "No school tomorrow, so I can sleep."

"I guess so." Interesting. Ursula hadn't noticed Rory was particularly fond of sleeping in.

"That means I get to stay up late."

Ah, that's where this was going. "Why do you want to stay up late?"

"I want to keep playing with Mac."

Well, why not? They both seemed to be enjoying it, and goodness knows, they deserved a little fun. Ursula smiled. "I guess we can play a little longer. I'm starting to get the hang of it now. Maybe I'll win this round."

She didn't, but it didn't matter. They paused the card game long enough to pop popcorn in the fire, and then Rory and Mac duked it out for the title of Concentration Champion. At the end of the night, Mac had won two, Rory three, and Ursula came in second once. By that time, Rory was about to fall asleep in her chair.

"Bedtime," Ursula announced. "You can skip a bath tonight, but you need to brush your teeth."

Rory managed to change into her pajamas and take a few swipes with her toothbrush before Ursula tucked her into bed. She was asleep almost before her head hit the pillow. She looked like an angel, blond hair shimmering in the nightlight, her mouth relaxed in a small smile. Peaceful.

Ursula returned to the kitchen, where Mac had put away the cards and was staring out the window. "Is she asleep?" He spoke without turning.

"Yes. She's resting easy tonight."

"I'm sorry if I upset her earlier, talking about Andi."

"You didn't. In fact, I think she found it comforting to realize she wasn't the only one who's lost family. It makes her feel less alone."

He continued to stare into the darkness. Ursula boiled the kettle. "I'm having a cup of chamomile tea. Want some?"

"No, thanks. Not a fan of herbal teas." Mac turned toward her. "How did Rory end up here, with you?"

Ursula added her teabag to the cup and settled at the table. "It's a long story."

Mac sat down in the chair next to hers and leaned forward. "I'm not going anywhere."

"Well, it started a little over eight years ago, when I was

still living in Anchorage. Rory's grandmother Gen Houston was a good friend of mine. She lived in Soldotna, but was in Anchorage having lunch with me when her son, Coby, called to say his wife, Kendall, was having their baby a little earlier than expected. We went straight to the hospital." She smiled. "Rory was beautiful, even as a newborn."

"I'll bet."

"There were complications, with an emergency C-section and ultimately Kendall had to have more surgery. They needed lots of help while Kendall recovered, so Gen and I took turns with baby care and housework. Coby couldn't afford to spend too much time away from work. They'd just opened a ski store a few months before."

"No wonder they made you godmother."

"Gen passed away a couple of years ago, so I'd sort of been filling the role of Rory's grandmother, too."

Mac frowned in concentration. "Coby Houston. Why does that name sound familiar?"

"Do you follow winter sports?"

"A Nordic skier, right? Seems like he did some human-interest stuff about Alaska. That would have been about ten years ago."

Ursula nodded. "He was on the team that took bronze in the sprint."

"Kendall—not Kendall Normand? The freestyle skier?"

"That's the one."

"I remember her. Amazing talent in the aerials. She could almost fly. As I recall, after she won the medal,, she was on every talk show for a while and appeared in a commercial or two. Then it seemed like she dropped out of sight."

"Yes. When she got pregnant, they decided to move to Alaska and settle down, to try to have a normal life."

"What happened to them?"

"Faulty furnace. They'd been living in an apartment but decided they wanted more room and a yard for Rory, so they moved into a rental house. It was old but had a lot of square footage. They didn't realize anything was amiss for the first month. Then the first real cold snap came along."

Ursula's throat tightened, thinking about what came next. A happy family, gone overnight. She took a swallow of tea to clear her throat before continuing. "Thank goodness Rory had heard a cat crying outside. She'd opened the window and it got stuck so she couldn't get it closed. That's what saved her."

Mac's face looked thunderous. "Didn't the landlord have the furnace checked? And put in carbon monoxide detectors?"

"Apparently not." Ursula shook her head. "His insurance paid a settlement. It's in an account for Rory when she's ready to go to college. Doesn't bring her family back, though."

"Didn't Kendall have family? I seem to remember her parents getting quite a bit of airtime during the big competitions."

"Parents." Ursula scoffed. "Yes. Kendall's parents were milking her success for everything it was worth. After she retired, they weren't interested anymore." Once, when she and Kendall were folding laundry together, Kendall had told her the story. "Her mother was a figure skater. Almost world championship caliber. Almost. She was convinced she would have been the best if only her parents had started her earlier and given her better training. She married a wealthy man, and from the time Kendall was born, her mother was grooming her to be a winner.

"When she was two, they had Kendall on the ice and learning gymnastics. They entered her in skating competitions as soon as she qualified. She was good, but not good enough. She would never be a world-class skater. Then they discovered she had talent for skiing. Freestyle was just taking off, and Kendall's mother was shrewd enough to see an opportunity there. So they moved to Colorado where Kendall could train."

"And she grew up to medal."

"She got silver. Not good enough for her mother. She informed Kendall she was to devote the next four years to perfecting herself. But for once, Kendall rebelled. She started dating this Nordic skier she'd met at the competition. Coby adored her. I think it was the first time in her life Kendall had ever experienced unconditional love."

"And she felt the same about him?"

"She did, but her mother was pressuring her to break it off with him and focus on her skiing. Then Kendall got pregnant. She and Coby decided they wanted their child to have a normal childhood, so they married and moved to Alaska where he'd grown up. Kendall's parents were furious. They squawked and threatened, and finally disowned her. They've never even seen Rory."

"Even after the accident?"

"They sent a lawyer, but Coby and Kendall had wills appointing Rory's grandmother Gen as guardian, and me as contingent. They didn't try to dispute it."

"I can't imagine they why wouldn't want to see their own granddaughter."

"I can't either. The only explanation I can come up with is to their way of thinking, she's what kept Kendall from going after that top podium."

"It sounds as though Rory's better off without them in her life." Mac laid his hand over Ursula's. "I'm glad she has you."

CHAPTER EIGHT

Mac woke and gazed upward into the darkness, debating whether to get up or burrow deeper into the comfortable bed and go back to sleep. The curtains at the window weren't quite closed, but no light showed through. He'd eaten well, enjoyed his evening with Ursula and Rory and slept through the night—simple pleasures he used to take for granted. He pressed the button to light up the face of his watch. Six twenty.

Blossom roused herself from the pallet Ursula had made for her at the foot of the bed, her tags tinkling, and padded over to Mac, taking the decision out of his hands. He greeted the dog, did his push-ups, got dressed and made his way to the kitchen, hoping for coffee to sip while he let the dog outside. When he opened the door, he spotted Ursula standing on a wooden chair, taking something from the top shelf of her kitchen cabinet. She spun around at the sound, dropping whatever she had in her hand. It hit the floor and scattered. The chair teetered.

Mac rushed forward and grabbed her around the waist. "I've got you, darlin'." He set her gently on her feet on the kitchen floor.

"Thanks, cowboy." She gazed up at him, her eyes wide, lips slightly parted.

Maybe it was because his hands were still around her waist. Maybe it was the look of trust on her face. Whatever it was, some long-buried instinct kicked in and he bent to kiss her lips. After the briefest hesitation, she responded, reaching up to wrap her arms around his neck.

It felt good, natural, and he realized he'd wanted this for some time now. He pulled her closer, deepening the kiss. His heart pumped as though he was on push-up number forty-nine. Finally, he lifted his head. Ursula traced her fingers along his jaw. Blossom nudged his leg but he ignored her to study the warm light in Ursula's eyes. Hazel eyes, he realized, green but with intriguing brown and golden speckles, like flecks of mica.

But suddenly, Ursula blinked and stepped back. She bent to gather up the batteries that had rolled across the floor. "I don't know what I was thinking, climbing on that chair. I was using the step stool upstairs yesterday and didn't want to take the trouble to go up and get it. Stupid of me. This would be the absolute worst time for a broken leg. They'd probably have to send the helicopter. Maybe I should buy another step stool for upstairs…"

Mac stood where he was, absently stroking the dog's head as he watched Ursula flutter around the kitchen. Apparently, they were going to pretend that kiss never happened. Part of him was relieved. This wasn't something he'd planned, and he didn't have a follow-up. Ursula was his neighbor and his friend, and he wanted to keep it that way. He shouldn't be complicating their relationship.

But a perverse part of him was annoyed. How could she brush off that kiss like that as if it were negligible? Like he'd accidentally bumped her hand when they reached for something at the same time. Didn't she feel what he'd felt?

She set the batteries on the counter and turned, her chatter finally trailing off as she met his eyes. Even in this light, he could see that her cheeks were flushed, and she seemed to be breathing more rapidly than usual. She wasn't unaffected after all. An almost shy smile was blooming when the kitchen door opened.

"Where's Blossom?" Rory galloped into the room, still in her pajamas, and slid across the floor in her fuzzy socks. Blossom almost knocked him down in her hurry to greet Rory.

"Good morning." Ursula laughed. "I guess we know where we rank around here. Mac and I are here, too, you know."

Rory looked up from petting Blossom and grinned. "Good morning, Mac. Good morning, Ursula. Can we make a snowman today?"

"I need to head over to the cabin soon to feed my wood-stove," Mac said, "or my pipes might freeze."

"Can I come?" Rory begged. "We didn't get to go snow-shoeing."

"If it's okay with Ursula."

"We can all go," Ursula said, "once we've had breakfast. After that, we'll see about building a snowman. What are you hungry for?"

"Oatmeal." Rory dashed toward the pantry. "I'll get the dried blueberries."

"Is that okay with you, Mac? I've got eggs and bacon if you'd rather have that." Ursula glanced at him and then looked away, a smile tugging at the corners of her mouth.

"Ursula makes real good oatmeal," Rory volunteered, popping out of the pantry carrying a jar.

"I'll bet." Mac replied, his eyes on Ursula. "I haven't found anything she doesn't do well."

AFTER BREAKFAST, they all bundled up and strapped on their snowshoes. Mac let Rory take the lead. The trip to the cabin was uneventful, other than watching Rory run rings around him. She moved with ease and grace, even on snowshoes. She'd obviously inherited her parents' natural athletic abili-ties.

Blossom, discovering it was much easier to run over a packed trail, stuck close to them, until she spotted a squirrel. She plunged into the woods, immediately vanishing as she sank into the snow. She leaped forward and sank again, making slow progress toward the tree. Meanwhile the squirrel had climbed the trunk and was watching her from just overhead, chattering. Mac and Ursula stopped to watch.

"How do sled dogs keep from falling through the snow like that?" Mac asked Ursula.

"Huskies have big feet with fur between their toes. They're probably three times the size of Blossom's feet, and the dogs weigh less. Besides, mushers tend to stick to packed trails."

Blossom reached the tree and the squirrel moved to the other side of the trunk. When Blossom followed it, it circled back to their side. Blossom gradually packed the snow around the tree, following the squirrel who, rather than climbing higher, kept circling the trunk at about the six-foot level, just close enough to give Blossom hope.

Mac laughed. "I never realized squirrels had such a sense of humor."

Ursula chuckled along with him. "They're wicked teases."

Rory, realizing she'd left them behind, retraced her steps. "What are you looking at?"

"Blossom's trying to catch a squirrel."

"It's not Frankie, is it?" Rory asked, her eyes wide.

"I don't think so. Don't worry. Even if it is, Blossom doesn't stand a chance."

Eventually, Blossom came to the same conclusion and returned to them. Rory led the way to Mac's cabin. They all left their snowshoes on the porch and went inside. The fire had been reduced to embers, but it was still well above freezing inside. Mac replenished the stove.

When he turned, Rory was holding one of the wood spirits he'd started on one particularly bad night. Although only roughed in, the expression on the spirit's face was one of intense anger. Maybe he should take it away before it scared her.

But Rory didn't seem scared. She studied the face, almost as though she recognized it. Ursula came to stand behind her and wrapped her arms around the girl's shoulders. "Mac made that. He carves faces in wood."

Rory pulled off her glove and touched the wood gingerly. "He's mad."

"Who's mad?" Ursula asked.

"The man in the wood. He's mad because his family went away and left him all alone." Rory stroked the wood. "But somebody will be nice to him and he won't be mad anymore."

"You think so?" Ursula asked.

Rory nodded. "And then he'll laugh, and the angels will be happy."

Mac took a deep breath and slowly let it out. The simple wisdom of children. Rory had lost more than he ever had, and yet she was brave enough to laugh again.

But there was a big difference between his situation and Rory's. Rory bore no responsibility for the death of her loved ones. She deserved to move forward and live a good and happy life. He wasn't sure he could say the same.

ONCE THEY'D MADE it back to the B&B and had lunch, Rory was itching to get started on the promised snowman. Ursula urged them outside. "You two go ahead and get started. I'll just tidy up and gather some accessories for Mr. Snowman."

"It's gonna be a girl," Rory declared.

"Miss Snowman, then." Ursula tugged Rory's hat down so it better covered her ears. "Have fun."

Rory led Mac and Blossom to an open area just past the deck, where her creation would be visible from the living room. Mac reached down and gathered a snowball. Fortunately, it had been relatively warm when it snowed, and the new snow stuck together nicely. He threw the ball at a tree, but missed. Blossom charged after the ball, digging furiously in the snow. She couldn't seem to understand why she couldn't find a snowball hidden within a snowdrift. Rory laughed so hard she hiccuped.

Once she'd caught her breath, Rory patted a ball together, set it on the ground and started rolling it, picking up snow as she went. Obviously not her first snowman. When the ball grew to the point she was having trouble pushing it, Mac helped her roll it to a spot directly in front of the windows. They stepped back, and Blossom jumped onto the snowball and stood there wagging her tail.

Rory giggled. "She thinks we made her a chair."

"Or maybe a throne. We'll let her enjoy it while we roll the next snowball." As soon as they turned their attention away, Blossom jumped down and scurried over to see what they were doing, snuffling along behind the ball Rory was rolling.

Once Rory declared it the right size, Mac lifted the heavy ball on top of the first one, and they patted more snow around the middle. Rory was rolling the ball for a head when Ursula joined them. She'd brought the traditional carrot for a nose, along with dark polished rocks, a couple of different hats and a hank of yellow yarn.

"Where'd you get the rocks?" Mac asked.

"They were in the pot with my ficus tree. I'll get more from the creek next summer."

Rory carried the last snowball over to Ursula. "Look what me and Mac made."

"It's a big one."

"The biggest one ever. Mac, can you put this on top? I can't reach."

Mac set the head in place and then held Rory up so she could arrange the carrot and rocks into a face for her snowperson. With Ursula's help, she braided the yarn into a long rope and draped it over the head, then added a winter hat and birch branches for arms. She stood back to inspect it. "She needs ski poles."

"There are some old ones hanging on the wall in the garage," Ursula told her. "Why don't you run get them?"

While they waited, Ursula came to stand beside Mac. "Nice job. Thanks for helping Rory build it."

"No need to thank me. I enjoyed it." And, to his surprise, Mac realized it was the truth. Rory's energy and enthusiasm were contagious. It had been a long time since he'd done any playing.

Rory came back, carrying a pair of black ski poles. Blossom tagged along beside her, apparently no longer concerned about sticks, at least as far as Rory was concerned. Rory hooked the poles onto the branch hands so that her snow girl appeared to be skiing. She looked it over and pronounced it good. Mac pulled out his phone and took Rory's photo, posing beside her snow creation.

Afterward, they went inside to sip hot chocolate and admire the view through the window. A raven landed on the snowgirl's hat.

"What's he doing?" Rory ran to the window. A minute later, the raven snatched the carrot and flew away. "Hey, that's our carrot. Bring it back."

Ursula laughed. "He probably needs it worse than you do. You can take another carrot out later. Or maybe a potato would be less tempting."

Rory returned to the couch while she thought it over. "Potatoes don't look like noses."

Mac tapped his finger on the end of Rory's upturned nose. "Yours doesn't look much like a carrot either."

"I have some hot peppers," Ursula said. "Maybe that would discourage the raven."

Rory accepted a green jalapeño and ran outside to replace the carrot. It looked good. Mac decided all snowmen should have pepper noses. "I can't wait to see the raven's reaction if he tries to steal it."

The sun had set and the three of them were in the kitchen washing the hot chocolate mugs when the motion-sensing light over the garage flashed on.

"Oh, good," Ursula said. "That means the power's restored. I'll go shut down the generator."

Mac set the last mug in the drainer. "Guess I'd better head home." Not that he wanted to. He'd found a little interlude of tranquility here at Ursula's inn with her and Rory. He realized, with a pang of guilt, that he'd almost forgotten about Andi's murder for a day. But he didn't want to forget. The killer was still out there. Mac hadn't been able to keep his daughter safe, but he was going to do whatever it took to make sure her murderer was caught and punished. He shouldn't be having fun while Joel Thaine was free.

"Stay for supper," Ursula urged.

"No. I need to go." Mac slipped into his coat and hat and shrugged his backpack onto his shoulder. "Thank you for your hospitality."

Rory ran to give him a hug. "I can build a snowman at your house tomorrow if you want."

"I don't think so." Mac patted her head. "But thank you for the offer. And thank you for sharing your home with me." He bent to fasten Blossom's coat.

"Bye, Blossom." Rory hugged the dog. "Remember to give Mac lots of kisses."

Mac almost let it go, but his curiosity won out. "Why should Blossom give me lots of kisses?"

Rory gave him a pitying look, like the answer should be obvious. "Because dog kisses make you laugh," she said. "And laughing makes the angels happy."

CHAPTER NINE

As soon as Mac had checked the cabin to make sure the heat and refrigerator were running, he pulled out his phone and called the private investigator. Chandler answered on the second ring.

"It's Mac. I've been out of touch for a couple of days, so I wanted to check in. Have you found anything?"

Chandler made a noncommittal noise. "Afraid I don't have much to report. I've followed every lead from the hotline, and so far they've all been mistaken identity."

"I've been thinking. The police believe Thaine is still in the US, so eventually he'll turn up. In the meantime, why don't you focus on background? When they catch him, I want to make sure he stays caught."

"The cops didn't find any previous arrests."

"I know. But people don't turn into killers overnight." Over the years, Mac had poured over the research regarding the psychology of murderers. "There's bound to be a trail. What have you discovered about family?"

"Parents are dead. A half-sister out there somewhere, but haven't yet been able to locate her. They were raised in separate households. No phone calls between them in the last three years."

"Neighbors?"

"Not much there. 'Kept to himself. Seemed nice enough.' The usual story." Chandler paused. "I do have a childhood address. I could see who's still living there, see if anyone remembers the family. It's a long shot."

"Do it. Let me know what you find."

"I'll get right on it."

Mac hung up the phone, trying to think of another string to pull, another lead to follow. He'd failed Andi. He'd recognized that she was pulling away, putting distance between them, but he'd been so busy writing books he'd failed to recognize it wasn't her need for independence but her boyfriend's manipulations that caused her to push him away. If Mac had been paying attention, he'd have been in time to keep her safe.

He wasn't going to fail her again. He didn't need to be spending his time building snowmen and kissing pretty innkeepers. Not with Andi's killer still on the loose.

URSULA MADE A final room check for the three couples arriving that afternoon, now that the Seward highway was clear. Two of the couples were repeat customers who came out every winter to ski. The third were first-timers. When the woman made the reservation, she'd mentioned they'd be on their honeymoon. She was so excited she'd insisted on telling Ursula the whole story. It was a second marriage for them both. The two couples had been good friends for decades. They lost their spouses within two years of each other and in comforting one another, they'd fallen in love.

Ursula loved stories like that. She put them in the best suite at the end of the hall and set out a bowl of chocolates. She hadn't had a chance to get into town for flowers, so she moved the biggest African violet from the kitchen to their room along with an iron candelabra and beeswax battery-powered candles. Instant romance.

As an innkeeper, she'd witnessed plenty of romance but hadn't experienced it herself in the past few years. Not until yesterday. She touched her finger to her lips, remembering Mac's kiss in the kitchen. He'd stayed with them less than twenty-four hours, and yet it felt like he belonged there. Rory clearly thought so. She'd asked about Mac this morning before school. Ursula had explained that Mac was busy, that they wouldn't be seeing much of him. She didn't want Rory disappointed when he withdrew into his shell once again.

For one day, they'd experienced the real Mac. The man who built snowmen and played cards with little girls and enjoyed life. For one day, he'd held his grief and guilt at bay and let himself live. But then, when the electricity came back on, reality returned and Ursula could almost see the dark rain cloud settle over his head. His grief was all he had left of his daughter, and he was holding onto it for all he was worth.

So why did he kiss her? Maybe it was a simple gesture of comfort after she'd almost fallen off the chair, but that's not what it felt like. There was heat in that kiss. It might have been awhile, but Ursula knew the difference between a casual peck and a kiss that meant something. A kiss that led somewhere.

"Aargh." Ursula shook herself like a dog. Why was she even bothering to think about that kiss? Whatever it might have been, it was over. It wasn't going to happen again. If she knew what was good for her, she'd keep Mac at arm's length. Because, as much as she liked him, in the long run Mac wasn't good for her or Rory.

Ursula had seen guilt and blame rob her family of happiness when her brother died. She wasn't going to let that happen to them. Rory deserved better.

URSULA'S RESOLVE LASTED a little over a week, until the first weekend of Cabin Fever Festival. Rory was excited about attending the fun winter event in Anchorage, and she insisted Mac and Blossom would want to go with them.

How could Ursula explain Mac wouldn't want to come, because he might accidentally have a good time? Rory couldn't possibly understand. She'd played with Mac, built the snowman; she knew he was capable of fun.

"I'll call him," Rory offered.

Well, why not? If Mac didn't want to come, he could explain it to Rory. Why should Ursula have to make excuses for him? She trusted him to be careful of Rory's feelings.

"Here." Ursula pulled up the number on her phone. "Go ahead."

Rory pushed dial and held the phone to her ear. It rang several times, and Ursula had just come to the conclusion that he wasn't going to pick up when he did. Rory jumped right in. "Hi, Mac. Do you wanna come to the Cabin Fever Festival with us tomorrow? There's a Ferris wheel and reindeer, and Sam and Dana and Griffin will be there."

She paused to listen. "Griffin is a baby. He's my aunt." Rory giggled. "I mean, I'm his aunt, 'cause Sam is my brother now… Uh-huh… Okay." She handed Ursula the phone. "He wants to talk to you."

He probably wanted to tell her no so he wouldn't have to let Rory down himself. Ursula accepted the phone. "Hello?"

"What is this about reindeer on Ferris wheels?"

Ursula laughed. "Two separate events. The Cabin Fever Festival is the winter fair in Anchorage."

"I've been reading about it in the newspaper. Outhouse races?"

"And snowshoe softball. They have it all."

"I don't think I—"

"It's up to you. Rory wanted to invite you."

"This is Rory's idea?"

"Yes."

He paused. "I don't want to leave Blossom alone all day."

"You can bring her along. We can leave her at Sam's house with his dog. Kimmik's a Labrador. He loves everyone and everything."

"I don't want to disappoint Rory, but…" He trailed off.

Ursula could have jumped in and assured him Rory wouldn't be disappointed, but it wasn't true. Rory wanted him there, and Ursula wanted Rory happy. Besides, if there was any chance for healing, Mac needed to get out, meet people, live. She let the silence build, waiting for his answer. Finally, he sighed. "What time?"

"We'll pick you up at eight. Dress warmly. We'll be outside most of the day."

"Tell Rory I'll see her then."

Ursula smiled. "I'll tell her." She ended the call.

Rory was already dancing around the room. "Mac's coming and bringing Blossom. And we get to see Sam and Dana and Griffin and Kimmik. Do you think Griffin will like Blossom?"

"I'm sure he will." Griffin laughed every time he spotted a dog.

"Will he remember me?"

"Of course. It's only been a month since he last saw you."

"Tomorrow's gonna be fun."

MAC CHECKED HIS WATCH. It would be a quarter to eleven in Kansas. He had time to check in with Chandler before Ursula arrived. On the other hand, if Chandler had anything new to report, he would have called. Until he did, there was nothing Mac could do to help Andi. But maybe there was something he could do for another little girl.

He wasn't sure about this outing, meeting a bunch of people and attending public events. He'd done everything he could to stay out of the public eye. But this wasn't about him. Any press he encountered today would be there to cover the festival, not him. All the same, he selected a muffler that could partially obscure his face if he felt it prudent. Maybe he should add sunglasses, as well. Or maybe just forget the whole thing.

Before he could talk himself out of going, Blossom

rushed to the window and barked at the sound of a car arriving. She stopped barking and wagged her tail, recognizing Ursula and Rory when they got out. Mac grabbed Blossom's leash and was out the door before they arrived.

Rory ran forward to greet Blossom. "Mac, guess what? We brought carrots to feed the reindeer. Marissa said we could."

More people. Just what he needed. But Rory looked so excited, Mac couldn't begrudge her. He managed a smile. "That's great. Who's Marissa?"

"She's Chris's wife. They're Sam's friends. They have a reindeer farm." Rory climbed into the back seat. She spent most of the drive chattering and singing to Blossom, so Mac didn't have to say much. Occasionally, Rory would address a remark to him. "I'm gonna ride the Ferris wheel, but not the Hammer. It's too scary. Do you wanna ride the Hammer?"

"No, I don't think so."

"Will you do the Tilt-a-Whirl with me?"

"Sure."

"Good. Ursula says she can't, 'cause her stomach doesn't like it."

He glanced toward Ursula. Judging by the twitching at the corner of her mouth, this was exactly what she'd planned to happen. He grinned. "Fortunately for Ursula, I have a strong stomach."

Once they reached Anchorage, Ursula pulled up in the driveway of a modest split-level that backed up to the forest. Before they could knock on the door, a dark-haired woman holding a baby opened it and ushered them up the stairs. She closed a baby gate behind them and they all hugged and greeted each other. Ursula took the baby in her arms before introducing Mac. "Mac, this is Dana MacKettrick, and this handsome young man is my grandson, Griffin."

Mac smiled at the baby and offered a hand to Dana. "Mac Macleod."

Rory was talking to the baby. Griffin leaned from Ursula's arms trying to reach her. Cute kid, with a thatch of dark hair and eyes already turning from blue to brown, like his mother's. Finally, Ursula set him on the floor, where he started crawling purposefully toward Rory.

"Oh, here's Sam." A dark-haired man carrying a large diaper bag trotted up the stairs to join them, followed by a brown dog. Mac held onto Blossom's leash until he was sure they'd get along, but they simply sniffed one another and wagged their tails. The man set the bag aside and rested his hand on his wife's back. Ursula introduced them.

Sam offered his hand. "Nice to meet you, Mr. Macleod. Ursula told me you'd bought the cabin next door. I've read some of your books."

"Call me Mac." Mac was never quite sure what to say when people mentioned reading his books. Asking if they liked them sounded insecure. *Thank you* seemed awkward.

Fortunately, Sam didn't seem to expect a response. He turned and opened his arms. "And here's Rory. How's my favorite girl?"

Rory stopped playing with the baby long enough to give him a hug. "Hi, Sam. When are we going to see the reindeer?"

"Just as soon as we can get Griffin's stuff packed up and his snowsuit on, which could take an hour or so with the way he wiggles."

It didn't. Dana packed a few diapers and snacks into the bag while Rory distracted the baby and Sam zipped him into his snowsuit. Fifteen minutes later, Blossom was curled up against the Lab on his bed in the corner, and they were on their way. Rory chose to ride in the car with Griffin, which left Mac and Ursula alone in her car for the trip downtown.

"Cute baby," Mac offered. "Does he look like your son did at that age?"

Ursula beamed. "Isn't he? I'm not sure if Griffin looks

like Sam did. Sam didn't come into our lives until he was ten. He was twelve when his mother took off and he moved in with us."

"What do you mean, took off?"

"Exactly that. We lived near Sam's elementary school, and we got to know him. My husband, Tommy, liked to build things, and Sam loved hanging around and helping. Occasionally he'd stay over with us when his mom went out. One day, she didn't come back for him. So we kept him."

"She never came back for her son?"

"No. After that, Sam was ours."

He looked at Ursula with admiration. "You must have done a good job raising him. He seems a fine man."

"He works hard and loves his family. I couldn't be prouder of him."

"And now you're doing it again. Raising someone else's child."

Ursula shook her head. "Not someone else's. They're mine. Both of them. I might not have given birth, but I love those kids with all my heart." Ursula drove on for a moment without speaking. When she stopped at a traffic light, she turned toward him. "My friend Marge seems to think by taking in Rory, I'm making some sort of sacrifice. She's wrong. I love that girl. I loved her parents, too, and while I wish they could have been the ones to raise Rory, I'm blessed to have her. She belongs to me, and I belong to her." The light changed, and she drove onward. "Sorry. I guess I'm a little touchy about the idea that Sam and Rory aren't really mine."

"I understand, and you're right. They're lucky to be yours."

"We're all lucky." Ursula parallel parked in front of a gift shop. They walked two spaces up to Sam's Jeep.

Rory jumped out of the car and bounced on her toes. "Where are the reindeer?"

"Over on Fourth. Just wait right there while we get organized," Ursula said. She helped Sam arrange the baby in a backpack while Dana gathered the baby's things.

Meanwhile, Rory's head swiveled. She was showing signs of bolting. Mac reached for her hand. "Rory and I are just going to walk over to that dog statue, okay?"

"Good idea." Ursula flashed him a smile.

He let Rory lead him to the statue of a husky. "Oh, it's Balto. I know this story."

"He's the dog who brought medicine."

"Right. For the diphtheria epidemic in Nome."

"That's why the Iditarod goes to Nome."

Mac chuckled. "How come you're so smart?"

Rory thought before she answered. "Because I ask questions. Mommy said that's the way to learn things."

"Your mom sounds like she was pretty smart, too."

Rory nodded. "She knew lots of stuff. She was pretty, too. And real good at skiing."

"I know. I saw her on television."

"You saw my mom?"

"Yes. I saw her when she was competing and won a medal."

"Daddy won a medal, too."

"I know. That's really cool."

Rory wrapped her arms around herself. "Mommy said skiing in the meets was fun, but not as fun as skiing with me and Daddy in Kincaid Park."

"I'll bet."

The group caught up with them. "Ready to find the reindeer?" Dana asked Rory.

"Finally." Rory grabbed Dana's hand and tugged her along the sidewalk. Mac wasn't sure she knew where she was going, but she was determined they were going to get there fast. Sam hurried to catch up with them.

Ursula dropped back to walk beside Mac. "You know, you should really be in this event. Very Hemingway-esque."

"Ah, such a shame I didn't sign up."

Her eyes crinkled in the corners. "I happen to have connections with the reindeer people. I could get you in."

"Into what, exactly?"

"The Running of the Reindeer. It's Anchorage's answer to the Running of the Bulls in Pamplona."

"Yeah, uh, don't they have a lot of casualties in Pamplona? Sounds like a young man's game."

"Well, the course here only goes five blocks, and the reindeer are much gentler than bulls. They're female, for one thing."

"All of them?"

"All the ones they bring for this event. The males have already shed their antlers."

"Antlers. That's what I'm avoiding."

Ursula laughed. "What kind of cowboy's afraid of deer?"

"The prudent kind." He could just imagine how a herd of cattle would react to this crowd. Mac was starting to notice a strange preponderance of elaborate fur hats among the people gathering. Of course, it was the fair. The crowd grew denser as they got closer, but Ursula led him through the throngs toward a roped-off area where Rory and the others were talking to a group of people, including a boy a year or two older than Rory.

A red-bearded man stepped over to raise the rope and allow Ursula and Mac under. "Thanks, Chris. This is Mac." Once they were inside, Ursula introduced Mac to the rest of the group. The oldest man, Oliver, who bore a striking resemblance to Santa Claus, explained to Mac that they were three generations of reindeer farmers. Mac let it slip he'd grown up on a ranch, and before he could find an excuse, he'd been pressed into service helping unload reindeer from the trucks.

Fortunately, they didn't seem to be easily spooked by the crowd, and Mac found he enjoyed working with the reindeer. Rory was in her element, petting one of them and feeding it carrots while the boy holding its lead rope told her the names of all the others as they came off the truck. Dana took Griffin and went to stand with the spectators, but Ursula and Sam stayed and helped.

"How do you get them running?" Mac asked Oliver as he handed him the lead of another reindeer.

"My wife and Marissa have a couple of the herd leaders at the other end of the course. Once we turn them loose, they'll hurry to their friends. We'll run them in batches."

While they had been getting the reindeer ready, some-one had gathered the herd of human runners up ahead. Most seemed to be in costume, dressed as everything from but-terflies to pirates. A group of cavemen wearing only fur loincloths and sneakers jogged in place, their skin slowly turning blue as they waited. Ursula pulled Rory back from the herd.

Someone gave the signal, and the crowd surged forward. After giving them a block or so head start, the reindeer han-dlers snapped off the leads and sent the reindeer on their way. They galloped forward, darting between the runners toward the end of the street. Cheers and laughter erupted from the crowd.

They repeated the procedure with the next herd of hu-mans and reindeer. Meanwhile the catchers at the end of the street brought the reindeer from round one back for an-other go. They managed a total of five waves. Mac was im-pressed. They had this down to a science.

Afterward, they walked a few of the reindeer among the crowds. Rory jumped right in to help, handing out treats for the children to feed the reindeer while their parents took pic-tures. Eventually, they helped load the reindeer back into the trucks and said goodbye to the reindeer farmers. The baby in Dana's arms was beginning to fuss. Sam took him and lifted him high in the air, distracting him for the moment.

Ursula slipped her glove under Mac's elbow. "Well, cowboy. What did you think of your first Running of the Reindeer?"

He grinned. "Whoever came up with that idea had been through a long winter in a small cabin."

"Probably so. Are you hungry?"

"I am," Rory volunteered. "Funnel cakes?"

"Maybe later." Ursula put her other arm around Rory's shoulders and gave her a squeeze. "We need real food for lunch. And Griffin needs his nap. So, what do you say we pick up something and take it to Sam and Dana's?"

"Burgers?" Rory asked hopefully. "From Arctic Roadrunner?"

Ursula looked questioningly at Mac. "I never turn down a good burger," he assured her.

"Burgers it is. Sam," Ursula called, "go ahead and take Griffin home. We'll bring food."

Mac enjoyed lunch. It turned out Sam was an engineer who worked shifts on the North Slope of Alaska and Dana was a math teacher, both with fascinating stories to tell. Mac's writerly instincts kicked in, thinking about how he could use some of these situations in a book, before he remembered he wasn't writing anymore. And why.

Ursula must have noticed that he'd suddenly gone quiet. She gave him a gentle smile and touched his arm before urging Rory to tell Sam and Dana about the snowwoman she and Mac had built while the power was out. Not for the first time, Mac wondered if Ursula read minds.

The rest of the day was like that. Mac and Ursula left Blossom at Sam's and took Rory to watch the people making snow sculptures from giant blocks of snow, and then to the carnival. Mac enjoyed his time with Rory, listening to her speculation about what the snow sculptors were making and her excited squeals at the top of the Ferris wheel. But at the same time, he couldn't help remembering days like this with his own daughter. Andi should have had the chance to marry, to have her own child to ride with on the carousel, to live her life.

But every time he threatened to sink into melancholy, Ursula was there, distracting him with some funny comment or encouraging him to accompany Rory for another turn on the Tilt-a-Whirl or on a quest to find the funnel cake booth.

The sun had set and the sky darkened long before Rory was ready to leave the carnival. After such an activity-filled day, Mac half expected her to collapse face-first into her plate of spaghetti at the Italian restaurant, but she held it together. It wasn't until they picked up Blossom, said their goodbyes and headed home that Rory fell sound asleep in the back seat.

Tires hummed on the highway as Ursula drove through the darkness. They'd made it past Turnagain Arm and weren't far from home when Ursula spoke in a soft voice. "Thank you for coming today. I know it wasn't easy for you."

Mac shrugged. "It was no big deal."

"Yes, it was." Ursula glanced into the rearview mirror. "It was a big deal for Rory. She loved having you along on the rides. You give her courage."

Mac looked back at the sleeping girl. "Rory is one of the most courageous people I've ever met."

"She is, isn't she?" Ursula drove in silence for a few minutes. "I was ten, when my brother died."

"I'm sorry."

Ursula kept her eyes straight ahead on the road. "Billy was only three. My father had come home for lunch. He was running late and had to hurry to get back to work on time. What he didn't realize is that my brother had slipped outside without my mother noticing and was playing behind his car."

"No." Mac's fists tightened, wishing he could stop what came next.

"They say he died instantly." She swallowed. "I used to hear my parents arguing at night, after they thought I was asleep. My mother would say it was an accident, that rehashing it didn't help, but my father would never let it go. He blamed her for not watching Billy more closely. He blamed himself for not checking behind the car before he backed up. Even worse was when the arguing stopped and there was nothing but icy silence."

"Did they divorce?" Mac knew a tragedy of that sort would put tremendous stress on a marriage.

"No. They stayed together. If you can call it that. Maybe it would have been better if they had." She sighed. "One day we were a family that played and laughed and loved. The next day, we weren't. And my father never healed, never let our family heal." She finally glanced over at Mac, her expression resolute. "I'm not going to let that happen to Rory."

"Why should it? Rory has no reason to feel guilty."

"Everyone has regrets when someone they love dies. She mentioned once that her parents moved from an apartment to a house because they wanted her to have a yard to play in."

"It's not her fault the furnace malfunctioned."

"I told her that. But sometimes we try to make sense of a tragedy by blaming ourselves." A car passed her and she slowed to let it into the lane ahead before continuing. "My husband died of a heart attack when he was forty. Turns out he had a congenital heart condition. His father died young, as well. I wish I'd insisted that Tommy go to a cardiologist to get checked. If we'd known, we could have adjusted his diet. There were medications he could have tried."

"Would it have made a difference?"

"We'll never know. That's the thing about might-havebeens. They can't change the past. But hanging onto them can impact the future."

Mac let that hang in the air for a little while. "I understand what you're saying, but…" He trailed off.

"But you're not ready to let them go. I understand that."

"It's not the same."

"Of course not. Every situation is different."

Mac shook his head. Ursula didn't understand. She couldn't. In order to write the kind of stories he wrote, Mac had researched the psychology of killers, of their different motivations. He wasn't just any dad, he was an expert. And yet, he'd overlooked the obvious red flags, and Andi had paid the price.

No, the regrets Mac carried around weren't so easy to leave behind. And he wasn't sure he wanted to. He owed it to Andi to see this through.

CHAPTER TEN

URSULA CRADLED THE phone against her shoulder and reached for a pencil. "Yes, your room is ready and I can be here at two for early check-in." The doorbell rang as Ursula was finishing up her conversation. She finished her note about the time before leaving the kitchen. "No problem at all. See you then. Goodbye."

She hung up the phone and hurried toward the door, but before she got there, it opened. A young man took one step inside. "Hello? Is this the Forget-me-not Bed and Breakfast Inn?"

Since that's what it said on the door and the sign at the highway, Ursula didn't see where there was much room for doubt, but she gave him her best hostess smile. "Yes, it is. Are you looking for a room?"

Hmm. Not her usual winter tourist. He wore a light coat over suit pants and loafers, the kind with thin leather soles that turned into ice skates on snow. He hadn't shaved that morning, and the circles under his eyes hinted at an overnight flight. His left hand clasped a battered leather satchel.

"No. I wanted to ask about someone who may have stayed here in the past couple of months."

"And you are?"

"Irwin Grimes, with the *National Bugler*. If I could just check your registration records—"

"I don't give out private information about my guests."

He pulled something out of his satchel and continued as if she hadn't spoken. "I'm looking for R.D. Macleod. He may have registered under another name. This is his picture." He thrust a five-by-seven headshot of Mac toward her, with a folded bill under his thumb. It looked like a fifty.

Ursula's first instinct was to throw the reporter out on his ear, but it wouldn't take him long to find Mac in a town the size of Seward. All he had to do was show that photo at the grocery or gas station and somebody would remember. Without reaching for the picture, she pretended to study it. "He does look familiar. Why, who is he? A criminal?"

"No, nothing like that. I'm just following up on a story." He flashed her a conspiratorial smile. "It's confidential. I'm sure you understand."

Ursula nodded as though he'd actually told her something. "I think I do remember him. He didn't stay here, though. Didn't like the rooms. Kind of snooty, if you ask me. I sent him over to the Caribou B&B just up the road. Don't know if he stayed there or not."

"Thanks." He quickly withdrew the photo and the money. Ursula resisted the urge to laugh. "This way?"

"Yes. Second driveway on the left. You'll see the sign."

He was out the door like a hound that'd caught a scent. Ursula peered out the window to watch him get into a black rental car while she pulled out her cell phone and dialed Marge's number.

Marge answered on the first ring. "Good morning. What's this I hear about you and Rory accompanying our novelist neighbor to the Cabin Fever Festival?"

Marge was a wonder, but Ursula didn't have time to play the who-told-you game. "So you've figured out who he is."

"Of course. Saw him filling that Mercedes at the Gas-n-go, and recognized him from the news. Penny made me promise not to tell, though." One thing about Marge. Despite her propensity for gossip, if she promised to keep a secret, nobody was prying it out of her.

"Good, because a reporter's about to turn into your drive-way and he's looking for Mac."

"Mac, hmm? You're on a first-name basis?"

Ursula ignored the question. "He moved to Alaska to get away from reporters. I have an idea on how to get rid of this one, but I'll need your help."

"What's the plan?"

Quickly, Ursula spelled out what she had in mind. Marge had a couple of suggestions. "You've got to work Terry at Tattered Tales into this somehow. You know how he loves a good caper story."

"I'll see what I can do. You know your part?"

"Sure. Delay as long as possible, and then send him to Penny. He just pulled up in front."

"Okay, then. Good luck. And thanks, Marge."

"Anytime."

Okay. Marge was on the case. Her next call was to Penny. It helped that Penny already knew Mac's story. Still, she hesitated. "You want me to lie to this reporter?"

"Well...yes." Maybe Penny wasn't the best choice for this assignment. For a tourist information volunteer, Penny was a stickler for the truth. Tourists in Seward knew exactly how many rainy days to expect in August.

"I suppose it doesn't have to be a lie," Penny mused for a moment. "If I call Mac now and tell him what's going on, I can honestly say I recommended he get in touch with Bill about his remote cabin. I don't suppose I'm under any obli-gation to tell the reporter when I recommended it."

"There you go." Ursula breathed a sigh of relief.

"Besides, it would give Barb a chance to make a little money. She's considering offering mushing tours. Do you think this reporter would buy it if I recommend he hire her to take him to the cabin, or would he realize a snow ma-chine would be faster?"

"Play it by ear, but I suspect he'll buy whatever you're

selling. Do them both a favor, though, and get him outfitted in better clothes first. Barb wouldn't want her first customer frozen solid."

"Okay. I'll talk to Barb if you'll call Bill."

Bill was onboard, always happy for a chance to put one over on an "outsider." After almost forty years in Alaska, the last six in Seward, Ursula had earned "insider" status with him, but only because Betty and Penny had vouched for her.

"I'll call Terry," Ursula told Bill. "He can dig up a used guidebook and a flyer for one of the lodges on Kodiak. I have a guest coming, so I can't leave right now, but I'll ask Barb to pick it up at the store. Then she can hide it on her sled and plant it in your cabin for the reporter to find."

"Tell her to circle the phone number on the flyer in case this reporter's not so bright," Bill suggested. "On second thought, I'll get the book from Terry. I've got skis on the plane. Once Barb's got that reporter on her sled, I'll hop over and leave the book on the kitchen table for them to find."

"You don't have to go to all that trouble."

"I need to check it out, anyway, make sure no critters have moved in. My brother-in-law wants to use the cabin next week. I'll see about leaving a few more clues around the place. What shoe size does this writer fella wear?"

Somewhere along the way, Ursula lost all control. She just had to trust her friends and neighbors could pull this off. Once she'd checked in her guests, who didn't arrive at two as promised but closer to three thirty, she called for an update. Penny verified that the reporter was riding in the basket of Barb's dogsled on a snipe hunt and Bill had taken off in his plane to ready his cabin.

She looked up the *National Bugler*. It seemed to be an online gossip column, mostly centering on innuendo and unflattering photos of celebrities. Their archives showed several blaring headlines speculating about the Andi Macleod case. Ursula felt justified in thwarting their reporter.

The next day, Ursula had just sent her guests out for a trip to Seward when Barb herself called with the good news. "It worked like a charm. Between that book on the table beside the empty pickle jar and the tracks Bill left, the guy was convinced he was hot on the trail. We made it back to town about midmorning, and before I even got the dogs stopped, he was on his phone scheduling an air taxi from Anchorage to Kodiak."

"Good. I've talked to the innkeeper there."

Barb giggled. "Poor guy. He did seem to enjoy mushing, though. Maybe he'll write about that instead."

"And you'll be famous," Ursula predicted.

Several more people checked in with Ursula throughout the morning, congratulating themselves and each other on a job well done. It was early afternoon when Mac appeared on her doorstep, grinning. "Penny tells me it's safe to come out of hiding." Beside him, Blossom wagged her tail as though she thought it a fine joke.

Ursula ushered them in.

"I can't believe you pulled this off." Mac hung his coat on a hook by the door. "So far, I've only gotten hints. Tell me the details of this devious and brilliant plan of yours."

She laughed. "It wasn't that brilliant. When the reporter stopped by asking for you, I sent him to Marge, at the Caribou. She told him you'd talked to Penny at the Tourist Information Office."

"Which is why I got the call from Penny telling me about a cabin owned by someone named Bill."

"Right. Bill has a remote cabin about fifteen miles in. On Penny's recommendation, the reporter hired Barb, a local musher, to take him to the cabin. Meanwhile, Bill flew out and planted a guidebook about Kodiak Island, bookmarked by a brochure with the name of a lodge there. Also, an empty pickle jar. According to Terry, the owner of the used book store, you're well-known for your love of pickles."

Mac chuckled. "I happened to mention in some interview I was fond of baby dills. Next thing I know, people from all over the world were sending me jars of their favorite pickles. I was even asked to judge the pickles at the Oklahoma State Fair. Everybody seems to think I spend all day eating pickles."

"Well it worked. Barb says he swallowed it hook, line and sinker. The story, not the pickles, although he got excited when he saw the jar. He scheduled a flight out of Anchorage and he's on his way to Kodiak Island."

"And what happens when I'm not there?"

"The innkeeper is a friend of mine. He's going to say a guest of your general description was tired of winter and talking about going to Seattle or possibly Hawaii. Which is true, except the guest happened to be an old friend of his from Anchorage."

"I can't believe they went to so much trouble to help me out."

"It wasn't completely altruistic. Barb got paid for mushing him to the cabin. She'd been playing with the idea of doing tours and so this was a trial run for her. She says it went great. Nate at the outfitters sold him bunny boots and arctic gear. And Bill has sprained his arm patting himself on the back about his success in setting up the cabin."

"I suppose the only drawback is that now they all know I'm here."

"Oh, they already knew. Terry says he spotted you buying groceries weeks ago. Word got around. It's just that Alaskans figure if you want privacy, they'll leave you alone."

He chuckled. "All but you, I guess."

Ursula shrugged. "I couldn't just leave that eagle stuck in the fence."

He stepped closer, his eyes fixed on her face. "No, if you see trouble, you just can't help wading in." He reached out to touch her cheek. "Thank you."

"You're welcome." Some magnetic-like force swayed her forward and she found herself wrapped in his arms. The scent of sawdust clung to the soft flannel of his shirt. She had a fleeting thought that she'd sworn not to let this happen again just before his mouth met hers. Then all thoughts fled. Warmth crept through her body, sweet and comforting.

When he finally broke the kiss, she felt disoriented, as though hours might have passed without her noticing. She should put an end to this. And yet, she couldn't seem to look away, much less step out of his arms.

Blossom finally broke the spell. She squeezed between them, strategically placing her head under Ursula's hand. Ursula laughed and scratched her ears. "The school bus will be here anytime now. Rory will be happy to see you." She looked up at Mac. "Both of you."

"How is Rory?"

"Good, I think. She's been eager to go to school lately. Regular teacher conferences are this week, so I'll find out tomorrow if she's doing better in class."

"She was having trouble in class?"

"Sometimes. Her teacher said she'd draw pictures instead of working on her assignment."

"What kind of pictures?"

Ursula stopped petting Blossom and thought about it. "That's a good question. I don't know. I'll ask tomorrow."

Footsteps rushing across the porch alerted them to Rory's arrival. Blossom broke away to meet her at the door. Rory squealed. "Blossom. Hi."

Ursula took her coat and backpack. "How was school today?"

"Good. And guess what? Maddy Wilson is having a birthday party in two weeks and she's gonna invite me."

"That's great."

"Hi, Mac." Rory didn't seem as surprised to see him

as she was the dog. "Did you see the northern lights last night?"

"No, I didn't."

"It's been a fine year for it," Ursula said. "And this weekend is supposed to be high activity."

"They were really bright last night," Rory said. "Their other name is Aurora, like me."

"Aurora borealis. I've heard of them but never seen them."

"Never?" Rory and Ursula asked in unison.

"Don't you go outside at night?" Rory asked.

"I do to let Blossom out before bed. I guess I've never looked up at the right time."

He never looked up. That pretty much summed up Mac's existence since he'd been in Alaska. All this beauty around him, but he was so weighed down by grief and guilt, he refused to look up and recognize it unless someone forced him.

Ursula pulled out her phone and checked the long-term aurora forecast. "What have you got going this weekend?" she asked Mac.

"What?"

"Plans? Appointments? Anything?"

"Uh, no."

"Good. Rory's teacher conference is tomorrow. It's supposed to be clear and cold across the state. I think we should take the train to Fairbanks Saturday and see the northern lights the way they're supposed to be seen."

"They're not the same as here?"

"No. Here they're usually low on the northern horizon. Fairbanks is farther north, so they're more overhead. I have a friend who runs a B&B there. She's stayed with me several times, and she keeps asking me when I'm going to let her return the favor. We can catch the train in Anchorage and fly back."

"What about Blossom? I don't want to leave her in a kennel."

"My friend Catherine always fills in for me at the inn when I'm away. Blossom can stay with her here. Catherine loves dogs. Actually, you met her when you came by to bring those flowers."

"Come on, Mac. Let's do it. I never rode a train before," Rory said.

He looked from one of them to the other. "Well, if Catherine is available to take care of Blossom, I guess we can go."

"Yay!" Rory danced around the room with Blossom chasing after her. "We're gonna ride a train to Fairbanks."

MAC ROLLED A sweater and added it to his suitcase. Ursula had warned him to pack warm, that Fairbanks was considerably colder than Anchorage. He was adding wool socks when his phone rang. Chandler, from the detective agency.

"This is Mac."

Chandler didn't waste time. "I may have a lead."

"What?"

"I've been talking to the neighbors from where he lived growing up. Most moved in after Thaine left, but one remembered he had a half-sister he used to visit and where her family lived. It's a small town about forty miles out of Tulsa. Anyway, I chased it down and found a teacher there who kept in touch with the sister. She knows where she lives, way out in the boonies. So I'm on my way to see what she knows, if anything."

"Good. Keep in touch."

"I will."

Mac set down the phone and took a deep breath. This might be it. The police hadn't been able to find the sister at her last known address. It was quite possible her brother was hiding out with her. It was hard to believe anyone would hide a murderer, but maybe he'd convinced her he was innocent. He seemed to be quite good at hiding his true nature.

Mac should cancel this trip to Fairbanks. If they did locate Andi's murderer, they might need him to fly down and…what? Testify? It would be months or years before it came to trial. They had enough evidence to make the arrest.

Still, he felt as though he was letting Andi down. Again. Going off for a fun weekend when her killer was still on the loose. What kind of a father was he?

Blossom padded into his bedroom from wherever she'd been napping and dropped a ball. Nothing subtle about her. "You want to go outside and play?" The dog wagged her tail and nudged the ball closer to his foot. "You need Rory here. She'd play with you all day."

Rory would be disappointed if he didn't go with them to Fairbanks. He checked his watch. She and Ursula would be at the teacher's conference right now. He hoped they were getting good news. Rory was such a great kid. She deserved a break.

Maybe he deserved a break, as well. As Ursula said, guilt and blame couldn't change the past. He owed it to Andi to catch her killer, but that wouldn't bring her back. Spending a weekend in Fairbanks with an energetic little girl and her godmother might be the most productive thing he could do right now.

RORY COULDN'T HIDE her excitement. If Ursula hadn't been holding tight to her hand, she might have bounced right off the rail platform. "Are we gonna ride in this car? Will there be other kids? Do they have a bathroom?"

Ursula patiently answered each question. "Yes, this car. I don't know. We'll have to see who else is in our car when we board the train. Yes, there are bathrooms on the train."

"Where do we eat? Do they know I don't like lima beans?"

Mac laid a hand on her head. "I'm sure they'll have something to eat that doesn't involve lima beans. Here, I have something for you." He pulled a paper sack from his pocket.

"What is it?" Rory pulled the sack open.

"A disposable camera. So you can take your own pictures of the trip."

"Cool." She gave a little eye roll in Ursula's direction. "Since I don't have a cell phone." Mac knew from experience those eye rolls would become ever more frequent in the next decade.

Rory pointed the camera in their direction. "How do I take a picture?"

"Just look through that little window, and once you like what you see, press the button."

A woman who had been watching Rory stepped closer. "Would you like me to take it so you can be in the picture with your family?"

"Yeah!" Rory handed her the camera and skipped over to Ursula and Mac.

Family. Mac almost corrected the woman, but thought better of it. It didn't matter what this woman thought. She couldn't know he'd lost his family, that other than a scattering of distant cousins, he was alone. Rory didn't seem to mind.

"Closer," the woman ordered. Mac put an arm around Ursula and a hand on Rory's shoulder to anchor her in front of them. The woman nodded. "Now, act like you like each other."

Ursula laughed, and Mac turned toward the sound. Rory looked up, her eyes sparkling. The woman snapped the photo.

"Let's do silly faces now," Rory suggested.

"You might want to save your pictures," Mac said. "There are only twenty-seven exposures on that camera."

She frowned at him. "Expo...?"

"Exposures. Pictures. You can only fit so many on a roll of film."

The woman returned the camera to Rory. After a nudge from Ursula, Rory thanked her and turned the camera over to examine the back. "Where's the picture?"

"On the film," Mac explained. "You can't see it yet. When you finish taking all the pictures, I'll send it to the developer and they'll print paper photos for you."

Rory didn't look convinced. "You can't see it at all?"

"Not until it's developed. It's old school." He squatted down beside her. "It's sort of like a secret code. The light goes through the lens, here, and leaves an imprint on the film, which looks like a long strip of plastic. The film processer has to expose the film to certain chemicals, kind of like getting the key to the code. Once the film is developed, the processer shines a light through it onto special paper, and it makes a picture."

"Oh, okay." Rory seemed to buy into the secret code scenario.

"Now, since you took a picture, you need to wind the film. Turn this knob until it stops, so the next section of film will be ready when you want to take another picture."

Rory wound the film, fascinated by the new toy. By the time she had the camera set, the train was boarding. Other than a couple with a baby, Rory was the only child in their car, but it didn't seem to bother her. She followed Ursula onto the train and plunked down in the seat beside her. Their car was about half full. Mac settled into his seat across the row, with an empty seat next to him. The train started. Rory gazed out the window as the city of Anchorage whizzed by outside. Her fascination lasted for about five minutes before she was digging in her backpack.

"Would you like to sit by the window so you can see better?" Ursula offered.

"No." Rory pulled a deck of cards from her pack. "I want to play concentration with Mac."

She'd already beaten him twice by the time the sky had lightened enough to see out the windows. They were out in the wilds now. Everything seemed stripped of color—the deep snow blanketing the meadows, the pale bark of birch trunks against the dark gray of spruce in the background, the silvery sky along the eastern horizon. As they rounded a curve, Mac glimpsed the front of the train, a splash of blue across a stunning white scene.

Stark. Cold. And yet there was beauty here, the lack of light and color putting the emphasis on form and shadow. Miles and miles of snow and ice surrounded them, but the train kept them warm and moved them forward. There had to be a metaphor in there someplace.

Up ahead in the car, the baby cried, and both parents jumped into action finding a bottle. Rory scrambled past Mac. "I'll go help."

"Rory, wait—" Ursula tried but before she could stop her, Rory was skipping up the aisle toward the baby.

Ursula scooted into the aisle seat and leaned outward to check on her, but Rory was already kneeling beside the mother's armrest. "Hi. I'm Rory. I have a baby named Griffin."

"That's a nice name. This baby is Alice."

"She's a girl? Hi, Alice." Rory smiled and leaned closer. The mother didn't seem to mind having her there.

"She's fine," Mac whispered to Ursula. "The mom has everything under control."

"Let me know if she needs rescuing," Ursula whispered back. "Rory's help can be a little overwhelming."

"I'll keep an eye out," Mac assured her. The mom spoke to Rory and allowed her to hold the bottle. Rory seemed thrilled at the responsibility. Mac leaned closer to Ursula. "How did the teacher conference go?"

"It went well. She's definitely doing better in school. And I did ask about the pictures she was drawing when she was supposed to be working. It turns out, she was drawing her mom and dad. She said she didn't want to forget what they look like. We have all her family albums. I don't know why it didn't occur to me to hang a picture of Rory's family in the kitchen, where she can see it before she leaves for school every morning. We did that yesterday when we got home."

"Do you think it will help?"

"I hope so. Her teacher says she's noticed a change in Rory. She seems less inwardly focused and is interacting more with the other students. She mentioned you."

"Who did?"

"Rory. She was there for part of the conference, and she told her teacher she'd met this man who needed cheering up, and we were all going to Fairbanks for the weekend to see the northern lights."

"So I'm Rory's good deed."

"I'm afraid so."

Mac turned the idea over in his mind. He didn't really like the idea of being someone's project but if it helped Rory… Still. "What about you?"

"Me?"

"Am I your project, as well?"

"No, Mac." Ursula looked amused. "You're not my project. You're my friend."

Before he could comment, Rory returned. "Alice is going to sleep now. She's six months old, and she doesn't have any teeth yet." She'd started to climb over Ursula to the window seat when her head snapped up. "Look! A moose!"

Everyone crowded to the right side of the car to snap a photo of the young moose gnawing at the bark of a tree not far from the tracks. Rory used her new camera, although Mac doubted she would record anything but a blur in the distance. Once they were past the moose, Rory talked Mac into moving toward the window so she could sit between him and Ursula. She picked up the pack of cards, but paused before she laid them out.

"At school, the teacher's reading us a book about a girl named Anne. She's an orphan."

Ursula smiled. "I remember that book. It's a good one."

"Yeah." Rory looked at Mac. "Ms. Longton says an orphan is a kid whose parents died. So I asked her if I'm an orphan."

Mac drew in a breath. Rory didn't look upset, but it was sometimes hard to tell. Before he could decide how to respond, Ursula asked, in a matter-of-fact voice, "What did she say?"

"She said yes, but that I'm not like Anne, 'cause I have a godmother. So I still have family."

"That's right." Ursula reached for her hand and squeezed it. "We're family. You and me, and Sam, Dana and Griffin."

"Yeah." Rory looked at Mac again. "So, I was wondering, are you an orphan?"

"Me?" Mac's parents had died when he was in his thirties, one shortly after the other. He was an only child. Other than a scattering of cousins, he had no family left. "I suppose I am."

"Because your daughter died."

"No, orphan means my parents died. But I was grown up when that happened."

"Oh." The tip of her tongue appeared at the corner of her mouth, which Mac had learned to recognize as a sign of deep concentration. "Then what do you call a daddy or mommy when their kid dies?"

What indeed? There were words for others left behind, for children without parents, wives without husbands, husbands without wives. But there didn't seem to be a word for parents living without their children. Was the situation so unthinkable that English had never seen fit to invent a word for it?

Mac shook his head. "I don't know, Rory."

"I don't know either," Ursula said, "but I think they're a mommy or daddy, still. When someone you love dies, they stay alive in your heart."

Was she right? Mac felt he'd lost his moorings, now that he was no longer a father, but maybe he was wrong. Maybe he'd always be Andi's father, as long as he kept her memory alive. There was something reassuring about that.

"Ursula, are you an orphan?" Rory asked.

"No, sweetie. My mother is still alive. She lives in a retirement home in Wyoming. I was thinking we might fly down and visit her next summer, so you can get to know her."

"More family?"

"Yes. More family."

Rory bounced in her seat. "Goodie. I like family."

Ursula gave her a smile that somehow expanded to include Mac in its warmth. "Me, too."

URSULA OPENED HER EYES, unsure what had disturbed her sleep. She squinted at the bedside clock. It was well after midnight. Across the room, tucked under a down comforter, Rory's even breathing assured Ursula she was sleeping soundly.

And no wonder. Rory had spent the entire train ride bouncing from seat to seat for a better view of the sights, or playing cards with Mac, or chatting with the various people. By the time they'd arrived in Fairbanks, she was on a first-name basis with most of the people on the train.

Rhoda and her husband had been at the station to meet them. Just as Ursula had predicted, Rhoda was thrilled to be able to return the hospitality Ursula had shown her. After a huge dinner, they'd all settled into the hot tub and watched the northern lights put on a show overhead. Rory's giggles formed a soundtrack to the dancing lights, but eventually she ran out of energy, and Mac had to carry her to bed.

Outside the bedroom, the floor creaked at the head of the stairs. That must have been the sound that woke Ursula in the first place. And she had a good idea who was sneaking down the stairs in the wee hours of the morning.

She slipped out of bed and pulled snow pants, a coat and a hat on over her pajamas. Carrying her boots in her hand, she tiptoed down the stairs, carefully stepping over the creaky board at the top. Sure enough, when she opened the door, she saw Mac standing alone in the clearing, gazing into the shifting sky. The lights had petered out about the time they went to bed, but they were active again, dancing across the heavens.

As her eyes adjusted, she could make out the details of the scene from the light reflecting off the snow. She slipped into her boots and went to join Mac, snow crunching under her feet as she walked. If he heard, he gave no sign. She stopped a few feet away. "Hi."

"Hi." He kept his gaze toward the heavens.

"Are you okay?"

He turned to look at her. "I am. For the first time in a long time. I don't know how long it will last, but right now, right here, I'm okay."

"I'm glad." And she was. She'd watched him today, going out of his way to make this a special day for Rory. Patiently playing cards, pointing out the sights, listening intently when Rory explained why the girl caribou still had antlers and the boys didn't. Mac was a good man, and he didn't deserve the pain he'd been carrying around.

She'd seen that today, too. Occasionally he would draw into himself, almost as if he'd suffered a physical blow. When a brown-eyed young woman asked her companion about vegetarian restaurants in Fairbanks, Mac had turned his head toward her and then quickly away, and the sadness on his face almost broke Ursula's heart.

But tonight, in the silence, he seemed to have found serenity. Maybe there was something healing about being alone in the night. "Would you like me to leave?"

"Actually, darlin', I would like very much for you to stay." He held out a hand. She took it and he pulled her closer and wrapped an arm around her. They stood together, staring upward as the green lights played tag among the treetops and streaked across the sky, accompanied by the occasional touch of violet.

Ursula wasn't sure how long they had been standing there, but her feet were beginning to get cold even inside her felt-lined boots. Time to go in. But before she could say anything, Mac turned toward her and tipped her chin upward. He stopped to study her face for a long moment before his lips touched hers, softly, tenderly. And Ursula forgot all about cold feet.

THE NEXT MORNING, Ursula was awakened by Rory bouncing on her bed. "Aren't you awake yet? We're gonna ski and then go see the ice statues today."

Ursula yawned. "Good morning. What time is it?"

"Seven thirty. Miss Rhoda already gave me chocolate chip pancakes and she said I should let you sleep in. But I told her you always get up earlier than me and you wouldn't want to miss breakfast because you say breakfast is the most important meal of the day."

Ursula laughed. "Absolutely. Just give me a few minutes to dress and I'll be down." She watched Rory scurry away. Goodness. She hadn't slept this late in years. But then she usually didn't spend an hour in the middle of the night watching the northern lights, or another sleepless hour lying in bed thinking about a kiss.

A kiss. A simple thing, two pairs of lips making contact.

No different really than a handshake, or even an acciden-
tal brush of elbows. But she'd never had a handshake that
stole her breath and set her heart pounding. Three kisses
was starting to become a habit. And, delightful though it
might be, it was a habit Ursula needed to break.

She probably shouldn't have suggested they spend the
weekend together. It was a spontaneous idea. Rory loved
the northern lights, being named after them, and Ursula
had been toying with the idea of taking her to see them in
Fairbanks one day, so when Mac mentioned he'd never seen
them, it all seemed to fall into place. Rory liked Mac. She'd
always been close to her daddy. Maybe Mac filled that need
for masculine attention that Ursula couldn't.

And spending time with Rory was good for Mac. He was
different when he was with Rory—relaxed, content, happy
to live in the moment. But was it wise, letting Rory get attached to Mac? He might throw it off from time to time, but
that darkness was still inside him, a threat to his happiness
and the happiness of everyone around him. Guilt and blame
had stolen much of Ursula's childhood, and she would do
whatever it took to make sure that didn't happen to Rory.

But she wouldn't think about that right now. Today was
for spending time with friends, and viewing the World
Champion ice sculpture competition, and making Rory
happy. So that's what she was going to do.

RORY'S EYELIDS DROOPED as she climbed into the back seat
of Ursula's car, hugging her pillow. Mac packed their suit-
cases into the back of the car while Ursula tucked a blanket
around her. Before they even reached the Seward Highway,
Rory was asleep.

Mac turned in the passenger seat to check on her. Pale
locks of hair escaped from the ponytail she wore and twisted
across her cheeks. Her head nestled against the pillow, her

lips pursed like a baby's as she slept. Mac smiled. "She's worn out."

Ursula laughed. "It's an illusion. Rory's never worn out, just recharging. Tomorrow morning, she'll be bouncing all over the house."

"I figured she would fall asleep on the flight."

"It was her first flight, ever. No way she was going to miss anything."

"She did seem extraordinarily excited over a cup of ginger ale."

"Well, I don't let her have soda at home, so it's a special treat."

"It was a treat for me, too, seeing Denali in the moonlight from the air."

"It was something, wasn't it? And those ice sculptures were incredible. Rory loved the Mad Hatter's tea party, and I couldn't believe that school of tropical fish. Beautiful."

Mac didn't reply immediately. Instead, he watched Ursula's profile as she drove, the lights on the overpass highlighting her cheekbones and the silver streaks in her hair. Beautiful, indeed. Yes, the talents of the ice sculptors far surpassed anything he was expecting, but he preferred the honest beauty of nature. The snowcapped splendor of Denali, the dancing colors of the northern lights and the face of a woman who laughed and loved and lived.

A beautiful woman, generous and kind. She'd been a true friend when he needed one. And holding her in his arms last night, even if only for an hour under the pulsing skies, he'd known she could be so much more. She filled a void he hadn't even known existed.

She glanced his way and smiled. "Tired?"

"Not especially. Just thinking over the weekend. I'm content."

"I know what you mean. I love visiting different places

in Alaska, but it always feels good to know I'm on my way home."

Home. That was the feeling Ursula created, wherever she was. That sense of comfort, of belonging. It was no wonder she was a success as an innkeeper. Even Blossom felt at home at the inn. He'd been concerned she might protest when he left her with Catherine, but the dog simply acknowledged his farewell with a thump of her tail before she curled up on her bed and went to sleep.

Rory didn't open her eyes until Ursula had pulled into the garage. Mac went around to retrieve the bags while Ursula shook her shoulder. "Wake up, sweetie. We're home."

Rory yawned. "Is Blossom still here?"

"I'm sure she is."

"I'll go see." Rory stumbled toward the back door.

Ursula came around and picked up her suitcase, while Mac grabbed his and Rory's. When they stepped out of the garage, Mac noticed the green glow against the treetops in the distance. "Looks like the northern lights followed us home."

Ursula stopped to watch. The lights were dimmer and lower on the northern horizon than they'd been in Fairbanks, but they still moved and pulsed like a living thing. "They were like this last week, too. It's been a good winter for aurora chasers."

"I can't believe I never noticed."

Ursula laid a hand on his arm. "You have to look up to see the lights."

Mac looked up, but after a moment he was compelled to look down, to watch Ursula's face. To remember that kiss. Somehow in his mind, the beauty of the lights and of that kiss had merged into one incredible memory. He was just about to taste her lips once again when she suddenly moved away. "Brrr. Let's get inside." She grabbed the bag and trotted toward the door.

He frowned. Was that just unfortunate timing, or was she deliberately avoiding his kiss? She'd seemed more than willing last night in Fairbanks, but now she seemed jumpy, unsettled. He grabbed the two other bags and followed her inside.

Rory was there, chattering to Catherine about their trip while rubbing Blossom's belly.

Ursula turned to Catherine. "We really did have fun. Thanks so much for filling in."

"It was no bother. I always enjoy it. Blossom and I had a good time, didn't we?"

Blossom finally spotted Mac and rolled to her feet to run greet him. He bent to rub her ears. "She obviously enjoyed her time with you, as well. Thank you. The northern lights in Fairbanks were spectacular."

Ursula smiled at him and Blossom. Mac wondered if he'd imagined her nervousness outside. Catherine slipped into her coat and picked up her bag. "I'm glad you had fun. I'd better head home. Rory, can I get a hug before I go?"

Rory obliged, and Catherine started out the door, but before she left, she handed Ursula a bundle of envelopes. "Almost forgot. These are from yesterday. Good night."

"Good night. And thanks again." Ursula flipped absently through the mail, but when she reached the third letter, she paused, frowning. She picked up a letter opener from the desk in the kitchen and slit the envelope. As she read the letter enclosed, color drained from her face.

Mac took a step closer. "What's wrong?"

She raised her eyes to him, her face stricken, but before she could say anything, Rory came to tug on her hand. "Do I hafta take a bath tonight?"

Ursula gave her a smile, but it was obviously forced. "No, you took one this morning. Brush your teeth and get to bed. Tomorrow's a school day. I'll be there in just a minute to tuck you in."

"Okay." She yawned again. "Good night, Blossom." Rory started toward her room, but she made a detour to come wrap her arms around Mac. "Good night, Mac. I'm glad you went." Before he could reply, she stumbled off toward the bath.

"Good night." Mac waited until Rory had disappeared before he turned to Ursula. "What is it?"

Without a word, Ursula handed him the paper. It appeared to be from a firm of lawyers in Colorado. Mac skimmed the letter. Then he read it again, more carefully. When he looked at Ursula, she swallowed.

"Sit down," he suggested. "Let's talk about this."

Ursula sank into one of the kitchen chairs. "What's there to talk about? They want to take her away."

"Not necessarily." Mac sat in the chair beside hers and laid a hand on her arm. "It just says they want to discuss custody. Maybe they want visitation."

Ursula shook her head. "They want control. I should have known it was all too easy."

"If they planned to dispute the will, why would they have waited? Why not act immediately?"

"I don't know." She sat up straighter. "But I do know they're not going to take her. Coby and Kendall trusted me to take care of their daughter. I'm not going to let them down."

"Kendall was a skilled and articulate woman. Her parents must have instilled a disciplined and competitive spirit for her to have achieved so much. Are they such bad people?"

"Kendall didn't want Rory to have the sort of childhood she had. Winning was everything to her mother, and if Kendall wasn't winning, she was worthless. Nobody is ever going to make Rory feel worthless." She straightened her shoulders. "Not if I can help it."

"I understand." Mac reached for a pad and a pen. "So what's our battle plan?"

"Our?"

He smiled. "You don't think I'm going to let you go into this all alone, do you? I care about Rory. I know she loves you, and that you love her. You've been there for me, and it's time I was there for you. So yes—our battle plan. Do you have a lawyer?"

"Not really. Fred Wilson handled the estate."

"He handled the property sale for me, too. Fred's a good guy, but you need a specialist in family law. Let's talk with Fred tomorrow and see if he might recommend someone in Anchorage to represent you."

Ursula nodded. "This is going to get expensive, isn't it?"

"It might." That was one area where he could offer some real help, but he was sure if he said so now, Ursula would turn him down.

"That's okay." Ursula folded the letter and slipped it back inside the envelope. "I have some savings as well as my annuity. I'll spend it all if that's what it takes to keep Rory safe and happy."

He didn't doubt it for a second.

CHAPTER ELEVEN

FRED READ OVER the letter. "I don't know what to tell you, Ursula. It's not real clear what they're after. But the will specifically appointed you guardian, and the judge honored that request. The bad news is the estate hasn't finished clearing probate, and decisions aren't final."

"So there's a possibility a judge might award custody to her biological grandparents? Even though she's never met them?" Ursula heard the note of desperation creeping into her voice. She glanced toward Mac, sitting in the chair beside her, his face a picture of calm strength. She sucked in a breath. "How likely is that?"

"Hard to say." Fred shook his head. "I don't know what arguments they might make, or even if they want full custody. Perhaps they only want visitation. Would you be amenable to that?"

"I..." She paused, considering. The wounds these people had inflicted on their daughter went deep. Kendall had spent most of her life fulfilling their expectations, and yet when she'd made the decision to go her own way, they'd abandoned her without hesitation. But they were Rory's grandparents, and family was important. "I don't know. I'd have to meet them first."

"Yes. Well, I suggest you get yourself a family attorney who knows the ins and outs of this sort of thing. I've made a list of my recommendations. Given a choice, Darlene Henderson would be my top pick."

"Thanks." Ursula tucked the list into her bag. "I'll give her a call."

"I'd do it sooner, rather than later. This feels like the opening salvo of a surprise attack to me."

Ursula looked up, startled. "What do you mean?"

Fred shook his head. "I'm not sure. It's just the vague wording of the letter. I get the idea this is just the formal required engagement before they spring something on you. I may be wrong."

Ursula doubted it. Fred seemed to have a sixth sense about which issues were likely to fizzle out and which ones might build into something major. He'd been able to head off trouble for several of her friends over the years. But a vague feeling didn't help her much. "I'll call her today."

"Good. Good luck, and let me know if I can help." Fred shook her hand and turned to Mac. Fred had raised an eyebrow when Mac had accompanied her into his office, but hadn't questioned her. No doubt he'd pass this on to Penny, who would draw her own conclusions, but right now Ursula was willing to endure a little gossip if it meant she had an ally in this battle.

Mac had hardly said a word during this consultation, but she could tell he was listening carefully, weighing Fred's advice. She was confident he'd remember the things she was too flustered to consider. He reached out to shake the lawyer's hand. "Thank you, Fred. We appreciate your help."

In the lobby, Mac helped her into her coat and rested a hand on her back to guide her out the door to the parking lot. "Coffee?"

Ursula shook her head. "More caffeine is the last thing I need right now. Besides, I have to get home to make that call."

"Herbal tea, then. We'll go to that little place with the flowers. Maybe you need a few minutes to collect yourself before you charge ahead."

He was right. At the moment, she felt too scattered to make a coherent call. But Mac in the Natural Teahouse? She laughed. "You hate herbal tea."

"I'll survive." He waited until she'd climbed into the passenger seat of his car to shut the door behind her before going around to the driver's side.

A few minutes later, they pulled into the parking lot in front of the white cottage with red painted poppies scattered across the siding. Light shone through the colorful bead curtains in the windows. They crossed the porch and stepped inside, the tinkle of sleigh bells on the door announcing their presence.

A young woman wearing a loose dress, wool socks and sandals glided in from the back of the house and graced them with a serene smile. "Sit wherever you like."

Ursula chose one of the mismatched wooden tables closest to the front window. "Hello, Shelly. How are you?"

"I'm at peace. And I go by Harmony now."

"Oh, right, I'm sorry. Harmony, what tea would you recommend for calm and purpose?"

"I have just the thing. I'll get you a pot." She turned her eyes toward Mac. "What are your needs today?"

"Umm." Mac looked around the room, no doubt searching for a menu, chalkboard or something to clue him in on what he might order. Shelly/Harmony didn't believe in listing her offerings. She thought of herself as more of an herbalist, who prescribed healing based on her customer's mental state.

Ursula decided to take pity on Mac. "Mac needs energy and focus."

"Very well." She disappeared into the kitchen, which was down the hall from the front bedroom she'd turned into her main dining room. It was probably just as well Shelly didn't have too many customers. The inefficiency of the layout would run her off her feet.

Mac's mouth twitched. "I need energy and focus?"

"That's the only way to get what you want around here. You can't just order coffee. You have to use the code words to convince Shelly—oops, Harmony—that coffee is what you need."

"I see. How do you discover these code words? Trial and error?"

"Pretty much. I think Terry over at the bookstore keeps a translation list. For instance, when someone discovered an upset stomach would get you mint tea, they told Terry and he wrote it down."

"So what are you going to get for calm and purpose?"

"I have no idea. It's a gamble."

Their hostess returned, carrying a tray. She set a blue-and-white teapot in the center of the table and a matching cup in front of Ursula. "It's a special blend of lemon balm, peppermint, and rose hips."

"Sounds lovely. Thank you, Harmony."

Mac received a red china cup of fragrant coffee and a plate with three small brown mounds on it. Harmony reached up to hang a pink crystal on the fringe of the pendant lamp over Mac's head. "Rose quartz. For healing and forgiveness."

Mac did a double take but she just smiled and sailed from the room, leaving them alone. Mac picked up one of the brown things from his plate and inspected it doubtfully. "Cookies?"

"Sort of." Ursula smiled. "No refined sugar or white flour, so I'd guess they're some sort of honey-sweetened wholegrain pastry."

"Hmm." Mac took a small bite, grimaced and returned the cookie to his plate. He took a sip from his cup and his face brightened. "That's good coffee."

"Kona beans. She always goes to Hawaii in January and brings back a supply."

"So the secret code to get Kona coffee is 'focus and energy'?"

"Correct." Ursula sipped her tea. "But she does know her stuff. I already feel calmer. This is just what I needed. Thank you, Mac."

"I wish I could do more."

"You're doing a lot, just being here. I don't know what's wrong with me. I'm usually good at handling the unexpected, but this has me flustered."

"It's because you don't know what you're dealing with. You don't know these people, or what they want. You're afraid Rory will get hurt. Anyone would be upset."

She traced the handle of her teacup with her finger. "I'm wondering what to say to Rory. Should I tell her about the letter, or wait until I know more?"

Mac took another sip of coffee before he spoke. Ursula liked that about him, the way he took the time to consider before he weighed in. "I'd tell her something. She's going to sense you're worried, and if she doesn't know why, she might make up reasons that are much scarier than the reality."

"What could be scarier than strangers taking you away?"

"That's not going to happen." He laid his hand over hers. "We won't let it happen. That's what you need to tell Rory. That these people want to meet, but she doesn't need to worry. We'll take care of everything."

"We?"

"Okay, you. Officially, you're the only one who can make that promise. But I intend to help in every way I can."

"Why?" Ursula felt hot tears gathering. She blinked them back. "You have enough on your plate. Why are you throwing yourself into the middle of this mess?"

"Because I care." He squeezed her hand. "I can't seem to help it. When I came here, I was completely wrapped up in my own pain. I couldn't see anyone else, and I wanted it that way. But you and Rory somehow slipped past the walls I'd built and became a part of my life. And I'm not going to let anything bad happen to that little girl, if I can help it."

"Thank you, Mac." Now the tears had escaped and were rolling down her face. "That means a lot to me."

"You and Rory mean a lot to me." He picked up his linen napkin and dabbed at her cheeks.

Harmony glided back into the room. "Ah, catharsis. Excellent." She placed a milky crystal on the table and left as silently as she'd come in.

Mac looked after her, the corners of his mouth twitching. He looked so out of place, an Oklahoma cowboy perched on a spindly chair surrounded by crystals and teacups. Ursula felt a giggle rising. She tried to control it, but it came out as a snort. Mac chuckled, and before she knew what was happening, Ursula was laughing. It may have been partly hysterical, but it felt good. Mac was laughing, too, a deep belly laugh.

The tears continued. She wasn't even sure if they were crying or laughing tears anymore, but she took the napkin from Mac and wiped her cheeks as she caught her breath. "Oh, my."

Mac chuckled. "Feel better?"

"I do."

"Maybe there is something to this crystal business." He picked up the shiny rock from the table, examined it and set it down. "Finish your tea."

"Actually, I've had all I want. Now I'm eager to get home and make that phone call to the lawyer in Anchorage."

He drained his cup. "How do I get the check?"

"Oh, Shelly doesn't bring a check. You just leave whatever you feel is the right amount."

He raised an eyebrow. "Interesting business model. How long has she been running this establishment?"

"Three or four years now. She inherited the house and

a nice nest egg from her grandfather. She considers the teahouse more of a public service than a business."

"That explains so much." Mac dropped some bills on the table and held her chair for her. "Everything's going to be okay, you know."

"I know." And somehow, looking up at his face, she believed it.

As soon as Mac opened the front door, Blossom ran to greet him, skidding across the floor to sit at his feet. He pulled off his gloves and reached over to rub her head, but she pulled back and sniffed his hands, wagging her tail. Only after she'd thoroughly inspected him did she allow him to pet her.

"Yes, I was with Ursula. I just dropped her off." Mac hung up his coat and settled into a chair in the living room. The dog laid her head in his lap. "She's worried about Rory." He scratched behind the dog's ears. There was a time when he would have questioned the sanity of a man who carried on conversations with a dog, but that time had long passed. "I'm worried, too. Fred seems to think they're up to something."

His cell phone rang. Chandler. "This is Mac."

"I found her. The sister."

"That's great. Did you learn anything? Is she protecting him?"

"No. She hasn't seen him in eight years, and she hopes to keep it like that. She didn't want to talk at first, but eventually, she told me her story."

"And what was that?"

"She was a half sister, four years younger. Thaine lived with his mother, but came about once a month to spend the weekend with his father's family. When she was little, she looked up to her brother, but as she reached her teen years and grew more independent, she began to notice a jealous streak. He didn't like it if she had any activities planned that took her away on the weekends he was there. She had pet hamsters, and once, when she returned from a slumber party, two of them had died. Thaine made some cryptic remark that it wouldn't have happened if she'd been home where she should be."

Mac's gut tightened. Animal deaths. A classic sign. "Why didn't anyone know about this? There's nothing in his school records."

"She didn't tell anyone. He said he meant they got sick because she didn't look after them properly, and she believed him. But several times later, he would mention hamsters as a subtle threat."

It was all too familiar. In his work, Mac had studied the records of too many psychopaths, too many manipulators. "Did it escalate?"

"No direct violence, but she felt threatened. She began to avoid being alone with him. She says a boyfriend broke up abruptly after one of her brother's visits. He wouldn't explain, and seemed afraid."

"And nobody else caught on?"

"The stepmother may have sensed something. At her urging, the father encouraged Thaine to attend college across the country. He did return for spring break his freshman year, with a chip on his shoulder about having been sent away. Midway through that week, the whole family experienced a nasty case of food poisoning, except for him."

"Details?"

"Family cookout. Thaine shunned the homemade potato salad, saying he disliked the dill. Nobody tested it. They wrote it off as an unfortunate accident. Thaine was helpful while everyone was sick, but his sister says he seemed smug. Anyway, it was enough to convince her to cut all ties with her brother once she was out of her father's house."

"Suggestive."

"Yes. But nothing anyone could pin down. He's slippery."

"You've talked to the stepmother?"

"Dead. Car accident, five years ago."

"Suspicious?"

"Not at the time. Winding road. Rainy night. Blown tire. Although the tires were fairly new."

"Have you given all this information to Detective Ralston?"

"I will. I wanted to talk to you first. Oh, and I doubt it will lead to anything, but the sister mentioned a conversation they'd once had. They were discussing a television show where a fugitive had been hiding out in Omaha. Thaine said Omaha was the perfect place to disappear. Big enough so a stranger wouldn't stand out, and not on anyone's radar."

"You think there's anything to it?"

"Not likely. He would have only been about sixteen."

"But his sister did remember after all this time. For some reason, it stuck with her."

"I'll certainly check it out."

"Good. And Chandler? I want you to stick to this case, but if you have someone else available, I'd like some background information on the parents of Kendall Normand Houston."

"Kendall Normand, the skier?"

"Yes. Kendall and her husband died in an accident a few months ago, and her daughter is living with a neighbor of mine. Her parents are challenging her custody."

"Does this have anything to do with Thaine?"

"No. Just helping out a neighbor."

"So you want leverage?"

"I...yes. I hope we don't have to use it, but..." He let the rest go unsaid.

"Got it. This neighbor's name?"

"Ursula Anderson. Runs a B&B outside Seward, Alaska."

Chandler paused, and Mac could sense his unspoken questions about his involvement in a neighbor's custody suit. Fortunately, as employer, Mac was on the safe side of Chandler's investigative skills. "I'll put someone right on it."

"Thanks, Chandler. And good work."

Mac set his phone on the table with exaggerated care. Thaine was a psychopath. Self-centered, jealous. After all the books Mac had written, all the studies he'd pored over, how could he have missed the signs? It was all there. Why hadn't he investigated into Thaine's background before, when it would have made a difference? When it might have saved Andi's life?

Blossom nudged his hand. She always seemed to sense when he was falling into despair and tried to help. She was a lot like Andi in that way, constantly trying to make things better. He stroked the dog's massive head. He wasn't giving in this time, wasn't going to sink into a well of self-pity and regrets. He'd promised Ursula he'd be there for her and Rory, and he intended to keep his promise.

Andi was dead. No amount of self-torture and regret would bring her back. Eventually Thaine would be found and brought to justice. Mac would do whatever he could to ensure that, but it didn't change the facts. Andi was beyond his help.

But Rory wasn't. He was humbled by the courage of that child. Courage to live on, to run and play and laugh. She'd lost her whole world, and yet she hadn't numbed herself to life. Ursula was a big part of the reason why. They belonged together, and Mac was going to do everything in his power to make sure they stayed together.

He'd promised Ursula everything would be all right. He just hoped that this time, he could keep his promise.

TWO DAYS LATER, Mac pulled his car into a busy parking lot in front of a cedar A-frame. The sign on the front read Snow Country. He and Ursula were there at Rory's request. She'd called last night to remind him she'd never given him that cross-country ski lesson, and when he pleaded a lack of equipment, she'd ordered him to go to Anchorage and get some. "Everybody needs skis."

Since he'd already planned a trip to Anchorage with Ursula for her meeting with the family lawyer Fred had recommended, he agreed. Rory seemed to be taking the news about the custody suit in stride. According to Ursula, her main response was curiosity as to who these people were and where they lived.

Mac felt like the visit to the family lawyer had been productive. Darlene Henderson was candid and friendly, insisting they call her by her first name. She seemed quite confident that Ursula's position as Rory's guardian was secure. Mac couldn't shake the feeling that this wasn't going to be as straightforward as it seemed. But there was no use upsetting Ursula with pessimistic premonitions.

Now here they were at what Ursula explained was Rory's ski shop. "Kendall and Coby put their heart and soul into the shop, as well as the majority of their money. Most of the staff here has been with them from early on. They were devastated over the accident. Kelly Lee, who was the assistant manager under Coby, is running it now. The trustees handling the estate are discussing whether it would be better to keep the store or sell it and invest the money."

"What do you think?" Mac asked.

"I lean toward keeping it. It's Rory's legacy from her parents. Once she's old enough, she can make up her own mind whether to sell it or run it. Of course, a lot depends on whether it can remain profitable without Coby and Kendall, and their star power."

An employee working with another customer greeted them as soon as they stepped inside the store. "Welcome to Snow Country. Someone will be right with you."

Mac looked around. The decor landed somewhere between rustic cabin and Scandinavian modern. Light wood floors gleamed under pendant lights hanging from the high ceiling. A circular staircase led to a loft above the main sales area. Several clerks were busy fitting customers with ski boots or ice skates, while other people browsed the clothing racks.

Ursula led him past a gas flame flickering in a stone fireplace to a rack of skis. He randomly selected a pair and picked one up.

"Those are skate skis. You'll want to start with classic."

"Classic. I like the sound of that." Mac chuckled. "I know nothing about cross-country skiing. I've only been downhill skiing a few times and always rented whatever the shop recommended. I put myself into your hands."

A slim woman with a long black braid hanging over one shoulder hurried over to them. "Ursula! How are you?"

"Kelly, hi."

"Great to see you. Is Rory still doing Anchorski with me next weekend?"

"Is that next weekend? Time flies. Yes, she's looking forward to it. Kelly, this is my neighbor, Mac Macleod. He wants to take up skiing."

"More accurately, Rory wants me to take up skiing," Mac said. "She's promised me lessons."

Kelly grinned. "Then you're in good hands. Let's get you fixed up."

Mac left the store an hour later loaded down with skis, boots and poles. Ursula followed, carrying two bags full of ski clothes and assorted waxes. "You should be all set. Betty gave away all their ski equipment, but I think there's a wax bench in your garage."

"Is that what that is? I thought it was some sort of jig for woodworking." Mac packed the skis and equipment into the back of the SUV. "I didn't know learning to ski would involve alchemy."

"Waxing isn't all that complicated. At least it doesn't

have to be. The racers all have their special formulas, but for casual skiing you just need to use the right wax for the temperature. Rory can tell you all about it."

"I'm sure she can." He glanced at his watch. "Speaking of Rory, we'd better head back if you want to beat her home."

"You're right. I'm sure as soon as Rory walks in the door, she's going to want all of us to hit the trails."

Mac chuckled. "I'll be ready."

CHAPTER TWELVE

MAC CARRIED A stack of dishes to the table, his body protesting every movement. Rory was an excellent ski instructor but a hard taskmaster. He'd thoroughly enjoyed spending the afternoon learning to ski with her and Ursula through the forest behind his house, but now muscles he never knew he had were stiffening up. Blossom, having accompanied them on their ski, had collapsed on the dog bed in Ursula's kitchen and looked as though she might never move again.

The exercise didn't seem to have the same effect on Ursula and Rory. Ursula danced around the kitchen, whipping up some sort of chicken and pasta dish while Rory assembled spinach salads for each of them. "Do we have any sunflower seeds?"

"Yes." Ursula reached into her pantry and pulled out a mason jar. "But ask Mac before you add any to his salad."

"Mac, do you want sunflower seeds? They're really good."

"Sure." Mac finished setting the table. Rory brought the salad bowls and set one on each plate. She'd arranged slices of peppers and cherry tomatoes to form a face on the top of each salad, with shredded carrots for hair. "Hey, very artistic salads."

She beamed. "You can take a picture if you want."

"I'll do that." Mac dutifully pulled out his phone to snap a photo. He noticed a missed message that must have come in while they were skiing. It was from the lawyer in Anchorage. Ursula was still cooking, so he opened it. Hmm, the Normands wanted to schedule a preliminary meeting for Monday. They weren't wasting any time.

He must have frowned, because Ursula had stopped cooking and was watching him, the wooden spoon still in her hand. "Is everything okay?"

Mac nodded. "I think so. Check your phone when you get a chance. Looks like things are moving forward faster than we'd expected."

Ursula's eyes darted to Rory before she resumed sautéing vegetables. "Can you pour yourself a glass of milk, Rory? Dinner's almost ready." While Rory was busy in the refrigerator, Ursula looked over at Mac, her eyes worried. But then she smiled. "Wine, Mac? I have a half bottle in the refrigerator."

"I'll pour." Mac followed her lead. They could discuss this later, when they were alone. No use worrying Rory.

Ten minutes later, Ursula set the food on the table and Mac gingerly lowered himself into his chair. Ursula smirked. "Did Rory work you too hard today?"

"Oh, yeah. It's going to take some practice before I can keep up with you two."

"What do you mean, you two? Rory can ski circles around me if she wants to."

Rory plopped into the chair beside him. "I'm skiing in a race in Anchorage this weekend."

"I heard about that. How long is the race?"

"It's a twenty-five K."

"Wow, that's a long way to ski."

"Rory was the youngest finisher in last year's Anchorski," Ursula said as she dished some of the pasta onto Rory's plate.

"Impressive."

"Last time I skied with Daddy, but this year Kelly's gonna ski with me. She works at the store."

"I met Kelly," Mac sad. "She seems very nice."

"She is. She has two huskies and she goes skijoring. She says when I'm older, she'll teach me how."

"What's skijoring?"

"It's a cross between mushing and skiing," Ursula explained. "You hook a dog to a harness around your waist and they pull you along the ski trails. I've never done it, but I hear it's lots of fun."

"Maybe you could teach Blossom," Rory suggested.

Mac pictured himself getting dragged through thickets and over logs every time Blossom spotted a squirrel. "Maybe I'd better perfect skiing under my own power first before I get her involved." He looked over to where the dog lay sound asleep in the corner. "Besides, I'm not sure Blossom is up to it. You wore her out, too."

Blossom opened one eye when he mentioned her name and immediately closed it again. Rory and Ursula laughed.

They finished dinner and Ursula sent Rory off to work on homework. Mac started to clear the table. Once Rory was out of sight, Ursula grabbed her phone and listened to a voice mail from the lawyer. She set the phone down and turned to Mac. "You're right. They are in a hurry."

"That's good, though. Better to get it over with, right?"

"I guess so." She picked up a plate to rinse and loaded it into the dishwasher. "But it worries me. My admittedly limited experience with legal things is that they always move slowly. The fact that the Normands can send me a letter arriving Saturday and arrange a meeting with lawyers just over a week later sounds like they have some clout."

"According to Fred, Darlene Henderson is one of the best family lawyers in the state, and she's ready to meet on Monday. Maybe when they coordinated their calendars, they just got lucky."

"Maybe. Does Monday work for you? If you want to be there, that is. I don't want you to feel obligated."

"Of course I'll be there. I told you—I'm committed to seeing this through."

She closed her eyes and let out a long breath. "Thank you, Mac. I could really use someone on my side. Sam's working on the slope this week, and I hate to ask Dana to take off work."

He rested his hand on her back. "I'll drive. You call tomorrow and accept the appointment."

"Thanks."

Rory burst through the kitchen door. "I finished my worksheet. Can you check it?"

"Just a second, sweetie. Let me get the dishwasher started." Ursula reached for another plate.

"I'll look at it if you like," Mac offered. He sat down at the kitchen table beside Rory and read over her English homework. "Nice job. But here, take a look at this sentence. 'The group were happy.' Would you say 'The girl were happy'?"

"Girl was happy."

"Right. I know group sounds like more than one person, but it's only one group, so you need a singular verb. Was."

"Oh, okay." Rory made the change. "Are you gonna come to the ski race on Sunday?"

He grinned. "As long as I don't have to ski in it."

"No, you can wait at the finish. You don't have to ski."

"I'll be there, then, cheering for you."

"Yay." Rory snatched up her homework and started toward her room, stopping on the way to pet the dog. "Can Blossom come?"

"I don't think so. She's not good in crowds."

"Oh." She stroked the pit bull's head. "Don't worry, Blossom. We'll take you skiing next week. Mac needs another lesson."

MAC TUGGED HIS hat lower over his ears. The temperature was in the high twenties, but a brisk breeze chilled the people standing around, watching the skiers cross the finish line. Dana was there with him, with the baby bundled up and cozy in a backpack.

Just past the finish line, Snow Country had sponsored a table where they were handing out water and some sort of goodie bag to all the skiers. The fastest racers had finished an hour ago, but the main body was streaming across the line now. The crowd still clapped and cheered for each racer. Mac caught sight of a familiar purple hat just as Ursula spotted him and waved. She'd accompanied Rory to the start of the race and stopped off to take pictures along the way. She hurried toward them.

Ursula gave Dana a hug. "She was going strong at the three-quarters mark. They won't be long. Hi, Griffin." She leaned in to kiss the two square inches of skin exposed on his face. He gurgled and cooed at her. She turned to Mac. "You doing okay?"

"I'm good." Mac no longer worried about being recognized. First of all, these were ski fans, not gossip columnists. Second, he was old news. And finally, his own mother would have been hard-pressed to pick him out of the crowd of parkas and winter hats.

"Oh, look," Dana said. "Here they come!"

Rory led the way, dressed in pink tights and a hat with kitten ears on top. Kelly was right behind her. They were both moving fast. Dana and Ursula cheered loudly and clapped as they crossed the finish line. Mac added a whistle and called out his congratulations. A voice on a loudspeaker announced that Aurora Houston was the winner of the eleven-and-under division, to more cheers from the crowd, especially the group staffing the Snow Country table. Rory and Kelly stepped out of their skis and accepted cups of water.

Rory waved at Ursula, Mac and Dana. Before she could make her way toward them, though, a woman with blond hair under a dark fur hat stepped out from the crowd and spoke to her. Kelly stepped forward to join the conversation. Ursula hurried toward them and Mac followed. The woman seemed to be congratulating Rory on her victory and asking about her plans.

Ursula smiled at the woman but herded Rory away before she could answer the questions. He suspected at some point in the near future, she and Rory would have a talk about giving too much information to strangers. Andi always had difficulty with that when she was Rory's age, her natural enthusiasm overriding any innate caution. But he wasn't going to think about that today. Today was Rory's day.

"Did you see me, Mac? I won!"

"I know. You're amazing."

"She did so well." Kelly slipped an arm around Rory's shoulders. "Pretty soon, she'll be leaving me behind."

"I'll wait for you," Rory promised. "It's more fun to ski together."

As the women chatted with Rory, Mac glanced across the crowd. There, several yards away, the blond woman was still watching Rory. She seemed vaguely familiar. A man leaned in and spoke to her. She pointed in Rory's direction. He shook his head. They seemed to be arguing over something, but finally they turned and disappeared into the crowd.

Why were they so interested in Rory? Maybe they were just fans, impressed that an eight-year-old could keep up with so many fine skiers. But somehow, Mac had a feeling there was more to it than that.

MAC STRAIGHTENED THE tie he'd packed more from habit than from the expectation he would need it in Alaska. He followed Ursula and the receptionist into an empty conference room. After offering coffee, the receptionist left them there, alone. Ursula sat motionless, her face pale against the stark black of her dress. Mac reached over and squeezed her hand. "It will be okay."

"I hope so. I just wish—"

The door opened and Ursula's lawyer came in, followed by another woman and two men, one with a newspaper folded under his arm. As they approached the conference table, Mac recognized the couple he'd seen talking with Rory at the race the day before. No wonder they'd seemed familiar. They still looked much the same as they had during Kendall's competition days, when they'd been the included in several interviews and special reports. Rory's grandparents, if you could call them that considering she was eight years old and had never met them until yesterday, settled at the table and eyed Mac and Ursula.

Why now?

Ursula's attorney made the introductions, labeling Mac as Ursula's friend which drew a sharp glance from Mrs. Normand. Mr. Normand, on the other hand, looked as though he might recognize Mac. It didn't matter. Ursula was there to protect Rory, and Mac was there to help. If his celebrity could help Rory's case, he was happy to use it. Otherwise, it was irrelevant.

Mr. Normand set the newspaper on the table. The photo on the front page of the sports section was of Rory crossing the finish line, a huge smile on her face. A few yards behind her, the Normands stood at the front of the crowd, watching.

The attorneys talked for a while, using a lot of words but saying little. Mac could see Ursula's hand tapping against her leg under the table, but the face she showed remained perfectly calm. Eventually, Jake Shepherd, the Normands' attorney, got to the point. "My clients have filed for a court date to determine permanent custody of Aurora Houston, their granddaughter. They're concerned about the current custody arrangements and would like more information."

"What do you need to know?" Ursula spoke directly

to the Normands, but they looked to their lawyer. He consulted a paper and directed a question to Ursula. "Aurora inherited a successful sporting goods store and received a sizable settlement. How are those assets being managed for her future care and education?"

Mr. Normand seemed to be holding his breath. Is this why they were here? They wanted Rory's money? But that didn't make sense. Drake Normand was a well-known real estate developer in Colorado. His daughter's estate would be chicken feed to him. Maybe he was concerned that Ursula might be an opportunist, taking advantage of her relationship with Kendall and Coby to gain access to Rory's money.

Ursula's lawyer gave him a bland smile. "Aurora's assets are being competently managed by a team of trustees from a local bank, as was spelled out under her parent's wills."

Mr. Normand let out a breath. Mac couldn't tell whether it was from disappointment or relief.

Ursula's lawyer straightened a stack of papers. "Any other questions?"

Mrs. Normand leaned forward. "Aurora is a very special child. Her parents were both world-class athletes. I want to know what steps you've taken to nurture her talent."

"Rory is special." Ursula gave a small smile. "She's sweet and kind and enthusiastic. And yes, she has natural athletic ability. She's been skiing from the time she could walk, and we go out at least twice a week, weather permitting."

"What are your coaching credentials?"

"None. I'm just a recreational skier."

"Then who is in charge of her training regimen?"

Ursula chuckled. "She's eight. She doesn't have a training regimen."

Mrs. Normand's mouth tightened. "When Kendall was eight, she'd already been training with a prominent coach for four years."

"I know. Kendall told me." Ursula sat up very straight.

"Kendall and Coby were adamant that Rory's childhood would be different. She skis because she loves to ski, not to win ribbons."

The whole time his wife was questioning Ursula, her husband had been gazing at Rory's photo in the newspaper. Mac remembered seeing Kendall when she won her silver medal, standing on the podium with her flaxen hair flowing over her shoulders, her bright smile. As a little girl, Kendall must have looked much like Rory did now. Mrs. Normand took the newspaper from him and pointed at the photo. "She won her age group yesterday."

"Yes, she did."

"And yet you say she's not competitive."

"I didn't say that. I said she skis because she loves to ski. The Anchorski is a long race for young skiers. There were only five kids, including Rory, in the eleven and under class. Don't get me wrong. Rory likes to win. When she's older, she may decide to train competitively, and I'll support that. But right now, she needs to be a child."

"You can't wait. By the time she makes up her mind, it will be too late. She'll be too far behind."

"Behind whom?"

"The other hopefuls. She might not even make the US team. Even if she does, how can she expect to medal against competitors who've spent their entire lives preparing?"

"And what if she never wins a medal?" Ursula asked. "What if she never makes the team? What if she simply grows up to be a happy, healthy, well-adjusted woman? Does that make her a failure as far as you're concerned?"

Mrs. Normand rolled her eyes. "You obviously don't have the experience to know how to raise a child with this sort of gift. You don't understand how important this is."

Mac had an idea Ursula understood all too well. He was beginning to see why Kendall and her husband had chosen to raise their family in Alaska, far from her parents' influence. He glanced over at Mr. Normand, expecting to see the same indignation his wife exhibited. Instead, Mac noted a suspicious sheen in the man's eyes, still locked on that photo of Rory.

"Mrs. Anderson is an experienced parent," Darlene pointed out.

"Yes, I see that." Shepherd flipped to another page. "Samuel MacKettrick." He looked up at Ursula. "At what point did you begin fostering him?" He seemed to place emphasis on the word *fostering*.

Ursula's body tensed. She sucked in a breath before replying in a steady voice, "Sam was twelve when he moved in with us."

"I see." The attorney made a note.

Ursula's attorney closed her folder. "Do we have any more business to discuss today?"

"I believe we're about done," Shepherd said. "You'll be notified when we get a court date. In the meantime, of course, my clients want to arrange visitation."

Darlene looked at Ursula, who gave a reluctant nod. The attorney made a note. "Supervised visitation would be acceptable."

"Supervised?" Mrs. Normand turned toward her lawyer, but at his headshake she replied, "Fine."

"We'll set up a schedule and be in touch." Ursula's lawyer stood, cueing everyone else to stand, as well. Mac noted the lack of handshakes as everyone filed out of the office. The two lawyers spoke briefly before Shepherd disappeared down the hall. Darlene motioned for Ursula to step away into a quiet corner to exchange a few words.

Mr. Normand held the door for his wife. He glanced back, and for a moment his eyes met Mac's. He nodded before following his wife outside. Ursula shook hands with her lawyer and crossed the lobby to slip her hand onto Mac's elbow. "Ready to go?"

"Yes."

Once they were in the car, Mac pulled away from the curb while Ursula called to check in. Mac would never have guessed, listening to her voice as she chatted with Rory, that she had a care in the world. She hung up and put the phone away. "She's fine. Her friend Madison's mom invited her to stay for dinner."

"Sounds like they're getting along well." Mac stopped at a red light and looked toward Ursula. The worry lines had returned to her forehead.

"Yes. I'm so glad they've made friends. It's tough to be the new kid at school, on top of all the other changes in her life."

"Rory's a tough kid."

She laughed. "She takes after her parents in that regard." Ursula's face sobered. "But everyone has their breaking point. She has enough to deal with without the added pressure of fulfilling someone else's athletic dream."

"Yes, and I'm sure a judge will see that."

Ursula didn't answer. The stoplight turned green and Mac started toward home. He gave her a few minutes of silence before asking the question that had been bothering him since the meeting. "What's the problem with Sam?"

"What do you mean?"

"Shepherd was insinuating something. Something that scared you."

She gave him a rueful smile. "Am I that transparent?"

"Only to people who know you. You don't have to tell me if you don't want to."

Ursula blew out a long breath. "When Sam was twelve, his mother abandoned him. Tommy and I took him in."

"Yes, I know that. It seems to me that would be a positive when considering custody. You've already proven yourself a successful foster parent."

"But it was never official. Sam's mother left him with us

overnight. She used to do that sometimes, when she went out at night. When she didn't come home the next day, we didn't worry too much because that had happened before, once or twice. After a week, Tommy thought we should report her missing, but I was afraid if we did, they'd take Sam away from us. His mother was gone. I wasn't going to let them stick him in a home with strangers when we were there to love him and take care of him. I convinced Tommy we should keep Sam until his mother returned."

"Then what happened?"

"She never came back. Sam lived with us until he went to college. He didn't reconnect with his mother until about a year and a half ago."

"Sam would certainly say you did the right thing."

"I don't regret what I did, but will a judge understand? Or will they be able to use that against me in this custody dispute? I'm afraid my decision might hurt Rory." Ursula's voice wavered on the last words. Mac glanced over to see her eyes shiny with unshed tears.

"It's going to be okay."

"You don't know that."

He pulled off the road and turned into an empty parking lot next to a Russian Orthodox Church. "Let's take a walk." There really wasn't anywhere to walk except on the plowed pavement, but it didn't matter. He just wanted to get her out in the open air, where she could breathe.

He led her to the far corner of the parking lot and then put his hands on her shoulders and turned her toward him so she would look him in the eye. "It is going to be okay," he repeated.

"How can you be sure?" The tears were starting to spill over.

"Come here." Mac pulled her into his arms. With a sob, she leaned onto his shoulder and let the tears flow. Mac held her and let her cry. He was just kicking himself for forgetting to grab the box of tissues from the car when she pulled one from her coat pocket and blew her nose.

"Sorry." She wiped the tears from her cheeks with a gloved hand.

"Don't be sorry. Everyone needs a shoulder to lean on once in a while."

Ursula managed a little smile. "Leaning on your shoulder is one thing. Soaking your coat with tears in freezing weather is above and beyond."

Mac patted the shoulder of his parka. "Waterproof fabric. If it makes you feel better, you can squirt me with a hose."

She laughed. "I do feel better. I don't know why. Nothing's changed. I'm still afraid that my decision not to report Sam's mother missing might cause a judge to consider me unfit."

Mac considered what she'd said. "It's not as though you kidnapped him. You had permission from his mother to act as his guardian while she was away. I don't know that there's any implied expiration date for verbal permission."

"So you don't think I violated any laws?"

"I don't know. I'd advise you to talk it over with your lawyer. But, if I were a judge, I'd have a hard time holding it against you. You made your decision based on what you thought was best for Sam. Isn't that exactly what parents are supposed to do?"

"I hope the judge agrees with you." Those worry lines in her forehead weren't gone, but they weren't as deep as before. "After the questions Mrs. Normand asked today, my lawyer suggested that if I promised to set Rory up with a professional ski trainer, that might convince them to back off. It's as if they don't see her as a child, just their ticket to fame."

"Are you considering it?"

"Only as a last resort. Kendall and Coby trusted me to raise their daughter. They wouldn't want her subjected to the kind of pressure Kendall grew up with. I don't want that either."

"But you're going to allow visitation?"

"Yes." She straightened the finger of one of her gloves. "I have mixed feelings about that, but they're the only blood relatives Rory has left. And maybe once they spend a little time with her, they'll see her as a person, not just a means to an end."

"If anyone can win them over, it's Rory."

"Is that a good thing?" Ursula sighed. "If she does win them over, they'll fight even harder for her. If she doesn't, and her only grandparents drop out of her life, it's bound to hurt her feelings. I don't know what to hope for."

Mac put an arm around her shoulders and gestured toward the church. "It looks peaceful, doesn't it?" The last few rays of sunshine illuminated the top of the timber building. Snow covered the roof and clung in patches to the onion domes, painted a clear sky blue.

Ursula leaned her head against his shoulder. "I've always thought so."

"How old is it?"

"I'm not sure. Not that old as churches go. Probably built in the sixties."

"Still," Mac said, "I'm sure there's been plenty of heartache inside those doors."

"No doubt. But it's also seen joy. Weddings and christenings and celebrations."

"There." Mac grinned. "I knew you'd find the bright side. You always do."

"Is there a bright side to the situation with Rory?"

"There must be. I don't know what it is yet, but I know we'll find it. I have faith in you."

CHAPTER THIRTEEN

FOUR DAYS LATER, they were in Anchorage again. Ursula had scheduled the visit for late afternoon, so that Rory wouldn't have to miss any school. She'd been in with her grandparents for half an hour now. Ursula was pretending to read a magazine, but Mac noticed she hadn't turned a page in the last several minutes. She was always doing that, pretending nothing was wrong. Today, she'd said there was no need for Mac to spend his time riding along, but when he'd insisted, she looked relieved.

She'd kept up a cheerful dialogue with Rory on the way in, explaining that her mother's parents were in town and wanted to see her. Rory didn't seem exactly eager, but not opposed to the meeting. She asked a lot of questions, most of which Ursula had no answers for.

Once the social worker had led Rory away, Ursula had lapsed into an uneasy silence. Now she sighed and set her magazine on the coffee table. "I saw a coffee kiosk in the lobby. Would you like something?"

"Sure." Mac set down his book and started to stand, but Ursula motioned him to stay where he was.

"I'll get it. Black coffee?"

"That would be great." He watched her walk toward the stairs, her usually light step stiff from the tension in her body. Just after the door closed behind her, Mac's phone rang. He glanced around, and since the waiting area was empty, picked up. "Hello, Chandler."

"Mac. Just wanted to check in. I'm in Omaha. I've been

looking for the sorts of spots Thaine might frequent. No sign yet, but I'm just getting started."

"Good, good. Anything on the Normand matter yet?"

"Nothing definite, but my people say there's some buzz about his development in Vail. Some group has been protesting, trying to stop the second phase from breaking ground and now they've filed a lawsuit to stop him. It's costing him. A couple of contractors are saying he's been slow to pay."

Mac straightened. This could be the silver bullet. Leverage Ursula could use to counteract the implied threat Shepherd had made about Sam. That is, if Normand didn't want his troubles made public. "You think he's in serious financial trouble?"

"From what I've heard so far, I doubt it." Chandler's words deflated Mac's hopes on that score. "The permits were all in order, so the group isn't likely to get an injunction to stop the construction. We'll dig a little deeper, but he's handled bigger projects than this. Probably just a blip."

"Okay. Well, keep me informed. Good work getting that tip from the sister about Omaha. Hope it pans out." Mac pressed the end button as he thought it through. From what he'd seen, Chandler had good instincts on this sort of thing. If he didn't sense Normand was in serious financial trouble, he probably wasn't. All the same, Mac had to wonder if there was some connection between this and their sudden interest in Rory.

Ursula returned. Mac decided not to mention Chandler's information yet. She had enough on her mind. If and when he learned more, he'd fill her in. She handed him one of the foam cups. "It's hot. Let it cool a little before you drink."

Mac grinned. "Yes, ma'am. It's not as though I've ever drank coffee before."

"Sorry." She chuckled. "I guess I've gotten used to looking out for Rory."

"You're always looking out for everyone." He set his coffee on the table and touched her hand. "Maybe sometimes you need to let other people look out for you."

"That's a hard one for me," she said, "but I admit, having you along on all this legal stuff has been a tremendous help."

"I haven't done anything." A fact he found increasingly frustrating. He should have been able to help her, to make everything better for her and Rory, but all he could do was sit by and watch the drama unfold.

"You've been there beside me lending me your strength. And you've acted as my sounding board. When I talk it over with you, it gives me confidence that I'm doing the right thing for Rory. I don't know what I'd have done without you."

Mac knew exactly what she would have done. She would have fought for Rory's well-being, no matter how hard it was. He was just glad if his presence made it any easier.

Before he could formulate a response, Ursula spoke again. "I took your advice and talked to my lawyer about not reporting Sam's mother missing. She said it would depend on the judge. Some are real sticklers for procedure. Others, not so much." She opened the drinking spout on her cup but set it down without drinking it. "I hate to think Rory's fate would be based on random judge assignment."

"I'm sure even the most regimented judges would weigh the pros and cons, not base their decisions on one incident."

Ursula nodded, and this time she did take a sip. She wrinkled her nose. "Bitter. Did I give you the one with the cream?"

"Can't handle the hard stuff, huh?" He chuckled and exchanged cups with her. "I've been known to drain multiple pots of strong coffee when I'm on a deadline."

"I've always heard writers drank, but I thought they were talking about whiskey."

"I've been known to take a medicinal sip now and again,"

Mac admitted, "but my vice is caffeine." To prove his point, Mac swallowed a healthy slug of the strong brew.

They'd almost finished their coffee when the social worker brought Rory back. As soon as she rounded the corner, she broke into a run and rushed to Ursula's chair. "Can we go see Griffin now?"

"Of course." Ursula handed Rory her jacket. "How was your visit?" Ursula made eye contact with the social worker over Rory's shoulder, who gave a reassuring smile.

"Okay," Rory said. "They said I could call them Grandmother and Granddaddy, but they didn't tell funny stories like Grandma Gen used to. Mostly they just talked about people and stuff. Coaches or something. They were nice, though. They showed me some pictures of Colorado, where Mommy used to ski. I told them about school, and my friends, and Frankie."

"That's good."

The social worker put a hand on the girl's shoulder. "Bye, Rory. It was nice to meet you."

"Bye, Wendy." Rory turned to Mac. "Are you going with us to see Griffin?"

"That's the plan. Then I hear we're all going out to eat." Mac collected the empty cups and crossed the room to throw them away. From his vantage point, he could see down the hall. Mr. and Mrs. Normand stepped out of a doorway and took a few steps toward him before turning down another hall. Busy with her phone, she didn't notice Mac standing there, but Mr. Normand looked toward him. The man seemed pale, shaken. They held eye contact for a long moment, before he nodded and turned to follow his wife.

"Come on, Mac. Let's go!" Rory called. Mac accompanied them down the stairs and held the door for Ursula and Rory.

He stepped outside in time to see the Normands crossing the street. Something about the weariness in the man's step struck a chord with Mac. Mac dug in his pocket for the keys and turned to Ursula. "Say, I just remembered an errand I need to run downtown. Why don't you and Rory take the car to Sam's, and we can meet at the restaurant later. We're still eating at Simon and Seafort's, right?"

"Uh, all right." Ursula eyed him suspiciously, but she took the keys.

"Don't you want to see Griffin?" Rory demanded.

"I do, but he's coming to dinner, isn't he? I'll see him then."

"Come on, Rory," Ursula said. "You and Griffin can sit by Mac at the restaurant. He'll love that." Her grin let him know she was kidding, but Mac didn't mind if he did sit between them. He liked being around the baby, almost as much as he enjoyed spending time with Rory. And if this hunch panned out, he was going to enjoy it a lot more.

IT WAS A long shot. By the time Ursula and Rory were in the car and on their way, the Normands were out of sight. Since they were walking, Mac assumed the couple was staying nearby, so he looked around for the nearest high-rise five-star hotel. He dialed the desk and asked to be transferred to their room.

"One moment, please." The call rang through and Mac hung up.

He gave it about twenty minutes, strolling through the square and in front of the downtown shops and restaurants. His breath turned white in the frosty air. Finally, he walked into the lobby of the hotel, past the mural of early Alaskan achievements, and took the elevator to the bar on the top floor.

It didn't take long to locate Mr. Normand, sitting alone at a table, staring into a glass containing a smidge of dark liquid. "May I join you?"

He looked up and regarded Mac. "My lawyer wouldn't like it."

"No, I don't imagine either of the lawyers would approve."

He shrugged. "I'm not all that enamored with lawyers just now. Have a seat."

"Thanks." A waiter popped over to take their order. Mac nodded at the glass. "Two more of those, please."

"Right away." He disappeared as noiselessly as he'd appeared.

Mr. Normand studied Mac's face for a moment. "You're that writer, aren't you? The one whose daughter was murdered." His voice was matter-of-fact, conveying neither shock nor pity. Mac appreciated that.

"Yes, I am."

"Why are you in Alaska? I thought you were in Oklahoma."

"I was. But I had to get away, after everything."

"So you know what it's like."

"To lose a child? Yes, I know what it's like."

Mr. Normand drained his glass and set it on the table. "How did you know where to find me?"

"It wasn't that hard. You looked like a man in need of a drink."

"Yeah." The waiter arrived with their glasses. Mr. Normand took a large sip before setting his on the table. "So why are you here?"

"Because of Rory. I've grown quite fond of her, and I don't want to see her get caught up in a power struggle between adults."

Finally, a brief smile broke through on Mr. Normand's face. "She looks just like Kendall did at that age. More talkative, though. Rory's quite a chatterbox."

"Yes, she is. Big animal lover, too." Mac tasted his drink and returned it to the table. "You won't be able to get at Rory's money, you know. The bank isn't going to let it go without a struggle, and before you could work your way through that, it would be too late for your project."

"I know." Mr. Normand curled the edge of his cocktail napkin. "I assumed that would be the case. The money was just an excuse."

"For what?"

He didn't answer immediately. Instead, he asked, "Were you closely involved in raising your daughter, or did her mother make most of the decisions?"

"Andi's mother died when she was a baby. I raised her alone."

The man scratched his chin. "Kendall's mother pretty much raised her alone, as well. I was around, but I was busy growing my business, especially once we moved to Colorado. Once in a while, I'd take Kendall out for some daddy time, but it was all too rare. Crystal was the one who made the parenting decisions. I didn't always agree with those decisions, but I didn't question her. She was the hands-on parent."

"I see."

"One of Crystal's biggest rules was that there should be no empty threats. If Kendall didn't follow the rules, she suffered the consequences. I remember her sixteenth birthday. Two days before, she was goofing off with her friends and showed up for practice half an hour late. Crystal grounded her for a week. We had a big party planned, and I tried to argue for a one-time exception, but Crystal was adamant. She cancelled the party."

She sounded like a tyrant, but Mac couldn't fault her basic premise. "Discipline is important."

"Discipline is everything, according to Crystal. And for the most part, she was right. Kendall excelled, both at sports and academics. She got a lot of attention, but it didn't turn her head. She was a sweet girl."

"Yes. I never met your daughter, but I saw her interviews and special reports when she was competing. Her personality sparkled."

"Sparkled. That's exactly what Kendall was like." Mr. Normand stared at some point past Mac's shoulder, no doubt lost in memories of his daughter. "She sparkled."

He still hadn't answered why he was here for Rory, but Mac had a feeling pushing him for more information wasn't the way to go. "As I said, I know what it's like to lose a daughter you love. I also know about regrets."

Mr. Normand returned his gaze to Mac. "Do you? Did you allow yourself to be separated from your daughter because she had the gall to want to live her own life?" He shook his head. "I always thought we'd reconcile. I knew Crystal wouldn't back down, but I thought Kendall would eventually reach out, smooth things over. She was good at that. But it never happened." His voice broke and he took another drink before continuing. "I shouldn't have waited for her to make the first move. I should have stepped in, done something. I certainly should have met my granddaughter before she was eight years old. That's inexcusable."

A familiar flood of grief washed over Mac. "I have different regrets. Things I should have seen. Things I should have done. It's too late. My daughter is gone. So is yours. But you're lucky. Rory's still here."

"I was useless as a father." Moisture glistened in his eyes. "I allowed myself to be pushed to the edges of Kendall's life. I had to make up this excuse about the money to convince Crystal we should check on our own granddaughter. She'd told Kendall if she moved away she was cut off from the family forever and she was sticking to that, even after Kendall died."

"She seems interested in Rory now."

"She wasn't. Said Kendall made her choice. It wasn't until

she saw Rory cross that finish line on Sunday that she suddenly changed her mind. She's still after that gold medal."

"But you'd filed for custody before that."

"It was a ploy. Get her guardian worried she might lose custody and then settle for management of the trust. At least that's what I told Crystal. Mostly, I just wanted a chance to see her."

"So you have no intention of taking Rory away from Ursula?"

"We didn't. But now…" He hesitated. "Crystal's seeing visions of gold. And how can I turn my back on my own granddaughter? Shouldn't we take her in, raise her? Don't we owe Kendall that much?"

Mac didn't speak immediately. When he did, he kept his voice gentle. "It's not about you, or Kendall, or what you might owe her. It's about Rory, and what's best for her. Tell me something. I understand your wife was a phenomenal ice skater. Does she still skate?"

"Crystal?" He snorted. "She hasn't put on a pair of skates since we married. After she didn't make the national team, she joined a traveling ice show. She hated it. To her, it symbolized failure. She was convinced if she'd only started earlier, gotten better training, she would have had the gold. Before Kendall was even born, Crystal was strategizing her career."

"From what Ursula tells me, your daughter loved to ski, and she and her husband shared that love with Rory since she was a baby. They skied for the joy of it."

"Yes. She did look happy on Sunday."

"She always looks happy when she's skiing. Don't take that joy away."

The man frowned into his drink and he shook his head. "You think we should just go away? Pretend we never met her?"

"No. You're Rory's grandfather. You should be part of

her life. But don't let your guilt drive you to do something that's not in Rory's best interest. Ursula was there the day she was born, and she's been a part of Rory's life ever since. They love each other. Let Rory stay where she's happy."

"Rory's happy? After all that's happened to her?"

"Yes." Mac was certain of this. "She has bad days and she misses her family, but in spite of that, she's happy. She's a remarkable child."

"But after all we've put her through, would Mrs. Anderson be willing to let us be a part of Rory's life?"

"I think you'll find Ursula has an amazing capacity for forgiveness. I warn you, though, if she thinks you're doing anything to harm that child, she'll fight you with everything she's got. She loves Rory with her whole heart."

Mr. Normand eyed him. "And you? You said you're fond of Rory, but it seems to me you have strong feelings for Mrs. Anderson, as well."

"Ursula is my neighbor and my friend. I have great admiration for her."

Rory's grandfather laughed. "Okay, if that's what you want to call it. I'll think about what you've said. It makes sense."

"Will your wife go along with your decision?"

"I believe so, eventually. She'd never admit it, but she's been miserable ever since Kendall left. It's time for her to let go."

Mac reached out his hand. "Good talking with you, Mr. Normand."

"Drake." He accepted Mac's hand and shook it.

"Drake. And I'm Mac. I hope we meet again."

"I'm almost certain we will. And this time, I'd like to think we'll be on the same side of the table."

"LEAVE IT, BLOSSOM. Come." The dog had almost buried herself in the snow under a tree, digging for a shrew or something she'd scented. She never caught them, but she enjoyed the chase. Mac adjusted his ski pole before continuing along the trail toward Ursula's B&B, where he'd been invited for dinner "to celebrate."

Ursula wouldn't say what they were celebrating, but Mac had a pretty good idea. Today was Tuesday. When he'd left Drake Friday evening, the man had been doing some serious thinking. He'd had the whole weekend to convince his wife that their best chance to stay in Rory's life was to get in the good graces of the woman Rory's parents had chosen, and probably talked it over with their lawyer on Monday.

Drake was more perceptive than Mac had given him credit for. After meeting Rory, he'd understood that she needed to stay where she was comfortable, that the constant pressure to perform wasn't what she needed.

Drake was perceptive about more than Rory. He'd easily seen through Mac's declaration of admiration for Ursula. And he was right. Mac hadn't wanted to admit it to himself, but the more time he spent with Ursula, the more he wanted to spend. She and Rory were rapidly becoming the center of his life, and he wanted it to stay that way.

Could it possibly work? Mac had decided long ago he wasn't husband material. He'd failed miserably at his one foray into marriage. A good husband would have realized from their phone calls that Carla was depressed, would have asked the right questions. A good husband would have done something to help before it was too late.

But that was a long time ago, and he'd been overseas when it happened. He'd matured since then. He'd raised a daughter, and while he regretted some of the decisions he'd made along the way, she'd grown into a woman he was proud of. Her death didn't cancel that out. Maybe he hadn't done everything wrong.

Would Ursula even want him? Yes, she seemed to care

for him, but then she was a kind and caring person. She'd responded to his kisses, but attraction wasn't the same as love.

Love? Was he really thinking about love? His mind had somehow jumped from friendship to marriage without giving a name to his feelings. Ironic for a man who made his living with words.

Did he love Ursula? What did it even mean? He was happier when she was around. He cared about her, wanted what was best for her. Frankly, he admired her more than anyone he'd ever known. But did he love her?

He thought back on their time together. The laughter around the kitchen table when they'd all played cards during the snowstorm. Her warm smile that welcomed him. The way she felt in his arms when she'd finally let go and cried out her frustrations and fears. As though his empty arms were finally fulfilling their intended purpose. To hold her.

Blossom ran over and planted her feet in front of his, staring up at him. He laughed and brushed the snow off her fleece jacket. "Yes, I'm daydreaming again. Sorry. If you'll get off my skis, we can head on over. I'm sure Ursula has a biscuit waiting for you."

At the mention of Ursula's name, Blossom's tail wagged. She turned and galloped forward on the trail, looking over her shoulder to make sure Mac was following. He chuckled. He wasn't the only one who'd fallen in love with Ursula Anderson.

Mac was panting by the time he arrived at the inn. In the distance from his cabin to the B&B, Rory would just have been warming up. Blossom sniffed around the trees surrounding the inn, no doubt looking for signs of Frankie the squirrel, while Mac caught his breath and removed his skis. He left them on the porch and whistled for the dog.

When he opened the front door, Blossom ran inside and straight across the room to where Rory was moving things around on the coffee table. She squealed and hugged the dog.

"Hi, Blossom." Two people seated on the couch in front of the fire turned to look at him. The Normands. What were they doing here?

Rory ran to greet him. "Mac. Come play. Granddaddy and Grandmother are gonna eat dinner with us, and I want to teach them concentration." She grabbed his hand and tugged him across the room.

Before he'd reached the sitting area, Ursula popped out of the kitchen, carrying a tray. "Oh, hi Mac. I'm glad you made it."

Mac stopped to take the tray from her. She smiled her thanks and hurried over to clear a space on the coffee table. Mac set the tray down and looked at the Normands. Drake gave him a friendly smile. "Good to see you again, Mac. You remember my wife, Crystal?"

Ursula flashed a questioning look at him, probably wondering why he and Drake were on a first-name basis. He hadn't told her about their conversation, just in case it didn't pan out. "Of course I remember." Mac turned a polite smile toward Mrs. Normand. "Hello."

Her return greeting seemed congenial enough. Ursula poured glasses of wine and distributed small plates. "Salmon dip to tide you over until dinner's ready."

Drake dished up some and handed the plate to his wife before filling his own plate. Crystal tasted it and opened her eyes wide. "This is excellent."

"Thank you. I smoked it myself."

Mac hid a smile, remembering how he'd turned down his first chance at Ursula's salmon dip and threatened to have her arrested for trespassing. They'd come a long way since then.

Rory ran to the kitchen and returned with a pack of cards. She frowned at the tray taking up the table space. "I was gonna show them how to play concentration on the table."

"Then why don't you move to one of the dining tables?"

Ursula suggested. For the first time, Mac noticed the round table in the dining area was set for five. "I need to check on dinner."

Rory ran to one of the other tables. "First, you have to shuffle." She separated the deck into two parts and tried to shuffle, but dropped several cards. "Here, Mac, you do it. Mac showed me how to play this game, but I usually win."

"It's true," Mac said, as he shuffled the deck and began laying out the cards in rows. "Rory has an amazing memory."

Rory explained the concept to her grandparents, and they cheerfully entered into the spirit of the game. To Mac's surprise, Crystal seemed to enjoy playing. At the end of the game, she and Rory were tied with eight books each. "We're twins," Rory declared.

Her grandmother laughed. "I think we are. Shall we play again?"

URSULA OPENED THE oven door, filling the kitchen with the scent of cinnamon from the apple pie she'd been keeping warm. Dinner had gone well. The Normands seemed to be enjoying Rory's company, and she was certainly enjoying entertaining them.

When her lawyer had called with the news they were dropping the custody suit, Ursula suspected there would be strings attached, but the lawyer assured her their only request was to see Rory once more before they left Alaska. How could Ursula refuse them?

She'd immediately called to invite them to dinner, and she was glad she did. The people who had seemed so menacing in the lawyer's conference room had somehow morphed into doting grandparents. Ursula wasn't sure why they had changed their minds about fighting for custody, but Drake's attitude when Mac showed up made her suspect Mac had somehow influenced their decision. She couldn't imagine how he'd done it, but then Mac was a man of many talents.

She dished up the pie and carried it to the dining room, where Rory was entertaining everyone with tales of the playground. "And Ian said boys were faster than girls, so I challenged him to a race, and I won. He said his snow boot came off and made him trip, so it didn't count. So I said I'd race him again."

"And did you win?" Drake asked.

Rory shrugged. "He said it wasn't fair because he couldn't run good in boots, and then the bell rang. But tomorrow when we go to gym, I'm gonna see if Mr. Todd will let us race inside."

Crystal laughed. "I predict Ian will have another excuse. But he probably won't be bragging about running faster than girls anymore."

Ursula set a slice of pie in front of Rory. "Did you remember to bring home your spelling word list?"

"It's in my backpack." Rory took a bite of pie. "Yummy."

"It is yummy," Mac said. "In fact the whole dinner was delicious. Thank you, Ursula."

The Normands murmured their agreement. Once they'd all finished dessert, Drake mentioned they should be getting back to their hotel.

"Don't go yet," Rory urged. "I want to play another game of concentration."

"You need to practice your spelling words first." Ursula stood and began to clear the dessert plates. "Maybe your grandfather could quiz you while I make coffee. Any takers?"

"I wouldn't mind a cup of decaf," Mac said, helping her stack the dishes on a tray.

"I'll get my spelling list." Rory shot off toward the kitchen. Blossom jumped up and ran after her.

"She never slows down, does she?" Crystal chuckled. "Here. Let me help you with the dishes."

"I can manage."

"Nonsense. Here, I'll carry these." Crystal picked up some of the wineglasses and followed Ursula into the kitchen. "Where do you want them?"

"There, beside the sink is fine." Ursula set her tray beside the dishwasher and reached for the coffee. "Thanks."

"You're welcome." Crystal picked up one of the wineglasses as though to inspect the etched pattern, and then set it down again and turned toward Ursula. "You've been exceptionally gracious, inviting us into your home to spend time with Rory. I doubt if our positions were reversed, I would have done the same."

"I just want what's best for Rory."

"That's what Drake said about you. We had a long talk this weekend." She gave a wry smile. "A very long talk. Not just about Rory but about Kendall, and about our marriage. Looking back, there are things I could have done differently. Should have done differently."

No kidding. Ursula busied herself setting out the cups to keep her sarcasm to herself. Instead, she kept her voice neutral. "Like what?"

"Drake pointed out to me that I kept him and Kendall from bonding. I didn't intend for that to happen, but she was busy with lessons and training, and he was working so hard. It was just easier for me to manage her life while he did his job. Drake resents the time they lost."

"Kendall missed him." Kendall had always sounded wistful when she spoke of her father to Ursula. It sounded as though they'd never spent much time together, but enjoyed each other when they did. "She could never understand why he didn't even try to get in touch with her after her marriage."

Crystal raised her chin. "I suppose Kendall told you I

was a wicked witch who kept her locked in a gilded cage and then threw her out to starve."

"Nothing so melodramatic. Kendall was aware of how you'd worked and sacrificed for her ski career, and she was grateful. She had some wonderful experiences that wouldn't have been possible without you. But she felt she was never good enough for you. She always had to do better, to be better."

Crystal's eyes narrowed, but she didn't argue the point. Ursula filled a cream pitcher and set it on the tray before she continued. "She'd fallen in love with a good man who loved her, unconditionally. They were going to have a baby. She chose to marry him and move to his hometown where they could raise the baby without pressure. Was it so unreasonable for her to expect her parents to support her decision?"

The back door flew open. Rory and Blossom raced in and Rory skidded to a stop in front of Crystal waving a crumpled piece of paper. "I finally found it. It was in the very bottom, under my hat. Do you want to go over my words with me, too?"

Crystal smiled at her. "You bet. You go show them to Granddaddy and I'll be there in just a minute to help."

"Mac will help, too."

"Of course."

The door swung shut behind the girl and the dog just as the coffee finished brewing. Ursula added the carafe to the tray and turned. "Are you ready to go in?"

"Not yet. I need to make you understand."

"Understand what?"

"I loved her. Kendall was my daughter. I loved her so much sometimes I felt like my chest would explode. That's why I drove her. That's why I made her train when she didn't feel like training. That's why I never let her settle for good enough, only the very best. Because I loved her. Nobody did that for me. I was never good enough to even compete at those levels. But Kendall was. She did."

"And she won silver." Ursula remembered watching the competition on television and witnessing the pure joy on Kendall's face when she realized her scores had moved her into medal contention.

"I wanted gold for her."

"I do understand." Ursula laid a hand on Crystal's arm. "You wanted her to have a gold medal because that was what you'd wanted for yourself more than anything in the world. But it wasn't Kendall's highest goal. She wanted a happy family. And she got it. She, Coby and Rory were one of the happiest families I've ever met."

"I'm glad." Crystal toyed with one of the spoons on the tray. "I just wish…"

"What?"

"I wish I hadn't been so hardheaded. I thought if I stood my ground, Kendall would return to her training after she had the baby. Once it became obvious that wasn't going to happen, I still wouldn't give in. It was stupid." She met Ursula's eyes. "So what now? I know you don't approve of the way I raised Kendall. Are you going to punish me by denying me access to my only granddaughter?"

Ursula hesitated. "You understand I will honor Kendall and Coby's plan to give Rory a childhood as normal and carefree as possible? You're not allowed to pressure her. This isn't negotiable."

"I understand, and I respect that."

"Then it seems to me that it could only be beneficial to Rory to have loving grandparents in her life. Maybe we can set up a regular video chat so she can keep you up to date on her activities. In fact…" Ursula paused.

"What?"

"Rory and I were planning to visit my mother in Wyoming early this summer. If you like, I could bring her to visit you, as well."

"You'd do that for us?" Crystal seemed truly shocked.

"Not for you, but for Rory. There's not a lot I wouldn't do for Rory."

CHAPTER FOURTEEN

IT WASN'T EASY getting Rory settled that night, but eventually Ursula coaxed her into bed and stroked the soft blond hair away from Rory's forehead. "Did you have a good evening?"

"It was fun. Granddaddy says he wants to come to Alaska again in the fall. I'll be in third grade then." Rory wiggled farther under the covers.

"That will be fun." Ursula tucked the quilt in around her. "Your grandmother and I talked about maybe visiting them this summer, as well."

"In Colorado? Goodie." Rory smiled, but then her face grew serious. "If they're Mommy's mom and dad, why didn't they ever come visit before? Grandma Gen was Daddy's mom, and she came over all the time."

"I know, but she lived closer. The truth is, Rory, your mom and her parents were angry at each other and they didn't speak for a long time."

"Why?"

"It's complicated. Your mother wanted one sort of life, but your grandmother thought she needed something different. So your mother moved here, with your daddy."

"They were mad at each other?"

"Yes."

Rory thought about it. "Once at school, I got mad at Madison because at reading time, she grabbed the book I was going to read even though she knew it was my favorite. But at lunch she gave me half of her orange, and we played together at recess."

"So you forgave her."

Rory nodded. "She's still my best friend. Why couldn't Mommy and her mom and dad forgive each other and be friends?"

"I don't know, Rory." Ursula smoothed a crease from Rory's pillowcase. "Sometimes grown-ups can be stubborn. Maybe we're not a smart as you and Madison. Now go to sleep. You have school in the morning."

Before she could go, Rory wiggled her arms out from under the covers and pulled Ursula into a hug. "I'm glad me and you don't get mad and stop talking."

Ursula hugged her back. "I'm sure sometimes you'll be mad at me, but I will never stop talking to you. Ever. I love you, Rory."

"I love you, too."

Ursula dropped a kiss on the girl's forehead. "Good night, sweetie."

"Good night."

Ursula drifted back into the kitchen. Mac was there, loading the dishwasher. He looked up. "You look thoughtful."

She crossed the room to stand beside him. "I was just marveling at the wisdom of children. Kendall and her parents lost years. When Rory and her friend fought, they made up in an hour."

"Rory is amazing."

"Yes." With a start, she realized he'd cleaned the whole kitchen while she was tucking Rory in. "You didn't have to do all this."

"After partaking of such a glorious meal, it's the least I could do."

Ursula laughed. "You act as though I'm a gourmet chef, rather than a plain home cook."

"There's nothing plain about you."

Something about the intensity of his gaze when he spoke made her cheeks grow warm. To cover her confusion, she pressed the start button on the dishwasher. Mac reached for her hand. "I know it's late, but I'd like to talk with you about something."

"Good. I'd like to talk with you, as well."

"Let's see if the fire is still burning." He led her to the living room and added another small log to the coals there before sitting beside her on the sofa. "Okay, you first."

"I want to know what strings you pulled to make the Normands change their minds about custody."

"What makes you think I had anything to do with it?"

"Come on. You and Drake were practically acting like old college roommates. That wasn't the case during the last hearing. What changed?"

Mac chuckled. "I should have realized I couldn't get anything past you. Okay, I'll confess. After the supervised visit, I went looking for him."

She frowned. "Wasn't that risky? What if he'd accused you of trying to intimidate him?" Her eyes widened. "You didn't intimidate him, did you?"

"No, we just talked, father to father. He knew who I was, knew about Andi. He misses his daughter."

Her mouth tightened. "He had years to do something about it."

"I know. That's his biggest regret. And he has plenty of others. I just helped him see that trying to take Rory away from you would be another regret."

"However you managed it, I thank you. But I still don't see how you convinced him."

"It didn't take that much convincing. He wants to do the right thing, but after losing his daughter, he had a hard time letting go of Rory. I convinced him letting her grow up here, where she was happy, didn't mean letting go forever. I told you were a forgiving person. I'm pleased to see I was right."

"I'm not sure I've completely forgiven them yet, but I

do understand them a little better. And I feel a bit for them. In spite of all her talents and wealth, Crystal hasn't lived a happy life. Her single-minded pursuit of that one goal caused all of them to miss out on so many of life's joys."

"Yes. Although I can see where Rory inherited her competitive streak."

Ursula laughed. "Did she beat you at concentration again?"

"She beat everybody. You know, I don't agree with Crystal's methods, but when Rory gets a little older, she's going to want to compete."

"I know. And I'll try to make sure she has the opportunities for coaching and training when she's ready. The important thing, the thing Kendall and Coby felt so strongly about, was that Rory knows her worth isn't tied to her achievement in sports. Coby trained hard, and his parents encouraged him, but he always knew he was loved and accepted no matter whether he won or lost. Kendall's parents didn't do that."

"You don't think they loved her?"

"I'm sure they did. But Crystal withheld her approval to manipulate Kendall. Kendall was determined, and so am I, that Rory would never experience that feeling."

"But you're still going to let them see Rory?"

"Yes. Maybe it's not too late for them. They did seem to enjoy being with her. But mostly, I'm doing it for Rory's sake. She lost her whole family in one night. Now, she's found new family members, and it makes her happy. That makes me happy."

"And you make me happy." Mac did seem happy tonight. Hard to believe that bitter, angry man she'd first encountered was the same person. His positive attitude throughout the stress of dealing with the Normands made it all bearable. She just hoped, now that the crisis was past, he was able to stay positive. He smiled at her. "I wanted to talk with you about that, actually."

"About happiness?"

"Indirectly. I've been doing some thinking about life in general, and the way I've handled it in particular. As you know, I have regrets. But life doesn't come with Control Z."

"What's Control Z?"

"The computer keyboard shortcut for undo. It undoes the last action."

Ursula sat up. "What, so if I accidentally delete a sentence and then hit Control Z, it puts it back?"

"Yes."

"Wow. This will save me all kinds of time on my next newsletter. I should write that down." Ursula pulled out a drawer on the end table, rooted around until she found a pen and jotted a note. When she looked up, Mac was watching her with a bemused expression. She sank back against the cushions and folded her hands in her lap. "Sorry. You were talking about something important and I got distracted with computer tips. Go on, please. Tell me the meaning of life."

He laughed and opened his arms invitingly. "Come here, darlin'."

Darlin'? He'd called her that before, just before he'd kissed her. Her cheeks grew warm at the memory.

No more kissing. That's what she'd told herself in Fairbanks, after that kiss under the northern lights. That it would be best for all involved to keep this relationship at the friendship level. But the fire was dying, the night air was chilly and his warm arms were right there.

She slid into his embrace and rested her head against his shoulder. It felt...nice. Solid and warm. Comforting. Just as he'd comforted her through this whole ordeal with his solid presence and good sense. And now he was trying to tell her something.

She put her hand on his knee. "Seriously, I want to hear what you have to say. Life doesn't come with Control Z, and what?"

He pulled her closer and brushed his lips against the top

of her head. "I could talk all night, but what it boils down to is this. I've made mistakes, and I've tried to learn from my mistakes. After my wife died, I took great care to avoid any serious relationships. I put all my energy into raising my daughter."

"It can't have been easy, raising a daughter alone."

"Not always, but it was rewarding. But that's not my point. What I'm trying to say, is that you and Rory have become very important to me. I don't know if I can be any good at a relationship but I want to try. If you'll have me."

"Mac?" She tilted her head back so she could see his face. "What exactly are you asking me?"

"I don't even know what it's called anymore." He gave a little chuckle. "When you were, oh, about thirteen, did you wear an ID bracelet?"

"I did. My aunt gave it to me for Christmas. But I exchanged bracelets with Bucky Herrington and he lost it. He admitted that to me just before he asked for his back because he wanted to give it to Jolene Potoskí."

"Bucky sounds like an idiot. Who in his right mind would choose Jolene over you?"

"Jolene was the prettiest girl in school. All the boys were after her."

"Let me ask you this—if I had an ID bracelet to give you, would you wear it?"

"Well, I don't know. How could I be sure you wouldn't be like Bucky and dump me for a prettier girl?"

"Don't be silly." He gave her shoulders a squeeze. "There are no prettier girls than you."

"Oh, my." She pretended to fan her face. "Spreading the flattery on with a trowel, are we?"

He winked. "Sorry." He smoothed a lock of hair from her forehead. "Seriously, though. I feel like there's something between us. An attraction I've been trying to ignore, but I can't. Is it completely one-sided?"

She smiled up at him. "No. I feel it, too. But just because it's there doesn't mean we have to act on it."

"Is there any reason we shouldn't?"

"Yes. Rory."

A flash of hurt crossed his face before he spoke. "Are you saying a relationship with me is bad for Rory?"

"Not at all. Rory adores you."

"The feeling is mutual."

"I know. When I met you, you were in a dark place. Being around Rory has helped you heal, but Rory can't fill the hole Andi's death left in your soul. She's just a little girl. She can't shoulder that kind of responsibility."

"You think I'm using Rory as a crutch." He paused, his face thoughtful. "I think you're wrong. Sure, sometimes Rory reminds me of Andi, but Rory is her own person. In many ways, they're polar opposites. Rory isn't anyone's replacement. She's important to me because she's herself." He took Ursula's hand in his. "So are you."

"But what if this doesn't work out? Right now you're a friend and neighbor. If you were to pack up tomorrow and move back to Oklahoma, Rory would miss you, but I don't think she would feel abandoned. But if you get closer to her..."

Mac nodded, slowly. "I understand. If it doesn't work out, she could get hurt. But what if it does work out? I've raised a daughter alone, and as you said, it's not always easy. Two parents make it easier."

She sat up and turned to face him. "What are you saying? We've gone from ID bracelets to co-parenting?"

"Exactly. I want to take this friendship to the next level, to explore this attraction and see where it leads. Because I'm betting it can lead to something wonderful. It took me by surprise, but I've fallen in love with you."

Love? She hadn't seen that coming. Perhaps she'd deliberately averted her eyes. She'd tried to pull back when she felt the attraction, but circumstances conspired to bring them together. Or maybe it wasn't circumstances. Maybe it was her own choices that kept pulling Mac closer into their lives. Maybe she wanted him to love her, because she was starting to feel the same for him.

"Mac." She reached to lay her hand against his cheek. "I don't know what to say. I'm tempted. If I only had myself to consider, I wouldn't hesitate. You make me feel things I haven't felt in a very long time. I'd love to see where we could go with this."

"But?"

"But there's Rory." She traced her finger along his jaw before allowing her hand to fall to her lap. "I told you about my father. He never allowed himself to be happy after my brother died, and his unhappiness weighed down the whole family. Just lately, I've seen you experience joy, but I've also seen you in despair."

"I can't just put aside Andi's death, as though it didn't matter."

"No one expects you to be happy all the time. But I know you're still—I won't say obsessed—but strongly focused at least. I know you're working with an investigator. I know you haven't given up on finding your daughter's killer."

"Are you asking me to give it up? To choose between justice for my daughter and a chance to be with you and Rory?"

"Of course not. I wouldn't ask that of you. It's just…" How could she explain it to him? She understood why he needed closure. She wanted his daughter's killer found and locked away, too. But what if they never found the murderer? Would Mac be stuck in that place for the rest of his life, unable to move forward? Even if the murderer were caught, tried and sentenced to prison, would Mac be able to let go? Or would his blame once again turn inward? Would he be like Ursula's own father, locked in a prison of his own making, unable to change the past and unwilling to forgive himself for it?

But Mac was starting to take back his life. She'd seen him with Rory, patiently playing cards and building the snowman. And no matter how dark his mood, he'd always been gentle with Blossom and with Rory. Could she trust him to keep it up?

He lifted her hand and brushed it with her lips. "You say I make you feel things. What sorts of things?"

She smiled. "You make me feel secure. Comforted. I feel like I can let down my guard, that you have my back."

"I do."

She believed him. He'd certainly proven it throughout this custody challenge. And when he fixed the generator. Her resolve was weakening "What, exactly, is implied in this exchange of virtual ID bracelets?"

"Well, I suppose that we'll spend time together. Maybe go out to dinner or a show now and then. Pitch in when either of us needs help."

"We're already doing those things."

"Oh, and I get to do this." He gathered her up in his arms and pulled her close. His kiss was warm and sweet and wonderful, creating a glow in her center that spread all through her. When the kiss ended, they were both breathless.

"You make a strong argument."

"Do you need another demonstration before you decide?"

"No. I've made up my mind. If you're willing to take it slow, to give Rory—well, all of us—time to adjust, my answer is yes."

"You won't regret it."

"I'm already regretting turning down that second demonstration."

"Well, we'll just have to do something about that."

"A DULL KNIFE is a dangerous knife. It's important to keep it sharp so that you don't have to force the cuts." Mac wiped the edges of the silver penknife he'd picked up for Rory along the whetstone.

Rory nodded solemnly, her full attention on his safety presentation. Ursula hadn't been too keen on a knife for an eight-year-old, but Mac had convinced her that teaching Rory to use it properly was the safest option in the long run. Besides, they'd already agreed that the knife would remain here, in Mac's cabin, and only be used under his direct supervision.

The three of them had been together almost every day for the past week, skiing, eating dinner, playing cards. Rory's grandparents wanted to take her to a movie before they returned home, so on Friday night, Ursula, Mac and Rory had driven to Anchorage to meet them. While Rory and the grands enjoyed an animated film about dolphins, Mac and Ursula took the opportunity to see a popular drama at the same complex. It was their first official date, and despite agreeing that the movie didn't live up to the hype, they'd both had fun.

Now Mac and Rory were sitting together on the couch in his cabin for a carving lesson while Ursula worked on an afghan for the church bazaar. Mac demonstrated how to hold the knife properly. "Always cut away from your body, and only try to remove a small bit at a time."

"Okay." Rory looked at him expectantly. "Can I cut something now?"

"Yes, if you think you can remember the rules." Mac pulled out a waxy white bar from the bin beside the couch and handed it to her. "We'll start with this."

"But it's soap."

"Exactly. This is how my grandfather taught me when I was your age. See how I've sketched out a picture on top?"

"It looks like a turtle."

"Uh-huh. Now hold it in your left hand, like this so your fingers aren't in the way, and use your knife to take off the parts around the turtle shape." Rory tried to cut a chunk from the edge but Mac stopped her and put his hand over hers. "Just a little at a time, remember?" He guided her hand to peel away a smooth curl of soap and let it fall onto the newspaper he'd placed on the coffee table.

Ursula's crochet hook stopped in midstitch as she watched their two heads bent over the project. Under Mac's tutelage, Rory quickly got the hang of it and went to work rounding off the edges of the soap.

Blossom apparently decided if Ursula's hands weren't busy working, they should be put to a better use. She got up from her dog bed and laid her head on Ursula's lap. Ursula set down her crochet project so she could use both hands to massage Blossom's ears.

Mac retrieved his own knife and a half-finished wood spirit from the bin. The gnome whose face was slowly taking shape had long hair flowing to one side as though wind-blown. Laughing eyes held a hint of mischief. Really more of a sprite than a gnome, the face was full of energy, rather like the face of the sprite sitting beside him on the couch.

A new throw hung over the back of the couch behind them. Ursula recognized it as her friend Demi's work, handloomed and sold in one of the local art shops. There was a new pillow, too, and even a houseplant on the table near the window. Mac was starting to feather his nest.

In the kitchen where he'd left it charging, Mac's cell phone rang. Since he was settled in beside Rory, Ursula gently pushed Blossom back from her chair. "I'll get it for you."

"Don't bother." Mac winked at her. "Everyone I want to talk to right now is already in this room."

Aw. Now Ursula just wanted to kiss him. That had been happening a lot lately. They'd agreed to keep this new relationship low-key, especially around Rory, but inside Ursula felt as giddy as she had the first time she ever fell in love. The phone rang three more times, and then it was silent.

Rory and Mac continued to work on their respective carvings. Now and then, Mac would set his down to show Rory the next step. Finally, she laid down her knife and went to show Ursula. "What do you think?"

"He's cute." The turtle's shell bulged a little on one side, but overall it was an excellent first effort.

"Now what do I do?" Rory asked Mac.

He picked up the turtle, turning it over to examine each side. "It looks good. If you like, we can smooth it out with a damp finger and then add markings to the shell, but let's do that next time. I'm hungry."

"Me, too." Rory jumped up. "Pizza!"

"Then you'd better clean up your workspace so we can go," Ursula told her. "Remember what Mac said about how to care for the knife."

With a minimum of grumbling, Rory cleaned up the soap shavings that had missed the newspaper and dropped on the floor. Twenty minutes later, they were sliding into the corner booth at Fireside Pizza. Rory pointed at the pictures in the menu. "Can we get pineapple on the pizza?"

"Pineapple?" Mac grimaced.

Ursula laughed. "Not a fan?"

"I like pineapple," Mac said, "but I feel it should stay in its designated slot on upside-down cakes. The best pizza I ever had was simply topped with cheese."

Ursula let her head drop to her hands in mock despair. "Oh, Mac. The flavor combinations you're missing."

"Welcome to Fireside." A young man with spiky blond hair brought glasses of water. "Ursula! Good to see you."

"Hi, Jude. Rory and I are trying to convince Mac he needs to be more adventurous."

Jude turned to Mac. "You're the writer, right? The one that reporter was after?"

"Yes. Mac Macleod." He offered a hand.

Jude shifted his order pad and shook hands. "Jude Jenkins. Welcome to Seward." He grinned. "Sorry I missed out on all the fun. Bill was telling me how he set the scene out at his cabin. He loves that he was able to put one over on the press. So what adventure are Ursula and Rory trying to lure you into?"

"We want pineapple," Rory said, "but Mac just wants plain cheese pizza."

"Whoa, there's nothing plain about my cheese pizza. I use a five-cheese blend, including an amazing pecorino from Sardinia I've recently discovered." He kissed his fingertips. "It will make a pizza purist like you weep with joy."

"There you go," Mac said.

"But Hawaiian." Rory spoke with longing.

Mac touched Ursula's hand. "What do you like on your pizza?"

She sighed. "I can never decide. I love them all."

Jude flashed a grin. "Leave it to me." He tucked the tray under his arm and disappeared into the kitchen.

Ursula waved to a couple from church sitting at the table near the fireplace. Only one other table was occupied. "When Jude has time to play, he comes up with some amazing ideas. They're all rustic-style crust, in a wood-fired oven. I've never had a bad one."

Mac glanced around. "I'm surprised he can afford to stay open with so few customers."

"You wouldn't recognize the place in the summer. He'll have a dozen waiters milling around out here, and tourists will be lined up halfway down the block trying to get in. We're lucky he uses the winter to refine his menu instead of shutting down seasonally like so many of the restaurants do here."

Twenty minutes later, Jude brought plates and a stacking rack to their table. On his second trip, he carried out a large tray. "First, we have a pineapple pizza with Canadian bacon on one side, barbecued chicken and shredded carrots on the other."

Rory's eyes grew bigger, but before she could reach for a slice, Jude slid another pizza onto the upper rack. "Mac, I've got your cheese pizza here. And Ursula." Jude placed a pizza in the center of the table. "This is something I've been working on. Tell me what you think."

She picked up a slice and tried a bite while he watched. "Mmm." She chewed, the savory flavors blending in her mouth. "That's incredible. I taste roasted garlic, apples, and is that plum sauce?"

"Yes."

"But that's not chicken. What is it?"

"Duck, infused with a ginger marinade."

"Oh, Jude. You've outdone yourself. Mac, you have to try this." She held out her slice. Mac's phone beeped with a text alert, but he ignored it and leaned forward to take a bite from the piece in her hands.

As he chewed, he raised his eyebrows. "I stand corrected. This is the best pizza I've ever had."

Jude gave a satisfied smile. "You've haven't tried my cheese pizza yet. Enjoy."

They did. Mac admitted even the pineapple chicken barbecue was excellent. Rory wasn't as enamored with the strong flavors of Mac's cheese blend, but she agreed that it was possible she might like it better when she was a grown-up.

They were walking out the door when Mac's phone rang again. "Someone really wants to talk to you," Ursula said. "Better take it or they'll call all night. We'll meet you in the car."

"I suppose you're right." He handed her the keys and pulled his phone from his pocket. When he saw the caller ID, his face sobered. "This is Mac."

Ursula led Rory to the car and started the engine to warm

up while they waited for Mac. He was still standing next to the door of the restaurant in a pool of light from the overhead fixture. His face was in shadow, but his posture seemed tense as he listened. Finally, he ended the call and put the phone in his pocket.

Slowly he walked over and climbed into the car, but he didn't put it into gear. He stared unseeing through the windshield for a long while before he turned to Ursula. "They got him."

"Who?"

"Andi's murderer. Joel Thaine is in police custody."

CHAPTER FIFTEEN

THE NEXT MORNING, Mac was up at five, hoping to reach Detective Ralston as soon as he came in for the day, but it was after seven before Russ returned his call. "We've got him, Mac. That detective you hired is good. Based on that tip from the sister and knowledge of Thaine's habits, he was able to locate him in a popular sushi bar in Omaha. Followed him home and the Nebraska state police made the arrest."

"How long until he's extradited back to Oklahoma?"

"Already done. He's in a cell here in Tulsa now."

"Is he talking?"

Russ gave a mirthless laugh. "He waived his right to remain silent and now he won't shut up. From what I understand, he confessed to the arresting officers, confessed to the US marshal who transported him here and probably confessed to the guard who fed him breakfast."

"Odd." Thaine had been steadfast in proclaiming his innocence before he disappeared. He'd even given a couple of media interviews, playing the role of wrongly accused to perfection. Why now would he suddenly confess?

"Very odd. I'm on my way to question him in fifteen minutes."

"Won't his lawyer shut him down?"

"He's waiving his right to an attorney, as well. I have a bad feeling about it all."

"You think he's up to something?"

"As I said, I haven't spoken with him yet. But I have to wonder if he's going for diminished capacity."

"Some sort of insanity plea?"

"Possibly. Apparently he mentioned voices and avenging angels."

Mac's gut tightened. "Angels?" A character in one of his books had claimed to hear voices from avenging angels. Could it be a coincidence?

"We'll get to the bottom of it. I've got to go now, but I'll call you back later today and we'll talk more, okay?"

"All right. Thanks, Russ."

Mac ended the call and stared through the window into the darkness. It was possible, he supposed, that guilt had worried away at Thaine's conscience, eventually leading him to confess to the crime. But he hadn't turned himself in. His conscience seemed content to let him hide out until they caught up with him. Mac suspected Russ was right, that this sudden burst of cooperation and refusing counsel was all part of Thaine's backup plan.

Avenging angels. If Thaine had simply said he was hearing voices, Mac would have written it off as an obvious ploy. But throw in the angels, and Mac had to wonder if it wasn't part of a larger scheme. What was Thaine up to? Mac squared his shoulders. Whatever it was, it wasn't going to work.

MAC TRIED TO READ, or whittle, or do something productive, but in actuality, he spent all morning and part of the afternoon pacing between the rooms of his house, waiting for the phone to ring. He'd just started a pot of coffee when Blossom jumped up and ran into the living room, tail wagging. Mac opened the front door just as Ursula raised her hand to knock. "Hi. Come on in."

"Thanks." She stepped inside, carrying a tote bag, and reached down to stroke Blossom's head. "Any more news?"

"Not much. They have him in Tulsa now. Can I take your coat?"

"No, I can't stay. Rory will be home from school soon." She reached into the bag and pulled out a plastic container. "I just came by to bring you some of this mulligatawny soup. I figured you'd be sticking close to home, and wasn't sure if you had food in the house."

At the mention of soup, his stomach rumbled, reminding him he'd never eaten lunch. Ursula laughed. "I guess I have my answer."

"I do have plenty of sandwich fixings, but this is much better. Thank you."

"You're welcome. You're invited for dinner tonight as well, if you like."

"Thanks, but no. I'm feeling unsettled tonight. I wouldn't be good company."

"I understand. I'll just—" Mac's cell phone rang.

He held up a hand to ask her to wait and answered the call. "This is Mac."

"Mr. Macleod, this is Detective Ralston."

"Yes, Russ?"

"Do you still have the personal items recovered from the crime scene? Including a silver bracelet?"

"Yes, of course."

"Could you please send that bracelet to me by overnight mail?"

"Why?"

"There have been some developments in the case and we need to take another look at it. Please don't disturb it any more than necessary before you mail it."

"Russ, what's going on? Talk to me."

"Mac, I'm sorry. I know this is hard." Russ paused for a long moment, and when he spoke, he was once again using his official voice. "After interviewing the subject and examining evidence found in his residence, we believe we know how he was able to locate Andrea."

In a flash, Mac knew. "A tracker chip. In one of the charms in the bracelet."

"Yes."

"A battery that small wouldn't last more than a few days."

"No. He must have known she was about to run."

Or he had the means to keep the battery charged. Just like a character in one of Mac's books. The same character that claimed he heard voices of avenging angels. The same character that managed to manipulate the system and almost get away with murder. Even though he was standing next to the woodstove, goose bumps rose on Mac's arms. "I'll be there tomorrow."

"You don't need to do that. It will be a while before this goes to trial. The bail hearing is tomorrow afternoon, but he won't make bail. I've no doubt the judge will order psychological evaluation."

"Trial? I thought you said he confessed."

"Yeah, he did." Russ gave a frustrated sigh. "But now he's claiming he's innocent, that the avenging angel took control of him."

"I see. I'll be there. Goodbye, Russ." Mac ended the call and tossed his phone onto the couch. He looked up to see Ursula watching him, her eyes wide with concern. For a moment, he'd forgotten she was there.

"What is it?"

"He's playing games. Claiming insanity." Mac strode to the coat closet and pulled out a suitcase. "I need to be there."

"What can you do?"

What could he do, other than deliver that bracelet which he was ninety-nine percent sure would contain a GPS tracker chip? Russ was right, if he was claiming to hear voices, Thaine would be going through psychological evaluation whether Mac was there or not. But Mac's gut was telling him to go.

"I need to be there," Mac repeated. He picked up his phone and pulled up an airline site. "I'll see if I can fly tonight."

"Book two seats." Ursula crossed to the kitchen and placed the container of soup in the refrigerator. "I'm going with you."

He stopped flipping through the flights and looked up. "You can't. Rory has school. And there's Blossom. I need to leave her with you."

"I'm sure Catherine can stay with Rory, and she can run the B&B and keep Blossom, as well."

Mac paused. On one hand, he wanted Ursula with him. She was a rock, and he needed that stability if he was going to keep on functioning. But if what he was starting to suspect turned out to be true, he wasn't sure he wanted her to know. Because all of this might be his fault.

Ursula came back from the kitchen to stand in front of him. "Mac, I saw your face when you were on the phone. You don't have to tell me what's upsetting you if you don't want to, but I'm not going to let you go through this alone."

It was probably selfish to take her away from Rory, but the next few days were going to be a lot easier to get through with Ursula beside him. Besides, she didn't look as though she was going to back down, and he didn't have time to argue. "All right. If you can get Catherine to stay with Rory, you can come." As he said it, he realized how ungrateful he sounded. "What I mean is, thank you. I'll call you with the flight information."

"That's fine. I'd better get home. I'll talk to Catherine and Rory and pack a bag."

He nodded, returning to his phone, but she made no move toward the door. "Mac?"

"Yes?" He looked up.

She stepped closer and put her arms around him. Instantly, some of the weight he was feeling seemed to lift from his body. She rubbed her hands over his back and then released him. "You're going to get through this. We'll do it together."

URSULA TUGGED HER roller bag around the pole in the security line at the airport. The queue was surprisingly long, considering it was almost midnight. An accident on the Seward highway had delayed them, and she was starting to get worried about missing the flight. Ahead of her, Mac stared at the wall. He'd been doing a lot of that since that phone call. Something had him rattled. Badly.

She wasn't sure why. Of course catching his daughter's killer would bring the memories to the forefront, but shouldn't Mac be feeling some sense of satisfaction? He'd been working toward this goal from the beginning. But from the time he spoke with the detective on the phone, he'd withdrawn into himself. That's why she'd insisted on coming.

Ursula had mixed feelings about this trip. Despite what she'd told Mac, she didn't like leaving Rory in someone else's care, even Catherine's. But Rory had been okay with it when Ursula explained that she and Mac needed to go to Oklahoma to take care of some business about his daughter. Especially once Ursula told her they'd be leaving Blossom with her.

"I'll take good care of her," Rory had promised. "She can sleep with me."

"She can sleep in her own bed," Ursula had said, but looking at those eager eyes, she softened. "Maybe you can have her bed in your room."

Rory had agreed, a little too quickly. Ursula suspected that before long, either Blossom would end up in Rory's bed, or Rory on Blossom's.

She and Mac shouldn't be gone too long. The bail hearing was tomorrow. Mac needed to deliver a bracelet that, based on what she'd overheard on the phone, might contain a tracking chip. Mac hadn't volunteered any more information, and she hadn't liked to push. He was having a hard enough time without added pressure.

They reached the front of the line, and Mac stepped aside to let her go first. She presented her identification to security and walked to a conveyer belt to send her carry-on, handbag, shoes and coat through the X-ray. A moment later, Mac followed her.

At security's direction, Ursula stepped inside a scanner and lifted her hands while the machine hummed around her. *This is how a microwave casserole must feel.* Once the scan was done, the guard waved her through to collect her belongings.

As soon as Mac finished his scan, he started to join her, but two guards stepped up to block his way. "Sir, please raise your hands so I can wand you."

Mac swore under his breath as he complied. "I forgot it was in my pocket."

Ignoring him, the guard ran a scanner up and down his body. It always beeped when it reached his pocket area. "Please remove the object."

Mac reached inside his pocket and pulled out a pearl-handled knife. His grandfather's knife. Ursula tried to step closer, to explain, but a guard barked at her to stay back. Another guard offered a plastic bowl, and Mac dropped the knife inside. Then he turned and trudged toward Ursula.

She laid a hand on his arm. "Is there some way to get it back when we return?"

"No." Mac's voice was flat. No emotion showed in his face.

"Maybe we could buy some stamps and mail it home."

"No time to get through security again. We board in fifteen minutes." He collected his bag, slipped on his shoes and started toward the gate, moving mechanically.

Ursula finished tying her shoe before hurrying to catch him. "Mac, wait."

He turned back, looking mildly surprised as though he'd forgotten she was there. "Sorry."

She slipped her hand into the crook of his elbow. "Are you okay?" Even as she asked, she realized what a ridiculous question it was. He was anything but okay.

Still, he managed a tight smile for her. "I'm fine. We need to hurry."

They passed an airport bookstore on the way. On the table in front, a pyramid of Mac's latest title anchored the display. He glanced at it and looked away. They reached the gate, where they found a pair of unoccupied seats. Across from them, a young girl with sleepy eyes leaned against her father's shoulder. An older boy played with a handheld toy of some sort, while his mother typed something into her phone. A few rows away, a news program flashed pictures of a crowd of protesters on the television screen hanging from the ceiling.

The airline employee announced that they would begin boarding soon. Ursula stood to stretch. Suddenly, a publicity photo of Mac flashed on the television screen.

Mac's image was replaced with Andi's smiling face. It was a snapshot, taken outside at what looked like a city park. The hand pushing her hair back from her face sported a charm bracelet—the same one Mac was delivering to the police. Closed caption ran across the bottom of the screen, but Ursula couldn't take her eyes off that face. Young, happy, with every expectation of a long life ahead of her. The picture changed, to a video of someone in an orange jumpsuit and handcuffs being led from a police car.

A woman a few seats down nudged her husband and pointed toward the screen. "They caught the guy that murdered that poor girl."

"Her dad was rich, right? Probably wouldn't pay the ransom."

"No, it was her boyfriend who killed her. Remember? They think she was running away from him."

Ursula looked back at Mac. He was watching the screen, his face like stone. Thankfully, no one around them seemed to have recognized him. The call went out for preboarding, and everyone began gathering their belongings rather than paying attention to the television. The news cut to a bus crash somewhere in the world.

Their boarding call went out. Mac still sat, his eyes focused on something far away from the airport terminal. Ursula put her hand on his shoulder. "Are you ready?"

He blinked and turned his gaze toward her. "Ready?"

"To board the plane. They just called us."

"Oh. Yes, I'm ready. Let's go."

URSULA SMOTHERED A yawn as the taxi wound its way through traffic. The six-hour flight from Anchorage to Dallas/Ft. Worth had been uneventful, but she could never sleep on airplanes. As far as she could tell, Mac hadn't slept either. Their layover had been just long enough for a cup of coffee and a muffin before the flight to Tulsa. Now they were on their way to Mac's house.

The taxi turned into a neighborhood of tall brick houses on large lots with mature trees. They pulled into a circular drive edged with boxwood and stopped in front of the pillared porch of an expansive red-brick home with a steep slate roof.

Mac paid off the taxi and unlocked the front door. "Just leave your suitcase here. I'll carry it up later."

"All right." Ursula took in the polished wood paneling in the entryway and the warm tones of the Oriental rug on the floor. A far cry from how he'd been living in Alaska. "Your home is lovely."

Mac grunted thanks and led her through a formal dining room to a kitchen, which opened into a family room and another dining area. The combined space of the three rooms was probably more than Mac's entire cabin in Alaska. A bowl of fruit and a piece of paper rested on the acre of polished granite that topped the kitchen island.

Mac opened a cabinet door and pulled out a bag of coffee. Ursula picked up the note. "Someone named Joan says she stocked the refrigerator."

"My housekeeper." Mac spooned coffee beans into a stainless-steel coffee machine of the type Ursula had seen advertised in upscale catalogs.

She crossed to the refrigerator. Eggs, milk, vegetables. Oh, and Mac's pickles. "Looks like she left a casserole, too. That was kind of her."

"She's a kind woman. She's been with me for, let's see, fifteen years." Mac started the machine and let it finish grinding the beans before continuing. "She was crazy about Andi. Always trying to fix her up with her son. He's a good kid. Smart, hard worker. Unfortunately, they never seemed to be unattached at the same time. I just wish…" He trailed off, but of course Ursula knew what he meant. If only Andi had been involved with his housekeeper's son instead of Joel Thaine, she'd be alive now.

"What would you like for lunch? Looks like there's deli meat and cheese, or I could scramble eggs."

Mac checked his watch. "I don't want to be late for the bail hearing."

"We have two hours. You need to eat. All you've had since yesterday is a bran muffin." And he'd tossed most of that away, uneaten. The last thing he needed was more coffee on an empty stomach. She played her trump card, knowing it was the only way to get him to take care of himself. "I'm hungry."

"Go ahead, then, and put together whatever you want for lunch."

She managed to get him to sit down long enough to eat

a turkey sandwich, but the second she took the last bite of hers, he was sweeping the plates to the sink and reaching into a drawer for keys. "Let's go."

He led her out the back door and across a covered patio toward a detached garage made of brick that matched the house. A wide lawn swept across the yard, dappled with shade from old oaks and edged with shrubby mixed borders. Across the yard, something glinted in the sun.

Mac frowned. "A photographer in the alley. If you don't want your picture on the news, you may want to shield your face."

Ursula held up a hand to shade her eyes and looked toward the fence in the far corner. Sure enough, a telephoto lens was trained toward them. How bizarre. She quickly turned away and hurried after Mac to the garage where he ushered her into a car. When they raised the door and drove out, someone was there, snapping pictures. She could certainly understand why Mac had fled to Alaska.

She waited in the car while Mac ran into the police station to drop off the bracelet, and then they drove on to the courthouse. Mac parked in the lot across the street. As they walked closer to the imposing building, Mac's posture grew stiffer. He couldn't have been more on edge if it were his own trial he was attending. Ursula reached for his hand. "Hey, are you okay?"

He stopped, closed his eyes, and sucked in a long breath. After a moment, he blew it out and gave her a soft smile. "I am." He squeezed her hand. "Thanks to you."

MAC CHECKED HIS watch again. This hearing should have started ten minutes ago, but there was no sign of judge or defendant. It was a good thing they'd arrived early, because the courtroom was packed, mostly with reporters. A couple of them looked his way, but with Thaine's capture, Mac was no longer their main focus.

One woman who had been particularly persistent in trying to schedule an interview with him kept staring at Ursula, no doubt trying to place her. He felt bad about dragging Ursula into this circus, but she'd insisted on coming, and truth be known, he was glad she had. It was reassuring that at least one person in this room was not here out of curiosity or to bump their ratings, but to support him.

The side door opened at the front of the room, and a group of people in suits came in and settled in at the table on the right. A few minutes later, the door opened again, and Joel Thaine walked through, accompanied by a guard.

Mac's stomach clenched. He studied Thaine's face, trying to decide what could be going on in that dangerous mind, but at the moment, Thaine only looked mildly confused until the bailiff directed him to the table on the left. He sat alone, shuffling through some papers.

A few minutes later, another door opened and the bailiff instructed everyone to stand for the judge. A middle-aged woman wearing judicial robes sat behind the bench, and the onlookers sat again.

It seemed to happen quickly. After some lawyerly talk, the judge asked Thaine why he had refused counsel. His reply, about being innocent because he'd been led by an angel, seemed to flow too easily, as if he'd rehearsed it many times. The judge asked more questions, and Thaine answered, his voice revealing little emotion. After several more probing questions that elicited the same bland responses, the judge remanded him for psychiatric evaluation.

As Thaine stood to leave, he looked for the first time over the bar at the reporters madly scribbling notes. His expression remained neutral, but there was a sparkle of excitement in his eyes. He was clearly feeding off the attention. His gaze traveled to the end of the row where Mac was sitting, and stopped as recognition dawned.

Mac locked eyes with him, and he didn't look away.

Thaine's expression revealed no sign of either remorse or guilt, just barely disguised smugness. He gave a little smirk before he allowed the guard to lead him away.

Ursula touched Mac's hand, and he turned to her. "Did you see that?" he whispered. "He knows exactly what he's doing. It's all a game to him."

"I saw." But her look of concern seemed more focused on Mac than on the situation. She glanced around. "Let's go before some of these reporters decide to ambush you."

As they filed from the courtroom, Russ met him at the door. "Mac." He gestured toward an unoccupied corner. Mac nodded and put a hand on Ursula's back to guide her away from the crowd. Russ flashed a questioning look at Ursula before addressing Mac. "Thanks for bringing that charm bracelet."

"No problem. This is Ursula Anderson, from Alaska. Ursula, Detective Russ Ralston. I've known Russ for years. His daughter Bailey and Andi were in school together."

"Nice to meet you, Ms. Anderson." Russ shook her hand and turned to Mac. "Bailey's in Japan now. She wanted me to tell you you're in her prayers."

"Thank her for me." Enough small talk. "Were you in there?" Mac gestured toward the courtroom.

"Yes. It went pretty much the way we thought it would."

"You know he's faking."

Russ shrugged. "Then let's hope the psychologists can figure it out."

"Did you find a chip?"

"Not yet, but the lab is doing a rush job for me. They should have some information for me later today. Can you come to my office at, say, four thirty?"

"Couldn't you just call?" Ursula suggested.

Mac shook his head. It wasn't just about the chip. He knew, from the way Russ wasn't meeting his eyes, there was bad news yet to come. "I'll be there," he assured Russ.

They made their way downstairs and across the lobby of the courthouse. One reporter made a halfhearted attempt to collect a sound bite, but he accepted Mac's "no comment" without argument. They walked to the car, and Mac started home.

He stopped at a red light and looked toward Ursula. He wanted her take on this. "Well, you heard him talk. You saw the way he looked at me. Do you think he's faking?"

"I'm no mental health expert, but I'm glad he'll be locked up, one way or the other." Ursula shuddered. "The way he spoke—to be so matter-of-fact about such a shocking crime—scared me. He's dangerous. Of that I have no doubt."

The light changed and Mac pulled forward. She hadn't exactly answered his question, but as usual she'd gotten to the heart of the matter. Thaine was dangerous. But he was going to spend the rest of his life in jail. Mac would see to that. He'd let Andi down, hadn't protected her, but he was going to make sure her killer paid his debt to society.

Ursula yawned, and although she tried to cover it up, Mac knew she must be exhausted after flying all night. He probably shouldn't have brought her, for her sake as well as Rory's, but it meant more than he could say to have her there beside him in court today. Everything was easier knowing that someone cared about him, cared for him. That he wasn't alone. Just as he'd supported Ursula through the custody challenge, she was there to support him now. It was a good feeling.

Still, he wasn't sure he wanted her at this upcoming meeting. There was something Russ dreaded telling him or showing him, and if it was that distasteful to a seasoned cop, Mac didn't want Ursula exposed to it.

Once they reached the house, he picked up her suitcase from the entryway where she'd left it. "Let me show you to your room." He carried the bag upstairs to the guest room he'd asked Joan to prepare. Sure enough, the curtains were open and cool spring sunlight streamed through the windows and fell on the pillows resting against the cherry headboard.

Mac set Ursula's bag on the bench at the foot of the bed. "There should be fresh towels in the bathroom. Why don't you have a nap before dinner?"

She plumped one of the pillows, clearly tempted. "Do I have time before we need to leave for your meeting?"

"You were up all night. Get some sleep. You don't need to be at this meeting."

"You have to be as exhausted as I am."

He supposed he was, but he was too wound up to sleep. "I'm fine. You rest."

She studied his face. "Are you sure you don't need me?" He had no doubt that she would forgo sleep for as long as it took if she thought she could help him. But it wasn't necessary.

He opened his arms. "Come here." He held her close, and it seemed as though her calming energy flowed into him. "I need you. But you don't have to be at this meeting. It's enough to know you'll be here when I get home."

And it was true. Whatever the news Russ had to share, Ursula would be there to lighten the load. And they'd get through it, whatever happened.

She smiled up at him, and he brushed a kiss across her forehead.

"Sleep tight, darlin'. I'm glad you're here."

RUSS WAS SHUFFLING through some papers when Mac stepped into his office, but quickly stuffed them inside a folder and closed it. "Thanks for coming in. Decided not to bring your friend along?" He indicated a chair.

Mac sat down. "She was tired. Took the red-eye from Anchorage last night. Did they find a chip in one of the charms?"

"Yes, in the heart. The battery was dead, of course, but it was a GPS tracking chip. A fairly expensive model, but easily obtained over the internet."

A sense of déjà vu ran a cold hand down Mac's spine. "You say the battery was dead."

"Yes." Russ met his gaze as though willing him to make the connection. "The battery life of a tracking chip with a transmitter that small is only a few days."

"But you found a miniature charging pack in the charm, too, didn't you? And a charging mat on a tray in Andi's apartment. The tray next to her bed where she would put her cell phone to charge before she went to bed. And she'd put her bracelet in the tray, as well."

"You remember seeing the mat?"

"No." Mac swallowed. "I wrote about it. In a book about five years ago. It was new technology then, but now it's commonly available." The transmitter in a piece of jewelry. The charging mat. It might still be a coincidence, but it wasn't likely.

"We didn't find a charging mat when we took photos of the apartment after Andi went missing."

"No?" Maybe Mac was wrong.

"No. I suspect Thaine got rid of it. But yes, we found the charging pack in the charm, and when we searched his apartment in Omaha, we found this." Russ reached into his desk drawer and pulled out a plastic bag. Inside was a familiar book, the design on the dust jacket worn and faded.

Mac's heart stopped, and then began beating wildly. "You found this with his things?"

"Yes."

"May I see it?"

Russ paused for a moment before he nodded. "It's evidence. Here. Wear gloves."

Mac pulled on the rubber gloves and removed the book from the bag. It fell open to a page toward the middle. A section had been highlighted, detailing how the antagonist had arranged for one of his victims to have received a charging mat for her cell phone as a gift, to recharge the tracking chip he'd hidden inside her favorite necklace.

Mac flipped back a couple of chapters to find other highlighted sentences and phrases, all in the scenes told from the antagonist's point of view as he made his plans. And then Mac found the section he was dreading. Yellow highlighter taunted him.

"Do you have the autopsy report?" He knew Andi had died of strangulation, but he'd never known the details. Never wanted to know. Until now.

"Mac, you don't need to see that."

"I think I do." He had to confirm the depth of his guilt.

"I'm not sure I have it here." Russ pretended to shuffle through the papers.

"Just tell me. She died like this, didn't she?" Like the victim in the story, whose killer had taunted her by tightening the garrote around her neck until she passed out, and then loosened it to allow her to regain consciousness so that he could make her beg for her life. He would pretend to consider letting her go, and then change his mind, over and over, before he finally killed her. A cat, playing with a mouse.

Russ didn't answer.

Mac stared into his eyes. "Didn't she?"

Slowly, Russ nodded. "The report is consistent with that scenario."

Mac closed the book. The shadowy figure on the cover blurred and quivered. Mac closed his eyes and waited until he gained control and his eyes could focus once more. He opened the cover and checked the flyleaf.

To Andi. All my love, Dad.

URSULA WOKE TO a birdsong alarm app Rory had downloaded onto her phone. They'd made a guessing game out of identifying the different birds. Rory had recognized the robins, chickadees and waxwings right away, but she'd never heard the soft coo of the mourning dove, so common in Wyoming where Ursula had grown up. Here in Tulsa, a meadowlark was singing outside her window. She'd have to try to record it for Rory.

The nap had done wonders for Ursula's energy and peace of mind. She'd been worried. Worried that being in court and actually seeing the face of the man who had taken his daughter's life would pull Mac into that dark place he'd inhabited when she first met him. He was hurting, she could sense that, but that hug had reassured her. He wasn't isolating himself. He was willing to let her help him. To let her love him.

And she did love him. She'd been hedging, not admitting it even to herself, but she couldn't pretend anymore. Somewhere around four in the morning last night, unable to sleep on the plane, she'd shifted in her seat and looked over to find Mac watching her. He'd reached for her hand, and the instant they connected, she'd felt better, stronger, and she'd known she couldn't deny it any longer.

No parent should have to go through what Mac had. To lose a child for any reason was an unthinkable tragedy, but for someone to have stolen her life away for his own twisted reasons was too much to bear. But Mac had to bear it, and she would do everything she could to help him get through it.

She checked the time. Rory should just be getting home from school. She called the inn and spoke with Catherine for a few minutes. Catherine assured her everything was under control and called Rory to the phone. "Ursula!"

"Hi, sweetie. How was school today?"

"Good. For science, we're growing worms. They eat paper."

"Really? Where are these worms?"

"They're in a box of dirt. We keep them under the art table."

"Cool."

"Are you in Oklahoma now? Is it snowy?"

"No, it's spring here. I saw daffodils blooming. Are you and Blossom being good for Catherine?"

Rory giggled. "We are but Van Gogh isn't. Catherine says she was eating lunch and had to stop and answer the door. When she got back her sandwich was gone and he was lying on the chair pretending he was asleep."

"Maybe it was Blossom."

"No, she was in my room."

"Did she sleep in your bed?"

"Uh, just part of the night. Is Mac there?"

Nice misdirection. "Not right now. Do you want me to tell him anything for you?"

"Just say hi, and that I'm taking good care of Blossom."

"Okay, I'll tell him. I love you, sweetie."

"I love you, too. Bye."

Ursula smiled as she hung up the phone. Mac still wasn't back, so she took advantage of the groceries Joan had left to make a salad to go with dinner. She was bent over the oven, sliding in the casserole dish, when the back door opened.

"I'm just putting in the casserole. It should be ready in half an hour." Ursula turned and stopped at the expression on Mac's face. He seemed to be in shock.

"What is it?"

He didn't answer, just shook his head.

She stepped closer and laid a hand on his arm. "Mac? Tell me."

"They took some of his things as evidence."

"Yes?"

"There was a book. My book. One I wrote several years ago. It was a copy I'd given to Andi."

"What about it?"

"Don't you see? He was using it. Highlighting the passages the killer in the book used to control his victims. The

GPS chip in the bracelet? In the book, it was a necklace. That's how he found her, when she ran away."

She brought her hand to her mouth. "Oh, Mac."

"And then he killed her. He tortured her. Just like the killer in the book."

"I'm so sorry."

"It's my fault."

"It's not."

"Sure it is. I dreamed up all those nightmares."

"That doesn't make it your fault." She had to make him understand that.

"I gave him the blueprint. I might as well have killed her myself."

"Don't do this, Mac. Don't let guilt drag you down again. You're not to blame." Ursula put her arms around him.

He stood stiffly, not responding. Soon, she reached up to take his face between her hands. "Mac. Look at me. I love you. Don't let this come between us."

He wouldn't meet her eyes. "I don't deserve your love."

"Yes, you do. You're a wonderful person. Kind. Talented. And patient with little girls who like to play cards. Rory says hi, by the way, and that she's taking good care of Blossom for you."

"Rory's better off without me."

"How can you say that? She adores you."

He shook his head. "Every relationship I have eventually ends in tragedy. I had no business getting involved with you and Rory." He pushed her hands away from his face. "We're done here. I'll make reservations to fly back to Alaska tomorrow. Thank you for making dinner, but I'm not hungry. Good night."

He turned and started for the stairs. She almost ran after him, but she knew it wouldn't do any good. The darkness they'd been fighting had returned. And it was winning.

CHAPTER SIXTEEN

THE NIGHTMARES WERE BACK. Mac sat up in bed, gasping for air. The details of the dream swept away, leaving his mind filled with swirling terror. The terror made him think of Andi and what she might have felt in her last few seconds of life.

Mac stumbled into the living room and reached for his grandfather's knife, only to remember it was gone as well, into a mass grave with box wrenches, mace canisters, bottles of booze and other forbidden items at the airport security checkpoint.

The small silver knife he'd gotten for Rory was there in the drawer, but Mac didn't pick it up. Wasting his time whittling on a stick wasn't helping anyone, especially Andi. He should give the knife to Ursula to keep for Rory. On second thought, maybe it was best if she didn't have anything to remind her of him. Because he wasn't going to mess up any more lives, especially Rory's. She'd suffered enough.

Blossom opened one eye and thumped her tail briefly before her snoring resumed. Rory must have worn her out in the three days he and Ursula were gone to Oklahoma. It hadn't been easy prying the two of them apart so that he could bring Blossom home. He was almost tempted to let her stay with Rory, but he needed the dog with him. Andi's last request was that he take care of Blossom.

His wife, his daughter, his parents—every person he'd loved was gone, and it was his fault.

He should have never let Ursula in the door, much less

fallen in love with her. He'd bought into the illusion of security and love she offered, but she didn't understand. She didn't realize how he, with the best of intentions, turned good things into bad. Maybe it wasn't too late. Maybe he could end this relationship before any more harm was done.

But he couldn't explain his reasoning to Ursula. If he told her she should avoid him for her own good, she'd laugh in his face. She'd say he was being ridiculous, that none of those things were his fault. Someone as fundamentally good as Ursula didn't see the danger, she only saw the need. Well, he needed her all right, but that was his problem. She shouldn't suffer.

He could simply move back to Oklahoma, but the thought of packing and organizing things exhausted him. Besides, knowing Ursula, she'd come after him. No, the only way to drive her away was to break it off slowly.

He'd have to convince her to go back to being just neighbors. The kind of neighbors who nodded when they saw one another, spoke about weather and escaped into their respective territories. He needed to focus on his daughter.

He could never atone for what he'd done, creating the story that Andi's killer had used to destroy her. He couldn't take back all those books he'd written, all those despicable characters he'd created. It was too late for Andi. All he could do now was make sure her killer was punished.

He opened his laptop, glad that Ronald had insisted on getting high-speed internet installed, because Mac intended to uncover everything there was to know about law and precedent for insanity pleas in the state of Oklahoma. Thaine was smart. Mac and the legal team had to be smarter. This was how he would be spending his time, from now on.

URSULA WAS IN the kitchen making a grocery list when the front door slammed. Rory's footsteps skittered across the living room before she burst through the door. "Can we ski today? Did you ask Mac?" She dropped a stack of letters, flyers and a small package on the kitchen table.

"Sure we can." Ursula deliberately used her cheeriest voice. "Mac still isn't feeling up to skiing, but we can go."

"Why won't Mac go? Doesn't he like us anymore? Can I call him and ask?"

"No. We need to leave Mac alone so he can rest up and get better. Do you want a snack before we go? I made brownies."

Rory accepted a brownie and a glass of milk, but much of her enthusiasm had faded. Why did that man have to be so stubborn? Ursula had spent the last two weeks since they'd returned from Oklahoma trying to reach him, but he wouldn't let her in.

She'd call; he wouldn't answer. She'd come by with food, which he would accept politely—probably because it was easier than arguing—before shutting the door in her face. She would invite him to ski or offer to take Blossom along, but he'd decline. It was clear he was trying to drive her away.

Ursula had tried and tried to engage her father after her brother died, but she could never reach him. She was never good enough. Intellectually, she realized the lesson she should have learned is that she couldn't fix other people, but emotionally she wanted to. She wanted to break Mac out of that horrible emotional prison and let him live, let him love.

Rory couldn't understand why he'd suddenly gone silent. It was only a matter of time before she began to wonder if Mac's moods were her fault. Just like Ursula used to wonder.

She picked up the package Rory had brought in with the rest of the mail. It had taken a lot of online searching, but she'd found it. One last peace offering. Tomorrow, she would make Mac talk to her, one way or another. They needed to settle this. He couldn't hang around the edges of their lives, pulling Rory into his vortex of destructive emotion. Rory would be hurt if he disappeared, but it was better than dragging her through years of depression. If Mac couldn't pull out of this, Ursula was going to have to let him go.

THE NEXT MORNING, Ursula wrapped the box with brown craft paper, tied it with a raffia bow and added it to a backpack already stuffed with homemade chili, cornbread and brownies. She was going fully armed.

Blossom met her at the front gate, tail thrashing madly, but Ursula didn't see any sign of Mac. He must have let the dog out for a potty break. Ursula stopped to rub her ears. "How is he today, girl? Any better? Or still hiding in his cave like a grumpy bear?"

Ursula could have sworn Blossom gave a little eye roll before she galloped ahead. She scratched on the front door, and Mac opened it just as Ursula arrived. "Oh, hello. I didn't know you were here."

"I just got here." She waited to be invited in.

Mac remained in the doorway. "What brings you here today?"

She met his eyes. "I brought you something. May I come in?"

Mac looked away. "I'm in the middle of some legal research right now."

"I see. When will you be finished?"

"I'm not sure."

She took a step closer. "Mac, I don't know what game we're playing, but I don't want to play anymore. Can't we talk?"

After a moment, he stepped back and gestured that she should come inside. It wasn't the most gracious invitation she'd ever received, but she'd take it. She carried her backpack to the kitchen and unloaded the food. Mac stood in the living room, watching her, his face impassive. Stacks of law books littered the coffee table beside him. Another book and a yellow legal pad rested on the kitchen table. Ursula placed the canning jar in the refrigerator. "I had some chili left over."

"Thank you."

"You're welcome." She crossed the room and handed him the small box. "This is for you."

He eyed the package as though it might bite. "What is it?"

"Just something I found on the internet and thought you might like."

"That's very thoughtful." He set the package on the coffee table. "But I really need to get back to my research."

"What, exactly, are you researching?"

"Oklahoma law as it pertains to diminished capacity or insanity. I've found a precedent that I think Thaine is using as a model to try to get off. I sent the information to the prosecutor."

"Good. Then why are you still working on this?"

"There may be other cases. We need to be prepared."

"You're not a lawyer. You could hire people to do this."

"I have. But how can I be sure unless I've looked at it myself?"

She touched his hand. "Mac, let it go. It's the prosecutor's job now, not yours."

"I owe it to Andi to make sure he doesn't get off."

"What difference does it make whether he's on death row, or locked up in prison for the rest of his life, or locked in some sort of mental institution? As long as he's put away where he can't hurt anyone else, why does it matter?"

"It matters. Andi's death matters."

"Absolutely it does. But more important than death is life. Andi's life. Our lives, yours and mine and Rory's." She grasped his forearms. "Mac, we need to talk about forgiveness."

He stared at her in shock. "You want me to forgive that monster?"

"Right now I'm more worried about you forgiving yourself."

"How can I do that, after what I've done?"

"What have you done? You wrote a book. Thousands of people read your books because they want to experience the triumph of good over evil."

"But in real life, evil triumphed. And Andi died."

"Mac, it wasn't your fault. You didn't kill her."

"I might as well have. I wrote the instruction manual."

"If it wasn't you, he would have found the information somewhere else. Andi wouldn't want you to blame yourself."

"How do you know?" He stepped back, away from her. "How could you possibly know what Andi would want? You never met her. You're never going to meet her, because she's dead. I wrote a book, and the killer read it, and she's dead."

"Mac—"

"Get out. I have work to do." He sat at the table, picked up a pen and spoke without looking at her. "Don't come back."

Ursula stared. Did he mean it? She waited for him either to apologize or to reinforce his statement, but he just ran his finger over the page of a legal tome and made notes as if she weren't there. Blossom gave an uneasy whine and touched her nose to Ursula's hand, but Mac never looked up.

Finally, Ursula turned and left, giving Blossom one last pat before she closed the cabin door behind her. How could this happen? A couple of weeks ago, Mac said he loved her. But that was before he talked to the detective in Tulsa, before he'd found another reason to blame himself for his daughter's death. Now there didn't seem to be any room in his heart for love.

He was like that eagle, lashing out at the person who was trying to help him. Too bad she couldn't throw a blanket over his head and cut him out of the tangle of despair he was in. Ursula shook her head as she retraced her steps along the snowy driveway. If it were just her, she might keep trying, but there was Rory to consider. Mac was drowning, and Ursula couldn't risk allowing him to pull Rory down with him. It was over.

MAC'S PHONE RANG, but he ignored it. If someone needed him, they could leave a message. He was busy with his research. Twenty minutes later, he jotted down one last note and closed the book. The case he'd just read didn't offer any particular insights, but he wanted to be thorough. It had taken far too long to read through that one case, because his mind kept wandering to Ursula.

She didn't deserve the way he'd treated her. She was trying to help, trying to make things better, because making things better is what she did. But even more, she didn't deserve to be saddled with him and all the baggage he brought with him. She and Rory didn't deserve to suffer the inevitable fallout when he screwed up, as he was bound to do, eventually. It was cruel, what he said, but it was the only way to convince her to let go.

He missed her already. Missed her laughter, her smile. Missed how she felt when he held her in his arms. Missed how her hair would smell like cinnamon or vanilla or whatever amazing thing she'd been cooking that day.

He picked up the phone. One message on voice mail, from the Forget-me-not Inn. Probably Ursula telling him off. Not that he didn't deserve it. But the recorded voice was Rory's.

"Mac? Ursula says I'm not supposed to call, but she's upstairs now so I used the kitchen phone. She said you don't feel good. I can bring you my blanket and a movie. They made me feel better when I was sad, but I don't need them anymore so you can have them if you want. Oh, she's coming, so I've got to go. Bye. I miss you. Tell Blossom I miss her, too."

The chasm in his chest grew a little bigger. Such a sweet

kid, willing to share her most precious treasures to make him feel better. He hated to hurt her. But she and Ursula were better off without him. He looked over to where Blossom lay watching him from her bed beside the woodstove. "I guess it's just you and me, girl."

Blossom didn't even bother to wag her tail. Instead, she gave a huge sigh and shifted, resting her chin on her paws and gazing toward the door. The door Ursula had walked out of. For the last time.

Mac set the book he'd finished on the coffee table, knocking something to the floor. He picked it up—a small box wrapped in brown paper. Ursula's present. He'd forgotten all about it. He debated returning it to her unopened, but curiosity got the better of him. He pulled off the string and unwrapped the box. Inside lay a pearl-handled penknife, identical to the one he'd left in the airport.

He opened the blade and tested it against his thumb. This knife had obviously had less use over its lifetime but otherwise it was exactly like his grandfather's knife. Probably close to a hundred years old. How had Ursula ever found it? He'd never met anyone like her, and he suspected he never would again.

He almost reached for a piece of wood to try it out, but he didn't. Just like Rory and her blanket, whittling was his way of working through his emotions. But what good did that do? Instead he picked up another book with a case he'd marked and started to read. He wouldn't let Andi down again.

Two days later, Mac was still reading. He'd been sending his notes to the paralegal he'd hired for research, but she said, in the most tactful way possible, that he was just spinning his wheels. Still, he had to do something. He was responsible for Andi's death; he had to be responsible for bringing the monster that killed her to justice.

The days were longer now, and by late morning, the sun

had risen over the mountain and was shining into the kitchen windows. Not that Mac noticed. Anyway, not until he heard a solid thump against a pain of glass and Blossom barked. Mac got up and went to the window. A tiny bird lay on its back atop the wooden table on his porch.

The poor thing had obviously crashed into his window. Mac shrugged into a jacket and went outside, leaving Blossom indoors. He picked up the lifeless body of the nuthatch and held it in his hands. Another innocent life, extinguished. He stared at the tiny body, thinking of Andi, of her mother, of his parents, all gone before their time. Just like this.

And then the bird moved.

At least he thought it moved. Maybe it was his imagination. But no, the wing was flickering a bit. And then the other wing twitched. After a moment, the bird raised its head. It seemed to look directly at him, not understanding how it got there, but somehow feeling safe cradled in his palms.

He waited, allowing the bird to gather its strength. It opened its wings, and Mac gently pumped his hands up and down, letting the air flow under the bird's wings, helping it get its bearings. Another minute, and it was off, the sun glistening off its feathers before it disappeared into the trees.

Mac's heart soared along with the bird and somehow the load of a thousand if-onlys flew away as well, leaving him feeling weightless. He inhaled the crisp air, noticed the sun sparkling on the snow. The bird was alive. So was he.

He came back indoors, where Blossom greeted him at the door and sniffed him, wagging her tail. Mac passed a hand over her head before going to wash his hands. "A bird, Blossom. I thought it was dead, but it was just stunned. It's alive." He spent several minutes going through the wood-bin, looking for just the right piece. Shoving the books from the coffee table, he set the chunk of wood on the center and picked up his whetstone. He sharpened the knife Ursula had given him to a fine edge.

In the meantime, he studied the wood. Once he was satisfied with his plan, he started. The knife cut through the soft wood and a long curl fell onto the table. Mac smiled.

URSULA WAS ON her hands and knees, scrubbing up the blueberry syrup a guest had dribbled on the rug under one of the dining room tables. It had been six days since Mac ordered her out of his house. Funny how her life seemed to be divided into before Mac, during Mac and after Mac. Yes, now she was dealing with the after-Mac, and it wasn't pretty.

Rory's feelings were hurt. Naturally. Ursula had been trying to keep her busy, thinking Rory would get distracted and forget to ask about Mac, but she'd underestimated Rory's tenacity. Every day after school, Rory wanted to see if Mac would go skiing with them or eat dinner or give her a carving lesson. Ursula had been telling her Mac was feeling bad and didn't want company right now. Eventually, she'd have to give Rory an explanation for why Mac didn't want to be around them anymore. Just as soon as she figured it out, herself.

She should have known not to get involved with him. Living with her father should have taught her a lesson. She was arrogant enough to think she could save Mac, but you couldn't save someone who didn't want to be saved, no matter how much you loved them. Loving them only led to heartache.

Two couples had checked out that morning and the third had been out skiing, so Ursula didn't pay too much attention when she heard the front door open. The blue stain was gone, so she blotted the damp spot with an old towel. It wasn't until she heard the click of nails on the hardwood floor that she realized it wasn't her guests that had come through the door. "Blossom?"

The dog galloped over and squeezed between two chairs to join Ursula under the table. Her whole body wriggling in joy, she climbed into Ursula's lap, almost knocking her over. Ursula laughed and took the big dog's head between her hands. Blossom's tail beat a quick rhythm against the floor. Ursula's heart matched the beat as a pair of jean-clad legs and wool socks came into view at the edge of the table. Mac's face appeared. "Hi. What are you doing under there?"

After a moment, she was able to find her voice. "Cleaning up a spill."

"Need any help?"

"No, I'm done."

Nevertheless, Mac scooted a couple of chairs out of the way and crawled under the table, too. Blossom rolled over on her back between the two of them. Mac obediently rubbed her tummy, but he never took his eyes off Ursula's face. "Hi, again."

"Why are you here? I thought you never wanted to see me again."

"I came to apologize."

She watched him through narrowed eyes. He'd jerked her around too many times. "No flowers this time?"

"Would it help?"

"Probably not. I'm not too happy with you right now." Ursula crossed her arms. "I've been dealing with a broken-hearted little girl who wonders why her friend doesn't want to see her anymore. Mac, I know you've had a rough time, especially after what you found out in Tulsa. I'm not minimizing what you've been through, or what your daughter went through. I just don't see how making yourself miserable makes it better."

"You're right."

"Pardon me?" She tilted her head. "I thought you said I was right."

"You are. You've been telling me the truth since the very

beginning, but I wasn't ready to hear it." He took a deep breath. "Now I am."

"Why?" She wanted to believe him, but he'd burned her before. "Not that I'm not delighted, but what brought on this epiphany?"

He stroked the dog's head. "A few days ago, a bird crashed into my window. I thought it was dead. I picked it up, held it in my hands, and then, I saw it move. So I cradled it in my palm, trying to keep it warm. Eventually it gained enough strength to fly away."

"That's great, but I don't see the connection."

He looked down at his upturned palms. "When that bird moved in my hands, it seemed like a miracle, like I had somehow brought the bird back to life."

"It must have been an amazing feeling."

"It was. But then, as it regained its strength, I recognized the truth. The bird was simply stunned. I didn't save its life. It would have been fine whether I'd been there or not."

"Did that disappoint you?"

"Just the opposite. I finally realized I'm not nearly as important as I'd made myself out to be. Whether the bird lived or died wasn't up to me." He gave a rueful smile. "I'm just a man." He looked down and scratched under Blossom's chin.

Ursula remained silent, waiting for him to gather his thoughts and continue.

"I've been turning these things over in my mind for the last few days, and I think I've finally reached some understanding. I didn't hold the power of life and death over Andi, either. Or Carla. Or my parents."

"No," she agreed.

"Bad things happened. I'll always have regrets. But I didn't cause their deaths, and I shouldn't spend my life atoning for them." He inhaled a long, slow breath and let it out. "I'm free."

"Oh, Mac." Ursula scrambled toward him.

He leaned forward and banged his head against the table support. "Ouch."

"Ooo." She touched the spot on his forehead and winced. "Come on. Let's get out of here." They crawled out from under the table. She led him to the kitchen and filled a bag with ice. "Here."

"Thank you." He pressed the bag to his forehead. "Oh, by the way. I didn't bring flowers, but while I was doing all this thinking, I made something for you." He reached into his shirt pocket and pulled out a small wooden carving.

She turned it over in her hand. A nuthatch, carved from birch. Its wings were spread wide, capturing the perfect freedom of a bird in flight. A clear thread ran through one of the wingtips, with a hook on the other end of the thread. She smiled. "It's beautiful."

"Not as beautiful as you." He touched her face. "It's as though you carry around a reserve of joy. It shines through your eyes and warms everyone around you."

She blinked back a tear. "That may be the nicest thing anyone has ever said to me." She turned to hang the bird from the curtain rod in her kitchen window. It almost glowed in the sunlight.

Mac set the ice bag on the counter. He came up behind her and wrapped his arms around her. "I love you, Ursula Anderson." He brushed a kiss across her temple. "I want us to be together, you and me and Rory."

She stiffened but didn't step away from him. "You said that before. And then you told me to get out of your house and never come back."

"I know, and I'm sorry." He paused before continuing. "You're the best thing that ever happened to me, but I felt like I didn't deserve you. That I didn't deserve the happiness you brought into my life, because all of the bad things that happened were my fault."

She turned to face him. "And now?"

"I still don't deserve you, but if you'll have me, I'll do everything in my power to make you and Rory happy. I love you, darlin'. Is there any chance you could come to love me, too?"

She sucked in a breath and reached up to touch his face. "I do. I tried to fight it, but it sneaked in anyway. I love you, Mac."

"Those are the words I wanted to hear." He pulled her close and covered her mouth with his. The kiss was light at first, tentative, but when she slid her hand into his hair and pulled him to her, it grew deeper. It was the kind of kiss a woman could get lost in. In fact, Ursula was so caught up she didn't hear the footsteps until Rory burst open the kitchen door.

"I saw Blossom. Is Mac better—eww, what are you doing?"

Ursula whipped her head around, but before she could come up with an answer, Mac laughed. "I'm kissing your godmother. And yes, I'm feeling much better, thank you." He didn't loosen his embrace.

"Oh." Rory stopped to think that over. "So if you're kissing, does that mean you're in love?"

Ursula's cheeks burned, but she tried to sound matter-of-fact as she wiggled out of Mac's arms. "Kissing doesn't necessarily mean people are in love."

Mac winked at Rory. "But in this case, it does."

Rory's eyes widened. "Are you getting married?"

Ursula swallowed. Mac chuckled. "Would you like that?"

"Yeah!" Rory bounced up and down. "'Cause if you get married, you can live here with us, and Blossom can live here, too, and we can play concentration and build snowmen and stuff."

"She makes a good point." Mac turned to Ursula. "We could move in here with you. That would leave my place free to develop that RV park you've been planning. This could all work out just the way you wanted."

"Whoa." Ursula held up her hands. "I'm not marrying you for your property."

"But you are marrying me?"

"Who said anything about marriage?"

"Rory did. But only because she beat me to it." He reached into his jeans pocket and pulled out a jeweler's box. "See? I came prepared."

"What's that?" Ursula's heartrate shifted into overdrive.

"Well, I was considering an ID bracelet, but I thought this was better." He opened the box. A marquise diamond ring in a rose gold setting winked in the light.

"Oh, Mac. It's beautiful." She gazed at the ring. Slowly, she raised her eyes to his face. "But, aren't you rushing this?"

"Not at all. I love you. You love me. We both love Rory and Blossom. The way I see it, I've already wasted far too much time on regrets. If you need more time, I'll give you all you need, but I'm ready."

"You're not going to change your mind again?"

"No, I'm not." He looked into her eyes. "I know I've made it hard for you to trust me. I can't promise I'll never have a bad day, never feel sad, but I will promise you this, I'm never again going to let past regrets dictate my future, and the future I want is with you and Rory."

She stroked his cheek. "You're sure?"

"I'm absolutely sure." He sank to one knee. "Ursula Anderson, you have my heart, now and forever. Will you marry me?"

Rory squealed and ran to throw her arms around his neck, which excited Blossom so much she jumped onto his knee. The combined weight of the girl and the dog toppled him over, and they all collapsed in a heap on the kitchen floor. Ursula stood above them, laughing. "Oh my goodness. Life is never going to be dull around here."

"Is that a yes?"

She dropped to her knees and crawled over to kiss the man who had somehow stolen her heart. "That's a yes."

EPILOGUE

Two MONTHS LATER, the sun shone over the mountain, shrinking away the remaining patches of snow that lined the drive to the B&B. Ursula had dropped off the other students who rode along on the field trip and now she and Rory were on their way home. Rory kept chattering away while Ursula parked the car and they went inside.

"Did you hear all those funny noises the magpie made? It scared Maddie when it squawked." Rory skipped ahead as Ursula pushed open the door to the kitchen.

Mac stood at the counter, screwing the lid onto a jar of pickles. At the sound of Rory's voice, he turned, and the expression of pure love on his face touched Ursula's heart. "How was the field trip to the bird rescue center?"

"Really good!" Rory ran to hug him without ever slowing down her narrative. "Did you know baby eagles are called eaglets? They use eagle puppets to feed the eaglets so they know they're eagles and don't think they're people."

"I've heard that." Mac picked a stray feather from Rory's hair. "What else did you see?"

"There was a raven with a missing wing, and he's so smart they have to keep him in a special place because he can open most of the regular cages." Rory trotted through the kitchen divider to greet Blossom, who had been beating her tail against the gate while she waited. Van Gogh jumped down from the window seat to rub against her ankles.

Ursula sidled closer to Mac and was rewarded when he

slid his arm around her waist and brushed a kiss across her forehead. "Hi, darlin'. Did you enjoy the trip, too?"

"I did. Our eagle was there."

"I wondered. How is he doing?"

"Very well. They're planning to release him later this month. They said if we want, we can be there to watch him fly away."

"I'd like that."

She stood on tiptoe to kiss him on the lips. "Thank you for holding down the fort today so I could help chaperone the field trip. Any problems?"

"Nothing I couldn't handle. The toddler in the Shooting Star suite decided it would be fun to flush his dad's socks down the toilet, so there was a minor flood."

"Oh, no."

"It's fine. A plumbing snake and a mop fixed everything."

She patted his cheek. "My hero."

Rory had finished greeting the animals and ran back into the kitchen to tug at Mac's arm. "We're gonna get a snack and then we're driving to town to see the new stuff at Andi's Animal Place. Wanna come?"

Ursula clarified. "Bill built a half dozen kitty condos for the shelter, and Rory wants to see them. And the good news is Penny has organized a full roster of volunteers, so if everything passes inspection next Tuesday, they're ready to open."

She watched his face to see his reaction. She'd wondered if this plan to establish an animal shelter in Andi's memory was a good idea. Would seeing Andi's name every time he drove to Seward be hard for Mac? But the community had jumped in with their usual enthusiasm, and working with the local people on a project his daughter would have loved seemed to be a healing journey for Mac.

He saw her concern and gave her a reassuring smile before patting Rory's head. "I would love to come along, but I was in the middle of something and I'd like to get a few thoughts down first. Why don't you get a snack, and I'll be ready to go in about half an hour, okay?"

"Okay." Rory headed for the cookie jar. Ursula poured her a glass of milk while Mac disappeared into their private living room. Ursula sat with Rory at the kitchen table and chatted about the field trip.

Rory swallowed the last bite of her cookie. "Is Mac ready yet?"

"I don't think so. Why don't you take Blossom outside and throw the ball for her until it's time to go?"

"Let's go, Blossom." Rory grabbed a tennis ball and the two of them galloped out.

Ursula went to look for Mac. He sat at the desk, typing on his laptop. He held up a finger to ask her for one more minute while he finished. He typed a few more words and then swiveled his chair to face her. "All done." He patted his leg. "Come here, darlin'."

Smiling, she went over to sit in his lap. He pulled her close, nuzzled her cheek and put his lips beside her ear. "Tell me something," he whispered. "What, exactly, is a kitty condo?"

She laughed. "I think it's kind of an enclosed tower with different levels where cats can climb around and play."

"Sounds useful."

"I'd imagine so." She tried to sneak a peek at his computer. "What were you working on?"

He rotated the chair so that the computer was out of her view, chuckled and swung back around so she could see the screen. "Some ideas for a new book I want to write. I just wanted to get some notes jotted down before I forget them."

She gasped. "That's fantastic, Mac. Can you tell me what it's about, or is it a secret?"

"No secret. It's about a crusty old cowboy who's reached

the end of his rope, and this aggravating woman too stubborn to give up on him." He paused just long enough to press a kiss to her temple. "And, just like ours, this story has a happy ending."

* * * * *

COMING SOON!

We really hope you enjoyed reading this book. If you're looking for more romance, be sure to head to the shops when new books are available on

Thursday
26th July

To see which titles are coming soon, please visit
millsandboon.co.uk

LET'S TALK
Romance

For exclusive extracts, competitions
and special offers, find us online:

- ⓕ facebook.com/millsandboon
- ⓘ @millsandboonuk
- ⓣ @millsandboon

Or get in touch on 0844 844 1351*

For all the latest titles coming soon, visit
millsandboon.co.uk/nextmonth